"Once in a great while, a book appears that gives voice to multitudes living just beyond our everyday scope. *The Poison Flood* establishes Jordan Farmer as a writer whose lyricism and unflinching search for truth place him among those artists who carry our deepest concerns and very best possibilities across time. This is a profoundly good book."

—Jonis Agee, author of *The Bones of Paradise*

"A fascinating exploration of character, with a story that captivates with suspense and heart, *The Poison Flood* is a book about the influence of music, the power of art, and the complexities of luck. Irresistible and original."

—Timothy Schaffert, author of *The Swan Gondola*

LIGHTHOUSE BURNING

OTHER TITLES BY JORDAN FARMER

The Poison Flood

The Pallbearer

LIGHTHOUSE BURNING

JORDAN FARMER

This is a work of fiction. Names, characters, organizations, places, events, and incidents are either products of the author's imagination or are used fictitiously. Otherwise, any resemblance to actual persons, living or dead, is purely coincidental.

Published by Thomas & Mercer, Seattle

www.apub.com

ISBN-13: 9781662509919 (paperback)
ISBN-13: 9781662509926 (digital)

Front cover design by Olga Grlic
Back cover design by Jarrod Taylor
Cover images: © Nitat Termmee, © Olga Siletskaya, © DenisTangneyJr / Getty Images

Printed in the United States of America

For my family

I

The Pugilist & The Painter

CHAPTER ONE

The only woman I ever loved told me secrets. These confessions always came at night, the bulbs of our empty wineglasses illuminated by the television's glow. I worshipped every inch of her body in those early days, but the conversations were my favorite part of our time together. She wanted to know all the things I'd sworn to never utter aloud.

Once, while we sat by the fireplace picking at leftovers, Gabrielle had asked me about the worst story I'd ever heard.

"The worst details or the worst delivery?" I asked. She normally would indulge that sort of deflection. That night, she pressed me.

"You know what I mean."

"I really don't. Like the grossest thing ever? I knew a kid in high school who passed a kidney stone. They found him in the boys' room, lying beside the urinal with his pants around his ankles."

I'd been rubbing her knee, so she stopped my hand from traveling farther up her thigh. I thought maybe she wanted a southern horror story. Gabrielle was a Black woman who'd been raised in Montana, and since I was a hillbilly from a coal-mining town, she might've wanted to know if I'd experienced any racist evil. Things another white man might have told me while feeling safe among his own.

"I want to know the saddest thing you've ever heard," she said.

"I'd have to think," I replied, but two contenders immediately came to mind. The first was something I'd done to a boy named Brandon a long time ago. The other was the time my father shot his best friend, Charlie, in a backwoods poker shack. They'd been drunk, and Dad thought Charlie had palmed a suicide king. My father tried carrying his wounded friend down the mountain and taxiing him to the hospital, but Charlie bled to death in the back of Dad's Impala before they descended the final hill. My father said it was the only person he'd ever murdered during his outlaw days. "I never killed anyone else," he told me. "But, if I'm being honest, that was mostly luck." He made no similar claims of innocence for his twin brother, Abbott, who maintained an even more notorious disposition.

Something had kept me from telling her this story. I didn't have the narrative power to explain what Dad must have felt, realizing the dark leak of blood from Charlie's liver would drain dry before they reached civilization. The story shamed me.

By that point I'd understood she just wanted to talk about her own tragedy.

"What's the saddest thing you've ever heard?" I asked.

The heaviness in her chest sailed out on a sigh.

"My brother threw his ex-wife out a fifth-story window. She wouldn't tell him where the car keys were hidden, so he pushed her through the glass."

I hadn't known if I should touch her, wipe away the tears that were coming.

"It hurts knowing that some part of him is part of me," she said.

Many years later, in the days of our second national economic depression, I was daydreaming about Gabrielle's smooth thighs when I drove up on the Dairy Delight and saw it looked like someone had been gutted in the parking lot. The ground was covered in a thick red sludge, but the smell wasn't right for blood. The night before, I'd driven out to Walton Richard's farm with my doctor bag because his boy had stepped on a nail somewhere behind the barn. I spent the evening chatting with Walton after irrigating the boy's foot with an antibacterial solution and bandaging him up. He really needed a tetanus shot, but that would've required a hospital visit. Walton had no gas or money for the trip. We'd stood out on the porch, Walton casting his eyes at the barn, which leaned sideways with age. I knew he didn't have any way to pay me, that even the normal alternative of fresh pork was gone since he'd slaughtered the last of his hogs. Cheaper to eat the animals than feed them. I'd left telling him not to worry, but the smell of the boy's blood hung in my nostrils all the way home like an omen. My newfound position as counterfeit country doctor had given me plenty of exposure to that sharp metallic tang. No, the smell from the mess in the parking lot was different, something sweet that reminded me of the festive dusks back when the summer fair still came to town. The sort of night made hotter by adolescent lust and carnival lights.

Out in the parking lot, the candy and toy machines I'd installed hung crooked from their metal poles. The glass fronts were busted out, the ground littered with the multicolored gumballs and little plastic orbs filled with spongy dinosaurs that grow in water. The damned things always came out deformed, one limb shorter than the rest or the tail shrunken. I sat in the truck and looked at my change bucket in the passenger seat. I'd hoped for a little bumper crop, but that was foolish. If my remaining patients couldn't even pay in meat, how did I expect my hobby to fare? I climbed out of the truck for a closer look.

The vandals had smashed open the coin mechanisms—considerable work since the machines were built with the resilience of old Buicks. Someone must have heaved hard with a sledge to cause such damage. I wondered about the use in loading everything up for repairs. It did feel good to take the pieces apart and reassemble them. I liked the grease on my hands, the security in knowing the broken gears could be replaced at my leisure. No matter the circumstance, each component would lock into place and operate smoothly. It calmed me, working on something sturdier than flesh. There was no fear that a slip or wrong decision would ruin the object's vitality. I suppose that's why I kept up the fruitless endeavor. Even with no one paying attention to the candy machines, it was a distraction from setting broken bones. Acts of healing were an obligation; the machines helped kill the remaining hours.

One of the milkmaids came outside as I inspected the glass shards on the ground. The girl looked sullen in her uniform. The white jeans and stained white smock caught the morning sun as she produced a hand-rolled cigarette from the band of her red visor, leaned against the restaurant's brick wall, and lit up. Like most vices, tobacco had become a cherished commodity in Coopersville. The lucky ones were sustaining on old bags of Bugler and rolling papers. An actual pack of Marlboros would've been worth spilling blood over. She was too young to be smoking, and while I could have listed plenty of carcinogen-laced parables, a hardness around her mouth kept me silent about the cigarette. I decided she wasn't the kind of girl to accept concerned warnings from a stranger.

The Dairy Delight was one of the last remaining institutions in Coopersville, West Virginia. Like so much of rural America in those days, my home had deteriorated into nothing more than the memory of a town. The economic collapse had hit us hardest in the southern part of the state. Basic infrastructure had evaporated in the wake of the following widespread migration. Most local businesses shuttered. You couldn't compare us with struggling American cities like Detroit or Saint Louis; we were more like the frontier mining camps of early westward expansion. Only less populated, without the prospect of gold in the hills or the promise of salvation by eventual statehood. Coopersville was suddenly in the strange predicament of being displaced from an America in a state of triage. With important places like Los Angeles, New York, and Chicago suffering, we were entirely forgotten.

"Got yours, too, huh?" the milkmaid said.

"It would appear so." I kicked away some Mike and Ikes and picked up one of the plastic orbs. Inside, a small triceratops lay imprisoned, waiting to be watered into something underwhelming.

The girl scratched an itch behind her visor. Horton Meadows, the owner of the Dairy Delight, exclusively hired blondes. This girl had chosen a platinum shade, but her dark roots were growing out.

"Assholes sprayed dicks on the side of Dalton Hardware and chucked a brick through the window at McGraw Tire," the milkmaid said. Both businesses were closed, but I'd heard rumors that old man Dalton still lived in the building. He slept in a cot set up in the plumbing aisle.

"I know the ones did it," she went on. "You want their names?"

My initial reaction was to climb back into the truck. I didn't need a list of teenage vandals and wouldn't know what to do if I did track them down. Still, I kept looking at the tiny fetus of that spongy triceratops, feeling the tacky pull of the sugary asphalt whenever I shifted my feet. The candy machines were one of my few remaining joys. I might as well tell them what they'd cost me.

"How much you want?" I asked, knowing that if anything had ever been free in this world, that time was long over.

The milkmaid considered the value of a premium informer. Just a little caution remained. Hustling had been bred into both of us. "Fifty bucks will do it."

Fifty dollars. She may as well have asked for a thousand. Wide portions of America were eating out of trash cans, reduced to a primitive sort of urban scavenging for survival. People might murder over fifty dollars—not that the dollar was holding its value.

I appreciated the rebellion in her, that teenage impulse for demanding the impossible. Even before the depression, a town like Coopersville, with its lack of opportunities and boring pace, would've felt like a trap. I liked the resilience—that even in such dire circumstances she still hoped, instead of resigning herself to the slow rot the rest of us endured. Something about that made me feel hopeful.

"Twenty," I countered.

"I got to live around here, man."

While we negotiated, a large white truck came around the corner from behind the abandoned pharmacy at the end of the street. As the vehicle approached, the milkmaid pitched her cigarette and stomped on the butt, concealing it with her white Converse. Considering the scarcity of smokes, it was the same as watching someone toss a diamond ring into the river.

When the truck slowed, I noticed the emblem of a large cross painted on the hood, the rendition of rough wooden timber giving off rays of golden light. The windows were tinted a presidential black that kept me from seeing inside, but the slowing pace told me I'd get a look at the occupants anyway. The truck stopped beside us. **The Lighthouse Community Watch** was written on the side door in crude spray paint that didn't match the professional work of the cross.

The window rolled down, and a young man with a thick red beard leaned his bald head out the window. Mirrored sunglasses hid his eyes. I'd seen him around town, a giant of a man I couldn't help but think of as Redbeard because of that copper curtain hanging off his chin. Redbeard emitted a violent air of agitation. His size, along with the K bar knife and sidearm displayed on his hip, made most keep their distance.

"What happened here?" he asked.

The sass ran out of the milkmaid like piss down a drunk's leg. She stood rooted in place, fake smile parting plum-colored lips as she shook her head a little.

"Just chatting," I said, keeping eye contact with the mirrored pools of his sunglasses.

I didn't like the intrusion, didn't like the way the man sat confident inside his protective suburban tank, scaring little girls. Most of the remaining community welcomed these patrols. There had been a rash of arsons around town—three buildings incinerated within a month. The worst had been an apartment complex on Culver Avenue where ten people died.

Some thought the community watch might prevent more fires. Others wondered if the zealots who lived alone in the hills might be setting the fires themselves, purifying all they deemed evil with flames.

"We've got reports of other incidents around town," Redbeard said. His attention turned back to the milkmaid. "Do you want to tell me what happened here, sweetie?"

"Just kids," she said, as if she weren't a kid herself. She managed a real smile. I wasn't as good with the charade. Despite how high the vehicle sat, jacked up on its raised suspension and mud tires, I saw the barrel of a shotgun poking up from the passenger seat. Men carrying Remingtons didn't seem like the kind who might turn the other cheek.

Redbeard looked out the opposite window while collecting his thoughts, turned back toward us, and lowered his shades, revealing pale eyes. It might've been meant to inspire trust, but something about the gesture seemed threatening, as if he could read our thoughts with a glance.

"I hate the idea of people going around, tearing up the community. It'd be nice to sit them down and explain why they should value this place. Just because things are hard doesn't mean we can't work together and make them better."

I snorted at the Boy Scout speech. All the ladled charity soup and prayers in creation couldn't fix a bottomed-out stock market or a nationwide unemployment rate near 20 percent.

As Redbeard leaned forward, I saw the outline of a bulletproof vest underneath his polo shirt.

"You promise to come by the church and tell me if anything else happens?"

"I promise," the milkmaid said.

"Good girl," he said with a smile.

The milkmaid stepped back as the window came up, sealing the man inside as the diesel engine roared, and he left us standing in a plume of black smoke. We watched the truck disappear in the distance until it turned a corner; then the milkmaid dug into her apron for another butt. The flame from her lighter wavered while she cupped a shaking hand around it.

"Those fuckers scare me, man."

Moments before, she had seemed like the sort of girl who couldn't be scared by anything.

"I heard they take people," she said. "A girl I know says they're eating them."

It wasn't the first time I'd heard such stories. As hopelessness grew, so did our penchant for myths. The original Lighthouse had been saving souls in Coopersville since before I was born. After years of quiet services on the mountainside and baptism revivals down by the creek, the congregation's numbers eventually declined. Probably nothing more than modernity prying people from the grip of old-time religion. That previous incarnation of The Lighthouse had closed for good when Pastor Abraham died four years ago. I've never been one for gossip, but the whole town circulated tales about how the patriarch's death changed the son. The whispers ranged from drug abuse to séances intent on contacting the father's spirit.

Best to just move on with my day and forget the holy men. But first, I thought I'd use the milkmaid's fear to my advantage.

"You gonna tell me who busted my machines?" I asked. "It's better I find them than the community watch."

"I believe we were discussing compensation."

I offered two crumpled fives and the few quarters from my pocket. The milkmaid took the money, her fingers cold and speckled with drops of chocolate.

"Melvin and Miranda Hill. They drive around in a black Toyota. Melvin and I used to date," she said as if that explained everything. "The other girls told me about you," she continued. "You're a doctor or something. Is that true?"

I'd been home so long it surprised me to meet someone who didn't know the whole sad affair. Towns like Coopersville revere their legends. The residents pass down tragedies and triumphs through the generations. I remained unique because my story fell into both categories.

Country life congeals, keeping you stuck in place. My fortune only changed because of an absolute collapse. With the depression, my role transformed from outcast with a cautionary tale to an unlicensed country doctor making house calls. Aside from tending to the Richard boy's foot, I'd recently set a fractured leg; stitched up a lacerated forearm; and broken the fever of an old man who died later in the night, despite my best efforts. Those in need knew they could count on me rather than drive thirty miles to the nearest hospital, where they'd incur bills none of us could pay. People might be forgetting my sins.

"What's a doctor doing this shit for?" she asked, gesturing toward the broken machines.

"I'm not a real doctor. I help people out if there's nowhere else for them to go, but I didn't finish school."

The milkmaid glared. The poor reserve a particularly strong disdain for the few among them who squander opportunity. We know privilege is too fickle a gift to waste. I wanted to explain how it wasn't that simple. Instead, I toed the candy scattered across the asphalt.

I was walking away when the milkmaid called out, "Hey, you want a cone or something?"

"Free with the price of information?"

"Tree fell on the line this morning," she said, and pointed to the shop's dark windows. "All this shit's going to melt anyway." Spring storms often blew over the birch and oak trees in our ancient woods, making power outages common in Coopersville. Without the constant reliance on modern conveniences, the isolation of the mountains set in. We lost track of things happening in distant cities, the miles between us more tangible without electronic signals breaching the distance. News traveled slower, resuming the old ways of tall tales and lies. Even the mail ran with a sporadic irregularity.

Not that it mattered to most. The internet was still up despite the unreliable Wi-Fi, but the remaining locals had grown so poor that images of American excess and the social media influencers populating our phone screens may as well have been beamed in from another planet. Why watch America's fall of empire when our own little world had been declining for years? The Lighthouse had spread that message of apathy around town.

I thought about the tubs of strawberry and chocolate liquefying, the machine leaking soft serve as if it were hemorrhaging milk. My own power had been off for weeks. Only a matter of time before we lost this place too.

"No thanks," I said.

The milkmaid nodded. "Just keep my name out of it. I gotta live here. Even if there isn't any here left."

I watched her slip inside to see how much Superman with sprinkles she could finish before the thaw.

On the days when my class dissected cadavers, I worried about the chemical smells from the bodies even though my hands were sheathed by latex gloves. I've never had proper surgeon's hands—just bulbous, broken knuckles and crooked fingers. The digits were malformed from my days as a grade-school pugilist and the thousand practice punches thrown in our basement. Many nights, Dad or Uncle Abbott would hold the heavy bag while I punched blindly through the swollen eyes received on the back of the school bus. After my third ass-whipping in a month, my father had come home with a punching bag and hung it from a support beam in the basement's drop ceiling. It wasn't new, just a castoff reinforced with duct tape that Murphy Charles's gym had been throwing out. My father, ever one to see signs in such coincidences, decided the bag was meant for my education in self-defense. Every morning before sunrise, we'd go downstairs and work the bag for close to an hour. I'd circle it, focusing on my footwork as I snapped jabs and uppercuts into the dense fabric that never gave, no matter how devastating my flurries became. Dad would offer encouragement or insults, based on the quality of my performance. I remembered the swat of his hand on the back of my head when I'd tire out. He'd grip the scruff of my neck and remind me that the holler boys wouldn't allow any breaks. Now I understood he was angry about the reputation I'd failed to uphold. By the end of each session, my hands would be full of a tingle that lasted through morning, too numb even to feel their impact against another boy's chin.

The fact that my hands worked at all was a blessing. Whenever I pulled the thin membrane of latex over them, I admired how they became free of scars. Gabrielle used to trace these marks, the divots between each swollen knuckle, the wrists that would only bend so far because of the breaks. She once said my perseverance in studying the difficult medical books showed "dogmatic vigor," but Gabrielle always had a way with words. Before opening the flower shop where I'd met her, she'd studied Victorian literature and used to talk about the fallible nature of language. "The only true human miracle," she once told me, "is this broken system of articulating ourselves."

Nights after class, I would touch Gabrielle with hands that had held dead hearts hours before and fear she'd recoil. It was the opposite, of course. She'd ask about the smells or textures, wonder aloud what it was like being elbow deep inside what had once been a person. I hadn't known what to say. The bodies never bothered me. There were no lingering clues about who the deceased had been or what kind of life they'd lived. All that I'd observed was the stark truth of absence. The idea that flesh was all we were and that flesh reveals no secrets once we depart. I was naive back then, so certain that all life's answers could be found in my textbooks.

One night, as we lay together in bed, Gabrielle spread out on the sheets.

"Show me where everything is," she said, pulling up her tank top. Her fingertips traced over the muscles of her stomach.

I circled her navel on my way toward her kidneys. I explained the spleen, the lungs, and moved my hand over the peak of her left breast atop the heart.

"What about skin?" she asked.

"What about it?" Every time we approached the idea of race, I feared she didn't trust me. My redneck raising would forever keep me from being believable, and like a dog taught to bite, people thought I was predisposed to an eventual act of prejudice. Even though the assumption hurt, I didn't blame her for being cautious. I'd seen plenty of hate in the men I grew up around.

"Well, historically, it's made a difference," she said. "Especially back in your part of the country."

"Not to me."

"Your people wouldn't have something to say if you brought me home?" Gabrielle asked. "I wouldn't have to sit on your porch and look at a neighbor's confederate flag?"

"My father wouldn't say a word," I lied.

I suspected she knew. We talked so little about my father it was clear I was hiding some dark secret. Gabrielle spoke often about the way her brother's drug addiction led to rampages and robberies, about the times she'd sat outside jail with him, listening to apologies that wouldn't last, or dropped him off at rehab centers he'd just escape to go on another bender. I never reciprocated. Gabrielle knew that I was emotionally estranged from my father. I hadn't seen the man since I'd moved away for school, but she didn't know the real reason. The stories about her brother were an acknowledgment that we shared a particular pain, but I never let her in. Until I could find a way to escape the pull of my family completely, I'd just lie. Of course, Gabrielle was too smart for that. If she pretended to believe, it was because she trusted that, eventually, I'd be honest about my past. Until that day, she'd seemed content to let me prune the thorns from roses or wrap bouquets in the silence of her shop. I had gotten decent at floral arrangements. She used to say she could always use another florist if being a doctor didn't work out.

That night in bed, I took her by the chin, ran a thumb over her cheek and lower lip.

"I'm not like those men," I told her.

The vandals' truck was parked in front of Eugene's gas station, dropped low on a flat tire. The station was still open, but the last gasoline shipment had come months ago, and the tanks were running dry. Not that it mattered. Gas prices had risen past most budgets in May. Now it was September, and nobody but The Lighthouse's community watch gassed up with any regularity.

I sat across the street, watching as the driver of the truck—a long-haired boy in a jean jacket and hiking boots who must've been Melvin—jacked up the ride. A girl, immediately recognizable as the young man's twin, sat beside him on the curb. She swigged from a bottle wrapped in a brown paper bag and counted a Ziploc baggie full of change. Her fingers sifted through the denominations, found the quarters, and stacked them into a row of little towers, each worth two dollars.

I needed a strategy. I didn't want to just walk up and start slinging accusations. I've never been good at confrontation. All my old schoolyard fights had been instigated by others who thought a smaller boy was easy prey. Their age made things worse. How does a grown man accuse two teenagers without drawing attention? I considered aborting the whole thing.

Melvin spilled the lug nuts. They rolled across the asphalt, hopping over cracks on their journey toward the road. He chased after the tiny wheels, trying simultaneously to run and scoop them up as his sister leaned back and laughed. A few of the nuts dropped sideways as their inertia petered out, but one made it all the way past the gas pumps and bumped into my shoe. I stamped down on it.

Melvin gathered the other nuts while I picked up the one underfoot. "Thanks, man," he said.

I looked at his unwashed hair and the sparse mustache he was cultivating. The boy might have been seventeen, but my gut said he'd only been driving legally for a few months. A blot of red paint smeared his shirttail.

"You need some help?" I asked.

"We got it."

"Come on, a little help never hurt." I kept the lug nut palmed so he couldn't object.

We walked over, and I pulled the tire off. The sister, Miranda, sat watching us, refusing to rise from her place on the sidewalk. She tapped her foot, her mud-crusted cowboy boot sucking at the concrete.

"I'm Harlan Winter," I said and offered a hand. Melvin's tight grip hurt my arthritic knuckles, but I didn't wince. I was good at disguising my weaknesses.

I knew they hadn't recognized me the moment I pulled up. There was no fear in their posture, and my last name always brought an aura of intimidation into each new meeting. People expected the mad blood of my father to be coursing through my veins. Melvin introduced himself, but his sister just went on counting my money. It had been a while since I'd changed a tire, but the steps came back to me.

After we finished, Melvin shook my hand again. "I appreciate the help," he said.

"You're welcome," I replied. "I just need those quarters." I pointed at the small stacks Miranda had assembled. Those shitty dinosaurs had done better than I'd thought.

"No way," Miranda said. If either of them would be trouble, it'd likely be her. She could bash me with a wrench if things escalated.

"That money belongs to me. You two busted my machines down at Dairy Delight. Considering I'm not asking you to pay for them, I think I'm entitled to that bit of profit."

"We didn't break anything," Miranda said.

Melvin's eye contact let me know they'd done it, and there was no remorse to be found. My options were dwindling. I could either fight with children or accept the loss.

"All that vandalism will attract attention," I said.

"Fuck the community watch," Miranda replied. She spit between her boots, emphasizing her disgust. "What are they gonna do to us?"

"From what I've heard, they may do a lot," I said. "Once upon a time, churches burned people at the stake and drowned them in the river. Punishment is fine with them so long as they can save your soul."

"He's just trying to scare us," Miranda told Melvin.

"You broke my machines," I said. "I can't prove it, but if I find them busted up again, I'm gonna send the watch looking for you two."

Not much of a threat. I wasn't even leaving with the money.

Miranda picked up each stack of quarters and dropped them into the bag to assert victory.

"Just leave my machines alone." I pointed at the red paint on Melvin's shirt. "And don't be drawing dicks on people's walls. It's childish."

I walked back to the truck. As I drove away, I saw Miranda finally standing, the light glinting off the change as she shook the bag at me. Through the rearview mirror, it looked like she held a small sun in her hands.

When I flunked medical school, I had to lie instead of admitting I'd ruined my future over a broken heart. I devised new narratives, spun tales to disappointed friends about how the human body was too much of a mystery. None of this was true. I was a catalog of illnesses and treatments. Most of what I lacked as a physician was the title.

Anytime I encountered someone who knew just how smart I was, I pretended I'd fallen into the juvenile traps of freedom and apathy. I said that booze and parties got the better of me. I fabricated mornings in bed, nursing a parched mouth and raw eyes that begged for darkness. If they wanted to be disappointed by it and picture me in some bathroom, cutting lines on the toilet lid like so many hillbilly delinquents before me, that'd be fine. I didn't mind being a stereotype. Others made assumptions for me. Women, some of the church ladies decided, had led me astray. All those morally loose college girls had become too much for a small yet handsome country boy. None of them ever knew how close they were to unraveling it or how much more severe my predicament actually was. Women—in the plural sense—would have been easier to forget.

My father was the only one who uncovered the truth of my heartbreak. It was stupid to bring the ring home, but I'd carried the meager gold band with just a sliver of diamond onto the plane, hidden it in my breast pocket until it could be stowed away in my mother's bureau.

On the morning Dad found the ring, he cornered me in the hallway, slammed my head into the wooden paneling, and demanded details. I tried sputtering out more falseness, but a few slaps loosened my tongue. I didn't delve into the final night when I'd dropped to a knee and received Gabrielle's quiet refusal. She told me she just wasn't ready, but something deep inside knew it was about my family. All those times she'd shared about her brother and I'd only responded with silence proved more revealing than any lies. I just hadn't had the courage to tell her I came from monsters. I'd been too afraid she'd think of my family heritage as a curse passed on, something that might infect our children.

I won't repeat the things my father said. After I finished with the story, he bashed my head into the paneling a final time. It would've been worse if Uncle Abbott had still been with us and not serving the second year of his decade-long sentence. The pair always fed off one another, escalating the other's capacity for cruelty into acts unthinkable when alone.

Years after my father's death, the dent remained unrepaired. Whenever I look at the splintered wood, it's a testament to the day I learned the real depth of the man's hate.

I was out in the yard, unloading the broken candy machines, when Melvin's Toyota pulled up. The sun had slid behind the mountains. Just enough light filtered through the trees to keep me from discerning if anyone else was inside the truck's cab, but Melvin climbed out alone. He kept his eyes low, head hung in supplication, and hands stuffed deep into the pockets of all that denim he wore. The dust of my driveway rose as his feet trod through the gravel.

"What are you doing here?" I asked.

"I came by to apologize and to thank you for helping me with the truck."

The boy didn't know how to lie. That familiar fear wafted off him, telling me the rumors had been circulating again.

"Who told you about me?" I asked.

"Mr. Hatfield at the gas station."

"What did he say?"

"That you weren't someone I should mess with. That you beat Brandon Flanders half to death when you were both fourteen. He told me that Brandon went blind."

Thinking of Brandon always made me remember that night when Gabrielle asked me about the worst story I'd ever heard. Out of all my fights, Brandon hadn't deserved it. I'd been trying to get the combination lock open on my bike, and he'd called me a dumbass the second time I rolled past the six. Once the combination lock was off, I'd beaten him with it till he bled out the ears and nose. Blindness had been the least of it. He had never spoken again and had to be fed by others till he died in a hospital at twenty-five. One of my father's bribes kept the police from prosecuting me. Officer Dillon—a dirty cop gone to his grave a decade ago now—pinned the blame on an older delinquent, but the locals all seemed to know the truth. No schoolyard bully ever stepped to me again. In fact, most other children didn't speak to me at all.

"Well, you and your sister were so rude before," I said.

"I'm really sorry. We didn't know."

"Didn't know what?"

"We didn't know how much respect you deserved."

I kept looking past him toward the Toyota.

"Where's the hammer?" I asked. "The one you used on my machines."

Melvin looked away again. "It's in the truck bed."

"Go get it."

He went around the back of the truck, opened the tailgate, and pulled a large sledge from the other tools. We stood silent a moment, just letting the heat extinguish, along with the last of the purple evening light.

"Don't stop till there isn't a straight spot on it," I said.

Melvin's face went slack. He wanted to plead, but I could see he was too scared. The sledge looked heavy. He emitted a grunt as he hefted it high and took the first swing. The door panel crunched inward, the black mirror image distorted until all its captured creation looked in ruins. Melvin huffed and swung again.

"The windows," I said, and sank down on my porch stoop, watching him work.

After a flood swallowed most of the neighboring homes, the previous owners of my house raised the foundation to create an expendable lower floor Dad and I always called "the basement." The rooms down there were cooler, dank, and filled with the lingering smell of long-dried sweat. Most nights, I descended into that darkness and never thought about the old days, but carrying the machine parts made me recall the weight of the lock I'd used to bludgeon Brandon. Its surface had been sticky with drying blood by the time I'd ridden my bike home and hidden it in the trash.

It was well past midnight when I finished working on the machines. The Hill twins had left little viable. All the internal components were spread across the card table where I performed my repairs. I sorted the pieces, leaving a small pile at the table's far corner for the broken bits that wouldn't serve anymore. The rest, I took time to admire. There was no satisfaction in the few repairs I managed. Most of the parts weren't even worthy of scrap. My hands hurt, and I couldn't focus. The shattered pieces just reminded me of my limited abilities and failures.

I tossed them aside, thinking about how there are things damaged beyond our capacity for renewal. After ten years of incarceration, Uncle Abbott was being released, and like some fool inviting a vampire into their home, I knew I'd be at the prison gate to receive him.

CHAPTER TWO

The next morning, I woke to a pounding upstairs. The sound was faint, but a childhood filled with my father's rages had left me a light sleeper. The slightest creak of floorboards or groan of a swinging door would jettison me into consciousness, throw open my eyes in the dark before whatever coming danger could grab me. In the basement, it was impossible to tell day from night, but my internal clock seemed to believe I'd slept past noon. Not that it mattered. My life had long ago abandoned any responsibilities I could oversleep.

As I climbed the stairs, I struggled with grasping the handrail. Sometimes, my hands refused to grip at all for the first hour of the morning. The knocking ceased as I crossed the living-room carpet. In the silence, a few birds resumed their singing.

"I'm coming," I called out.

I opened the door and found a man standing on my porch. Well over six feet tall, with thin wisps of dandelion-white hair fluttering atop his otherwise bald head. Despite the thinning white hair of a prophet, the man looked formidable. The charcoal work shirt he wore stretched over a wide chest.

"Harlan Winter," he said. "I'm Pastor Nathaniel Logan from The Lighthouse. May I speak with you a moment?"

I'd heard about Pastor Logan. On the Sunday when the leadership duties of The Lighthouse would've transferred to him, Nathaniel Logan arrived at morning services still shit-faced after an all-night debate on faith officiated by a bottle. He took the pulpit and cast the congregation from their pews, saying he was unfit to guide them, barred the door of the sanctuary, and was practically unseen for two years. It wasn't until a few months into the national depression that The Lighthouse's truck began making patrols around town. It delivered meals, offered rides to those without vehicles and small cash handouts for the destitute. Often Logan rode alone, stopping to ask people what services he might provide in these harsh times and promising a grand reopening of the church. On other occasions, it was only the red-bearded man, whom no one in Coopersville recognized. Their efforts seemed friendly, but some had grown suspicious after Logan's long hermitage.

Outside, the truck with the cross painted on its hood sat parked in my driveway. I expected a similar gold crucifix peeking out from between the man's unbuttoned collar, but in its place hung a circular medallion with a strangled conglomerate of lines. A series of circular markings was etched at each far margin, like the points of a cross or directions on a compass. Most Coopersville residents would've already sold any jewelry, but The Lighthouse seemed to sustain without need of money. Things like this only added grist for the rumor mill.

"What do you want?" I asked.

"We heard you had an altercation yesterday evening with two young vandals. I wondered if you'd be willing to talk about the encounter."

I didn't like the way he said "we." It carried an air of superiority, as if God Himself were waiting in the truck.

"I don't know what you're talking about," I said.

Over Logan's shoulder, bits of glass from Melvin's busted windows sparkled in my yard. Talking my way out of bad situations was something I'd been doing since childhood, but none of that offered much comfort.

"Mr. Winter, there's no reason to lie to me. We simply want to help these kids. Why don't I step inside and we can discuss it?"

I tried slamming the door in his face, but Logan extended a leg. The door rebounded off his shin with a force that should've cracked bone. He didn't even grimace, just pushed more of his body inside my doorway.

"Get the fuck off my porch or I'm going to the police," I said.

"Deputy Smith is a supporter of our community watch, Mr. Winter. Believe me when I tell you that our outreach has her blessing."

Something unstated accompanied the pastor's stare. My last name wasn't the sort that inspired confidence in law enforcement. Everyone knew I'd gotten away with too much in my youth.

"I know Melvin Hill came here after you confronted him at the gas station. Why don't you tell me about it?"

My knuckles tingled, followed by a tensing in my arms and legs always present in the moments before a fight. I tasted something metallic on my tongue and realized I'd been biting my cheek.

"If you don't get off my porch, I'm going to hit you so hard you'll swallow your goddamned teeth. You're not the law around here, even if you'd like to be."

I wasn't sure my statement was true. The police department had shrunk to nothing more than two deputies and a sheriff. If Deputy Smith was one of The Lighthouse's pilgrims, that comprised a third of the dwindling police force.

Logan raised a hand in surrender but kept his leg inside the door. He reached into his shirt pocket and produced a small business card with a cross pressed into the margin. I couldn't stop staring at the medallion around his neck. I'd never seen anything that resembled the bizarre design.

"I don't expect I'll hear from you, but I'm leaving this in case you change your mind."

Logan extended the card, arm stiff and unmoving until I accepted it. Only then did he remove his leg from my doorway. He crossed to the center of the yard and bent low, hands sifting through the tall grass to examine whatever he'd stepped over, then stood and slipped a small object into his pocket. Watching from my porch, I assumed it was a piece of glass from Melvin's truck. I kept my eyes on him until he departed.

Sipping the last reserves of my morning coffee, I sat at the kitchen table and looked at the card. **The Lighthouse**, it said in small calligraphy. **Come Seek Salvation!** Nothing ominous in the cheap stock paper or the quaint cross. Still, I remembered the fear in the milkmaid's eyes when the truck pulled up. Logan hadn't looked like a cannibal—just an entitled preacher.

I couldn't remember a time when I'd trusted church. Maybe it was my father's contempt for small-town religiosity, but I'd never understood the impulse to let another man—and it seemed to always be a man—tell you they had all the answers, not only regarding life but even secrets locked on the other side of death. My father had believed in the law of survival. While I saw the wickedness in that nihilism, just as much evil remained in assuring other mortals that heavenly decree wasn't only a code you followed but also one they must adhere to or suffer eternal hellfire. Living with con artists had helped me recognize all the potential abuses for such power. Even before The Lighthouse tightened its grip on our town, I knew what was coming. Now it was at my front door.

I slipped the card into my wallet and began preparing for my day. I was going by Wildcat's to serve drinks with Shannon. It would be a long evening, with little relief and no respite from the few loyal drunks with their familiar sad stories. I hoped the pain in my knuckles would ebb away before I dealt with that bullshit, but I suspected I'd be denied even that small grace.

Wildcat's was the last reliable bar for hard drinkers in Coopersville. By "reliable," I mean it was the only dive around that guaranteed the proper mix of darkness and silence an alcoholic seeks when they need a good, contemplative binge. The sort of dangerous deep drinking that only happens while pondering circumstances that have led one to a dead end. With the depression on, most people needed that. They just couldn't afford it. Not that lack of funds was ever a real problem at Wildcat's. Shannon Pierce, the owner, carried a soft spot for charity cases, even in the days before we'd all fit that bill. By that autumn, payment had been replaced by optional donations that kept the hangout going. I might've debated such a poor business policy with Shannon but knew Wildcat's couldn't last long anyway. Expenses wouldn't allow her to restock the bar. Until the booze ran out, the place functioned like an oasis where patrons barred the door against their troubles.

I'd spent many nights slinging brews at Wildcat's. Bartending made my feet hurt, and the fights were a plague. A few drinks after a hoot-owl shift in a soul-sucking job cracks some men open, but unemployment and foreclosures let all the poison buried deep ooze up to the surface until violence is all that keeps you from drowning in self-loathing. I knew that feeling. I just didn't like being around it anymore.

Aside from the brawls, there was no boisterous behavior in Wildcat's. No pool tables, karaoke, or darts. The main floor lay empty as a black ocean between the corner tables illuminated by just a few strands of colored Christmas lights. The jukebox was full of solemn, classic country, rarely played, and the volume could only be turned up past a whisper. In Wildcat's, this was usually loud enough to hear every word. During the five years I'd been bartending, I'd rarely seen anyone drop a quarter in the machine, aside from an old gin-blossomed man named Walsh who liked George Jones to sing "The King Is Gone" near the end of each night. We hadn't heard the song in a while. The electricity had been off for nearly a month, leaving us with nothing but Shannon's scented candles to light the establishment. The mixture of soothing scents—with names like Fresh Summer Rain, Paradise Mornings, and Tropical Relief—mingled until the pungent sweetness made me nauseous. Walsh was absent as well. Rumors floated that he'd hitchhiked out of town rather than stay in the small tent city erected under the sergeant's bridge. With gas at such a premium, I thought he'd probably just drunk himself to death out in the woods, but it didn't really matter how far he'd made it. Whether dead under the forest canopy or in an alley in some surrounding city, the result remained the same. The depression sped up how fast society eats its castoffs.

When I arrived at Wildcat's, Shannon was already wiping down the bar. She was the perfect owner. Always smiling and enduring the profane jokes and embellished stories from the men who'd made the place home after the American Legion Hall under the bowling alley had closed. She had a tender way of handling the most depraved and destitute of drunks, enabling them with kindness and free shots. It didn't hurt that she was beautiful. Dark eyes and hair that shone in either candlelight or, in earlier days, the Christmas lights wrapped above the bar. Some days I thought we were all in love with her. Shannon was good for Wildcat's, but the place was slowly sucking away her vitality, the way it did everyone who came through the door.

"You're early," she said as I walked in.

"Just thought I'd get an early start," I said, picking up a damp rag from the sink and helping her wipe down the bar top. Shannon gave me a concerned look but didn't press the issue. I was thankful. My hands were aching again, and I didn't know if I had the concentration needed for lies. I just wanted the burn of some room-temperature bourbon, to get a little drunk and chat mindlessly until I could escape into the blue darkness of dusk. Too many of my days operated that way, hours drunkenly weathered until time for sleep.

"You see the artwork outside?" Shannon asked.

I shook my head. I'd been in such a fog that I wouldn't have been surprised if I missed an elephant in the parking lot.

"Big grim reaper–looking motherfucker spray-painted on the wall out there."

"Really? On the side of the bar?"

"Yes, on the side of the bar. The thing's only eight feet tall."

"What do you mean by 'grim reaper'?"

"I mean a skeleton in a hood with a scythe, like on the front of some Megadeth album. Looks like a giant biker tattoo."

Shannon retrieved the bottle of Old Grand-Dad from the rail and poured us both a double shot. The amber liquid made me salivate, my hands trembling just a bit as I reached for it. Shannon clinked our glasses together and tossed the shot back. I let the whiskey roll slow over my tongue.

"They must have used a stencil or something. No drippy lines."

"You want me to scrub it off?"

"Don't much see the point," she said. "Nobody showed the last two days. The Decline has ruined us."

When Shannon talked about the Decline—as she'd named it—I knew she was thinking of shuttering the bar. Her sister was running some sort of shelter in Louisville. The city had reached a record number of evictions, and her sister said they'd taken to putting tents in the parking lot because of overcrowding. The staff rationed meals, only serving twice a day to feed all the residents. If Shannon wanted to go where she could offer something more substantial than a drink, I couldn't blame her, but losing my bartender gig at Wildcat's would rob me of another needed distraction.

Our first patrons arrived thirty minutes later—an unemployed coal miner and two grease-stained mechanics. They took a seat at the bar, where Shannon poured drinks and laughed at their banter.

Melvin Hill arrived an hour later. He slunk inside, shaking rain out of his hair, his split-sole boots slopping mud across the floor. Something about him looked diminished. The dark peacoat he wore swallowed him around the shoulders and neck. He didn't come directly to the bar, just stood by the entrance, waiting on someone to acknowledge him.

"No way," I heard Shannon call out. She held a highball glass aloft, the liquid inside sloshing as she thrust it in the boy's direction. "We still got standards in my bar."

For a moment, I was ready to let Shannon toss him out—the little shit had caused me enough trouble—but I raised a calming hand.

"It's cool," I said. "I got this."

When it was clear Shannon wouldn't protest, I approached Melvin. His eyes remained low, like when I'd made him take up the hammer.

"You're pretty popular," I said. "I had a visitor asking about you."

"I'm sorry," he said, still not making eye contact.

"What do they want from you? I doubt this is just about dicks on walls and my broken candy machines."

"Can we go somewhere and talk?" Melvin asked. He'd finally looked up at me, hazel eyes hidden behind dark bangs. Something in the glance was so pitiful I decided to accommodate him. I retrieved a bottle, a candle that smelled like a piña colada, and two glasses from the bar, then led Melvin toward a table in one of the back corners. He didn't even bother to take off his sodden coat when we sat.

"Where's your sister?" I asked as I poured.

Melvin shook his head. "She's not sure we need your help." The boy tossed the whiskey back like a professional.

My help? I thought. *What could the kid possibly want with my help?*

"That's strange for twins," I said. "Usually they share a personality."

"Where'd you hear that?"

"Twins run in my family. My uncle Abbott was just like my father."

"How's that?"

"Cruel," I said. Just because I'd be picking the man up the next day didn't mean I wanted to spend my afternoon talking about him. "Why would you come to me for any sort of help? I'm the one who made you demolish your truck."

"It wasn't my truck. It belonged to our older brother, Franklin."

"I'm sorry about making you trash your brother's ride. I didn't know that it didn't belong to you."

Melvin reached across my side of the table for the bottle and took a quick snort. It seemed like a fortifying act, something to give him the necessary courage to say what he needed to say.

"The Lighthouse doesn't really care about me or Miranda. All that stuff about vandalism is just an excuse. They're looking for Franklin."

"Why? He egg some houses with you two?"

"Franklin's a painter. Logan had commissioned some work from him—stuff to show at their upcoming revival. But they fell out once the pastor saw some of Franklin's other work."

"Like what?" I asked.

"He does a lot of fantasy."

I imagined Frank Frazetta's Conan. Muscular barbarians and nude elven girls. I suppose the polite thing would've been to ask, but I didn't really care.

"Franklin and his girlfriend, Alice, have both disappeared. I'm worried The Lighthouse might have something to do with it."

"Maybe Alice left, and your brother's just laid up heartbroken somewhere," I said.

Melvin shook his head. "You don't know these people. They wouldn't be above hurting Alice to get at Franklin—or maybe just to punish him for what he paints."

I shook my head. "Nobody's getting hurt over some watercolor wizards." But I wasn't sure I believed that. Not after the pastor knocking on my door that morning, and not after seeing the milkmaid's fear when she spoke with Redbeard.

Melvin watched Shannon and the men drinking on their barstools, as if looking for some secret surveillance.

"Everyone in town is afraid of you," Melvin said. "If there's anyone who can make them answer questions—or maybe back off—just by showing interest, that's you."

The old anger sparked inside me, but I suppressed the urge to drag Melvin across the table, throw him on the floor, and stomp his soft parts until the rage subsided. Even after so many years, the possibility of such great violence was as real as coming rain and passed with the same unanswerable fickleness as the weather. One moment, I wanted to murder the boy; the next, I was simply weary with the truth of what he was saying, sad that my reputation would never be outgrown.

"I think maybe you should see some of Franklin's work. It might make some of this easier to explain."

"I don't know how hobbits and ringwraiths will help me understand your brother."

"Not just those," Melvin said. "These are stranger. We got a little money that Franklin saved from selling pet portraits online."

Despite the bottomless absurdity of the internet, there couldn't be much cash involved in something as bizarre as pet portraits during the best of times. Many Americans didn't have enough disposable income to hang a new painting on their wall. I decided to see if he really had any money.

"Two hundred," I said. "A thousand if things go further. Agreed?"

The price wounded him, but Melvin nodded. If nothing else, the money might pacify Uncle Abbott. There'd be the usual vices of a man just released from prison to quench, and cash might delay the mayhem of his schemes. I doubted looking at the brother's paintings would help, but I thought I'd just pocket the initial money and be done with it.

"Let's go," I said, downed a final shot, and stood, wiping my mouth with the back of my hand.

I stopped at the bar to explain things to Shannon. "I gotta take care of something. Is that okay?"

She sighed, frustrated to be abandoned, but waved me out the door.

Rain splattered on the windshield as we drove. We'd left Melvin's abused truck in the parking lot, preferring my equally old but cosmetically sound Chevrolet. Even with a spare gas can in my garage, I decided I'd need to charge for the expense. Desperation severs the charitable impulses.

The roads in Coopersville are treacherous, blighted with rim-bending potholes and cliffside curves absent any guardrails to save you from hydroplaning off the mountainside, but they'd become even worse with the past few years of neglect. The narrow lanes were ragged, the paint almost gone from the center line. It felt as if we were driving on some forgotten highway after the apocalypse. The silence in the cab didn't help. Melvin just chewed his fingernails while the rain on the hood and the smack of the windshield wipers created a constant rhythm.

"Here on the left," he said.

I turned down another poorly paved road. In the distance, I saw the shabby one-story structure of the old Wyatt Grade School. The place had been closed for the better part of a decade after the population of Coopersville became so sparse the district couldn't justify the school's continued existence. Once it closed, the children were bused twenty minutes in the opposite direction toward the county line. Local teenagers considered the building haunted and shared a legend about an old schoolmarm who hanged herself in the auditorium. Occasionally, some of the braver ones would sneak in through a gymnasium window and screw under the bleachers.

"Your brother paints here?" I asked, parking in the empty lot.

Melvin nodded. "He worked out a deal to rent one of the classrooms from the county commission. Eventually, they just forgot about him."

"How do you know he's not still in there?" I asked. "Plenty of classrooms to hide in."

"Because Miranda and I have been crashing out here."

Melvin sorted through the jangling mass on his key ring until he found the key for the front door. Crossing the threshold, I took in all the confined scents of a long-absent education: chalk dust and pencil shavings, the greasy waft of a thousand meals of Tater Tots and cafeteria pizza with sauce more like ketchup than marinara. The stench made my stomach flip. As we passed the empty cafeteria and its long tables, I noticed a clown painted on the far wall. His bulbous red nose and crimson smile were startling in the fresh dark.

Melvin opened a door near the end of the hall, and we entered what must have once been the band room. A full drum set had been pushed into the back corner. It sat surrounded by cases for clarinets, oboes, and tubas. The paintings were in the opposite corner, hundreds of canvases propped against one another.

"This is the old stuff," he said.

Oil paintings of dogs and cats, some posed naturally—like the calico sitting on its master's lap, or the corgi stretched out on a sunlit kitchen floor. The rest had been painted from the chest up, their furry heads emerging from the uniforms of nobility. Hanging medals were pinned to the tunic of a Doberman. Pearls adorned the neck of a Pomeranian. After Melvin finished sorting through the dogs, some of the fantasy art emerged. Horned dragons broiling knights in their plate armor. Necromancers with crooked staffs, conjuring shadow demons from black tar pits. I couldn't understand how something so childish could bring out the ire of The Lighthouse. It was almost precious in its innocence.

Just as things were feeling fruitless, Melvin brought out another canvas.

The first thing I noticed was the fire. Long columns of flames descended from the puffy white clouds that parted in the upper portion of the canvas. The raining brimstone looked real, as if the flames might furrow everything painted beneath them. They continued down the canvas in a straight fall, ignoring all natural laws as they covered ancient buildings in some city from antiquity. A woman stood in the painting's foreground, looking back at the burning earth. She'd melted away from the waist down, her legs transformed into crumbling pillars of salt.

"That's Lot's wife, watching the town of Sodom burn," Melvin said. "This was the first of the religious paintings commissioned by Logan."

Neither of us could avert our eyes. Every brushstroke here was precise, the quality so much better than the pet portraits it seemed crafted by another man. I felt like I could see every grain of sand hardening into glass in those dusty streets. If I closed my eyes, maybe I'd taste the salt wife blowing away on the wind. I'm no critic, know nothing of the mechanics of art. Still, there was the undeniable truth that talent, once noticed, is irrefutable. I hated seeing such skill devoted to angry religious parables.

"Franklin did a whole series on what he called *Horror Stories of the Bible* for Logan. Noah watching from the ark while his neighbors drown in the flood. Job covered in boils as he huddled around the bodies of his dead children. Jonah swallowed by the whale. Eventually, Franklin started focusing on something else."

Melvin shuffled through the stack until he found a smaller painting. The framed piece was perhaps twelve-by-fourteen inches yet as realistic as a photograph. It was a portrait of a male face: the eyes almost closed, the forehead obscured by a wet tangle of hair, and the nose bisected with a deep line of scar that mushed the highest point of the bridge nearly flat, spreading the flesh unevenly across the puckered cheeks. The man wore a sparse beard, with scars marring the barren patches until it looked more like the face of a sick animal stricken with mange. Two large fangs emerged from a mouth absent any lips.

A cold wave enveloped me. When the chill passed, nausea took over, my stomach aching in that dull, delayed way that comes after a punch in the dick. These feelings kept me from commenting on the painting, but I sensed Melvin didn't expect any other reaction. He dropped it back on the pile of canvases.

"There are dozens. Worse faces, more monstrous. When Logan inquired on why the newest painting was taking so long, Franklin showed him these. Logan called it blasphemy, told Franklin to go back to work on his commissions, but Franklin refused. He said these were his most important work."

"What are they?" I asked.

"Something Franklin saw in a vision."

Melvin pulled a Polaroid from his coat pocket. After seeing the monstrous portrait, I prepared myself for some deformity, but the man in the picture was typical. Puffy cheeks and slick hair receding from a large forehead. His inviting smile showed no elongated incisors, just a gap between his front teeth. The woman with him was striking. A dark-haired beauty with green eyes and skin so pale it suggested her hair might've once been red. Her mouth was smeared in black lipstick, eyes circled in dark mascara.

"Alice?" I asked, pointing to the girl.

"I don't know if she's cut out the Elvira look, but that's her. Listen, Franklin posted some of the fantasy stuff online. It grabbed the attention of a collector in New York. He's putting together a role-playing game called *War Wizards*. He asked me if Franklin would do a set of prints for the first edition. Over sixty paintings."

The whole thing sounded ridiculous. The rich stayed rich by bunkering down, forgoing investments that didn't involve other people's money and exploiting the poor harder until the bad times were weathered. They didn't sink their resources into foolish projects. If someone could do that in such a weak market, they must have more money than I could comprehend.

"You think something like that can sell when people are living so lean?" I asked.

Melvin shrugged. "I don't know. All I know is, it's Franklin's last chance. Who among us gets to do what you love for money? Besides, it's more than just the money. I know that sounds crazy when everyone is so broke, but I think mostly I'm just glad to tell Franklin the news. He needs some purpose. Get him back to painting things that don't scare me."

At home that night, I lit a few candles and sat in the dark kitchen, eating cold beans from the can. Whenever I closed my eyes, I saw the lipless mouth and fangs protruding like boar tusks from the sullen underbite in Franklin's portrait. I imagined my spoon encountering the serrated teeth of a predator instead of clicking against the dental bridge installed after Sam Hawkins knocked out three of my teeth on the school bus. I pushed the can away, too troubled to finish eating. Maybe it was knowing I'd be pulling up to the prison gate in only a few hours. I'd told myself I was ready for the reunion with Uncle Abbott, but maybe nothing prepares you for moments like that.

I was drinking the dregs of a lukewarm Coca-Cola when a pounding reverberated through the kitchen. I looked out the window to see if The Lighthouse's truck had returned and was still gazing out across the empty lawn when the sound came again. Closer this time, a *thap, thap, thap* that swatted the air beside each of my ears.

Another series of knocks followed. Each blow surrounded me until locating their origin became impossible. A dull pain like an abscessed tooth throbbed in my forehead. I waded through the sound until I found myself beside the basement door. The noise was coming from downstairs, but I distinctly heard it in two places: the first, an outside echo dulled by traveling up from the basement and through the thin wooden door; the second, as if a creature had invaded my skull, creating a fullness behind my eyes.

I put my ear to the door, wondering what kind of animal might be trapped down there. Probably just a racoon. Varmints are a hazard of country life.

The candle provided little illumination when I opened the door, so I found myself leading with my toes on the descent, stretching them out to assure the location of the next step before committing my weight. As I reached the bottom of the stairs, I recognized the flat packing of knuckles on canvas. Someone was beating the heavy bag.

I watched as the bag swung in a lazy arch, back and forth like the pendulum inside a grandfather clock. The rattling chain made the familiar music composed whenever delivering uppercuts and solid body shots. As the bag came to rest against my palm, I felt the damp heat of the canvas and the little droplets of perspiration left by a fist. I hadn't worked the bag since the night before. It couldn't be my sweat, yet I was alone. Nothing in the basement but my machine parts, the old couch, and the greasy musk that always lingered after a long training session. I smelled tired bodies despite their absence.

I turned and stepped on something hard with my bare foot. Between my toes peeked the metal dial of a combination lock. I picked it up and examined its numbered face. It was the same kind I'd used to secure my bike as a kid. I twisted the dial and listened to it clicking as I rolled clockwise past the six. Something tacky coated my fingers. I brought them to my nose and smelled blood. My toes hurt from stubbing them against the metal, but I wasn't bleeding. This was old blood, half-dried and coagulated to clotted brown. The same consistency as the blood on the lock I'd hidden in the trash after bludgeoning Brandon all those years ago.

Examining it closer, I saw the lock had the worn blue dial and identical little dent in the metal from the time I'd dropped it down the concrete staircase outside my school. I turned it over, praying to find nothing but unmarked metal on the back side. Yet there, scrawled with a black Magic Marker in the precise hand of my father, were my initials: *H. W. W.* Harlan Walton Winter.

I dropped the lock onto the floor. The dial began slowly turning without my touch. A methodical *tick, tick, tick*. It stopped on 25 and changed directions, clicking counterclockwise. Above me, the heavy bag started swaying again. Every time the lock passed a new number, the bag jerked as if struck by an invisible punch.

I smelled fresh blood in the air. The ache in my forehead flared, and my mind's eye went back to that sunny morning with Brandon Flanders, his crooked smirk and braying laugh as he called me a dumbass after I'd fumbled so long with the lock's combination. I remembered walking calmly over and striking him in the temple with the lock secure in my palm. He'd never had time to protest or raise a hand in defense. The shock wave of impact had traveled up through my elbow as the lock reverberated off the side of his head. I hadn't hesitated, only brought the lock back down again with more force, feeling the dome of his skull crack and watching the blood pour through his hair. Brandon had taken a deep breath, mouth opening as if to speak, but any objection stalled as he snorted out a mist of blood. I'd hit him one last time before hopping on my bike and riding away.

While invisible strikes continued raining on the heavy bag, something unseen pummeled me. A quick jab made my nose sting and eyes water. My jowl pressed in against my teeth with the force of a harder right hook. I put up my hands to protect my head and retreated toward the stairs like a weak-legged fighter seeking the stability of the ropes. I stayed on my feet. If I collapsed in the basement, there'd be no ten count. My vision blurred, but I could see the imprint of fists on the heavy bag again. The canvas sank around the invisible knuckles, rotating as the beating continued.

A man stood on the other side of the heavy bag. He wore all white. A bright smock and wrinkled cotton pants that reminded me of the milkmaid's uniform but absent the chocolate smears on her denim. A trickle of blood dribbled from his right nostril, trailing down to circle his upper lip like a one-sided mustache. His head was shaved in the hurried fashion of the institutionalized, and his gaunt cheeks bore stubble, as if he lacked the responsibility to be trusted with a razor. There was some girth to him; the flabby, softening muscles of the bedridden lay underneath his shirt. The only part of him that never grew into manhood were the candlestick legs. I remembered the power in those legs from boyhood, the way they were always colt-fast as he rounded the bases of the baseball diamond. Even though I'd never seen him as an adult, I was looking at Brandon Flanders. Brandon Flanders eternally twenty-five years old, wearing the hospital uniform he'd died in when the aneurysm broke loose in his brain.

I bolted up the stairs, the clicking from the spinning lock and *thap, thap, thap* from the bag louder with each step I climbed. The man was gone when I turned to look, but the sound stayed right behind me, as if someone just a few feet away had turned the lock's dial, trying to crack my sanity the way one might a safe.

CHAPTER THREE

The next morning, I prayed Uncle Abbott's Mustang wouldn't start. As a kid, I used to sit behind the wheel of that 1973 Mach 1 and imagine myself in a Steve McQueen–style hot pursuit. The car felt like some conduit of freedom back then. As I grew up learning about the drudgery of outlaw life, the bright sheen of the red paint and black racing stripes dulled. I recognized the car for the vain luxury it truly was. Easy marks and rubes want flashy wheels. Working men like my relatives needed reliable, inconspicuous transportation.

I had ignored the Mustang after my father died. This neglect should have diminished it, but my father had spent his final years caring for the car the way a man might nurse a loved one confined to a hospital bed. He stayed in the garage for hours, the motor growling as he pressed the gas, fortifying the mechanical horses under the hood with promises. Despite this careful pampering, the car had been through a reconstructed transmission and a busted carburetor, and was an absolute lush for Valvoline. All the years sitting idle should've been enough to kill the damned thing, but when I sank down in the refurbished black leather seats and turned the key that morning, the car started right up. Listening to the engine, I couldn't believe I hadn't let some wealthy buyer take it off my hands, but something inside me still wanted to possess that final luxury. The idea of a rich collector owning my legacy was too much. Before that, I promised myself I'd total the beast.

—

The prison was a two-hour drive north, located at the top of a plateau that had once been a large mountain. One of the strip-mining operations had blown the top off and razed it bare of trees in their efforts to get at the coal underneath. Giant slabs of limestone protruded through the dirt like bone breaking through skin. Hard rains had washed away the remaining topsoil, taking the weak-rooted vegetation with it. Living in West Virginia my whole life, I'd watched the mountains eroded down by the men who inhabited them. The slow theft of resources was long over by the days of the Decline, along with any promises of restoration.

I pulled into the visitors' parking lot and waited. It was empty aside from two guards coming off their shift. They wore the starched-polyester uniforms with pride and stood next to their trucks, burning stubby hand-rolled smokes with an authority only granted kings. I'm sure that simply having a vocation was enough to lift their spirits. I rolled my window down and lit a home-rolled smoke of my own. It steadied my nerves after a sleepless night.

There were two possibilities for what had happened: either someone from The Lighthouse had staged an elaborate prank or I'd suffered some kind of stress-induced hallucination. The most troubling factor was the lock. I'd gone back down into the basement in daylight and found it on the floor where I'd dropped it. The blood was gone, and the dial didn't turn of its own accord, but it was real. Even my smudged initials remained written on the back side. I left the lock on my kitchen table, as unwanted a reality as a tumor clouding a CT scan. There was no sign of the man with the nosebleed; I searched each room with a kitchen knife just to be certain.

It hadn't been Brandon. I knew the truth about death the spiritualists and religious could never admit. Open a body. Remove all the organic machines inside like unpacking a suitcase. Take their weight and measurements. You'll see there's no place for belief in a soul. Organs have mass. Tissue has texture. Blood leaves a stain and smell. Where are all those quantifiable and documented aspects of the soul? Even the most frightening ghosts are just hopeful fantasy, a desire that something remains after our consciousness winks out. What I couldn't explain was the sensation of fists on the bag, the dampness of fresh sweat, and the sting of something striking my face. I'd felt those things, each one as real as the lock resting on my kitchen table. While my mind scrambled to explain this, I reminded myself that it didn't mean something supernatural. A logical explanation would occur so long as I didn't lose my reason.

I suppose the third possibility was madness. The specter of it lingered in my family. Despite a lack of diagnosis, my father's lust for crime had certainly been some form of derangement. There were days he would disappear entirely, leaving me with Uncle Abbott for so long both of us wondered if he was coming back. He'd always return with money and new scars, never offering a word of apology or explanation. I'd inherited the man's rage. Perhaps other ailments like hallucinations were now manifesting. Guilt-induced ghosts in place of Dad's werewolf urges. I might also have a tumor in my brain the size of a grape.

After I waited nearly twenty minutes, Uncle Abbott staggered out the front gate, wearing the only suit I'd ever known him to own. It was gray, wrinkled beyond repair, with a black ink stain on the outdated, oversize lapel. Uncle Abbott had married his first wife in that suit, and I felt certain we'd bury him in it. His face hadn't changed much over the decade. The scar bisecting his chin looked red in the morning air, and his eyes sank a little deeper into their sockets, receding as if blindness might be preferable to all they'd witnessed.

"Welcome home," I said as he climbed into the car. I handed over a pint of whiskey I'd taken earlier that week from Wildcat's. Uncle Abbott twisted the top off and took a long drink. A bit of the amber liquid dripped onto his chin and followed the tract of scar down to his shirt.

"Drive," he said.

We went a full five minutes without uttering a word. I couldn't think of anything proper to say. Some shared stories came to mind, but happy memories were so few it seemed false to mention them. I counted the cars we passed on the curving road. I've always played counting games with myself. These often have an incentive, a promise that a certain number will result in good luck. These desired outcomes almost never came true, but the real purpose of the game was distraction. Sometimes when fighting, I'd monitor my punches, force myself into delivering a few excessive blows on an opponent because I felt the bout must end on a specific number of strikes. A count made it beyond my decision—a quota to be filled like any other task.

"You look good," Uncle Abbott said. He'd finished a quarter of the bottle and hadn't even developed a slur. It made me wonder how a man could keep such a powerful tolerance imbibing only jailhouse hooch. He'd also held on to his ability to lie. I'd put on fifteen pounds of flab since my uncle went away. Appraising myself in the rearview mirror, I could see that it was plain my arms had softened. The skin under my chin hung loose, ready to elongate and dangle like a neutered hound's empty scrotum. My hands hurt.

"Let's stop for a drink. Get reacquainted."

"I came to drive you home. That's all I'm doing."

Uncle Abbott took another sip from the bottle. "I've been inside nearly ten years. Least you can do is sit down somewhere and share a drink with me."

"You don't need another drink. We can talk while driving."

"Maybe you need a drink," Uncle Abbott said. "It might get that stick out of your ass."

The truth was, I didn't really want to go home. As much as I hated admitting it, the scene in the basement had scared me. I thought about the lock waiting on the kitchen table. I saw the dial spinning. Blood leaking from the mechanism as it opened. I imagined showing Uncle Abbott the combination lock and trying to explain what I'd witnessed down in the basement. Better I drink myself to oblivion in some bar than endure that ridicule.

"A single drink. Then I'm taking you home."

We stopped at a place called Smith's Pub, a two-story building situated low on a wide curve off the mountainside. The owner had tried making the establishment look respectable with cream vinyl siding likely installed right before the Decline, but I knew a honky-tonk when I saw one. A surprising number of rusty pickups and battered Dodge sedans several decades old filled the parking lot—diseased things with engines full of mismatched spare parts, rusted frames held together by a combination of prayer and Bondo. The neon sign in the window was out, but a small gas generator hummed beside the front door. I thought the decay of the outside world would shock Uncle Abbott, but if any of this seemed strange, he didn't show it.

Inside, the lights were out, as I'd anticipated, but one of several orange extension cords snaked from the generator outside to the jukebox in the corner. Johnny Cash sang from its speakers for a group of men wearing either work shirts and jeans or overalls, along with a few tired-looking women. Cowboy boots tapped the floor in time with the tune while barstools creaked as the men shifted on top of them. I wanted to turn around and head out the door.

"This shithole will do," Uncle Abbott said. "As long as they turn the hick music down."

We sat on a pair of stools at the bar. Uncle Abbott watched the lone bartender. The place reminded me so much of Shannon's. The same men with nowhere else to be, sipping warm beer near its expiration date, all of them hideously aware that without the purpose of family or jobs, the truest human endeavor was just wasting time. That's something I learned when I first came home defeated from school. Those jobless days were filled with so many hours to ponder the fragility of my previously constructed purposes. Without them, I could see how flimsy those important lies we tell ourselves become. Not much keeps men from the bottle or the needle when that happens. I'd tried creating purpose with my rounds as a country doctor and was probably seeking another distraction with my search for the painter. Still, money was as real a need as water. That made any endeavor that produced a little cash worth my time. I just needed to keep the profits hidden from Uncle Abbott. He couldn't be trusted.

An old man in a weathered flannel coat approached the bar, set down his empty glass and a dented can of refried beans. The bartender took the can and placed it beneath the counter before producing a milk jug filled with clear corn liquor. He poured a finger of the home brew into the man's glass.

"Guess it's all profit anyway when you make your own."

Uncle Abbott didn't hear my words at first. He still stared at the bartender as if his eyes could smother the man. I repeated myself, and Uncle Abbott turned his gaze toward the dirty reflection of us in the spiderweb-cracked mirror behind the bar.

"We had the news inside," he said.

"Maybe you should've stayed inside, then. My power's been out all month."

"I did consider that. Three hots and a cot. Heat in the winter and AC in the summer. It's almost a shame that us crooks had it so good inside compared to other folks. Still, I needed out in the world again. Even if it's on fire. You hear things, but it's not the same as seeing the local businesses running on a barter system. It's all been a long time coming."

"How so?"

He gave me the look of one suffering a stupid child. "When's the last time anyone in this country had any real choice about anything? Do you think people would choose to work for a minimum wage that hasn't matched inflation in decades? Think people would choose insurmountable college debt if they didn't need it to earn half the salaries of their parents? People wouldn't live in rat-shit hollows like this if they had a way out. This is America. Only real choice has been Coke or Pepsi. And now people are seeing what this country really is."

"You think so?"

After a beat of silence, Uncle Abbott turned on his stool. "Did I ever tell you why I quit the mine?"

Uncle Abbott had dug coal for one year when he was just nineteen. I always figured that a penchant for easy money and a job that didn't involve subterranean labor were his reasons for leaving, so I waited on an explanation with the same skepticism as any of the man's stories.

"One day I was underground and passing the shift boss's office. We called it an office, but it was just a place where he'd hung up a curtain and made a tiny desk out of some crates so that he could rest while we did the work. I was on the other side of that curtain and heard him talking with one of the other bosses. The guy I didn't recognize was going on about how ingenious the little hideaway was and how our boss ought to get a raise for being such a smart thinker. Well, our boss said he didn't want a raise. The other guy didn't understand this. Everyone likes money, right? So he asks the boss man why he's got such a lack of ambition. And the boss says, 'My only real ambition in life is to work some poor son of a bitch to death.'"

Uncle Abbott paused here. When I didn't reply, he frowned and launched back into his story.

"I knew right then he was talking about me. I was one of those sons of bitches he wanted to work to death. I quit and haven't worked an honest day since."

"Good to see they're teaching philosophy inside," I said, but only because I didn't want him to know he made sense. There was no point in feeding his arrogance.

"You saying you still believe in choices?" he asked.

I shrugged. "Maybe."

"Did you have a choice when your dad and I took you down in the basement and made you a fighter? The bigger kids at school would've gone on beating you senseless. The only choice we had was to toughen you up."

The comment was meant as a source of solace. A way to move sharklike through life, secure in the idea that neither virtues nor transgressions matter. If I'd looked at my youth as an inescapable destiny, one where I'd been forced into those violent circumstances, perhaps I'd have found the same comfort as my uncle. Only I couldn't help knowing that whether programmed for violence by heredity or molded by my surroundings, my body still inflicted all that pain. I'd ruined others and felt pleasure doing so. Even if I had no other choices, I could at least choose guilt.

Uncle Abbott held out a hand. "Give me some cash, will you? I hope it still spends. I ain't got any canned corn to trade."

I handed over two crumpled dollars. Uncle Abbott rubbed the wrinkles from each bill on the bar top and fanned out the cash. Exposing the money in a place where men paid for drinks with canned food made me nervous, but I decided we'd be cool if I pretended it was the last of our funds.

"Hey," Uncle Abbott called out. "Is the only green around here that matters peas?"

Down the bar, a young girl watched us. The curly tips of her hair had been fried by a bad perm and dyed cotton white. Hip bones jutted out from under the pale skin visible in her low-rise jean shorts. She twisted on her stool and sipped from a longneck bottle of Coors.

"Get this lady another, and give us both a shot of that white lightning," Uncle Abbott ordered.

The bartender gnawed on a toothpick that he'd been digging into his molars. He gave me a look of warning to keep my shithead uncle in line and fetched the drinks.

"Awful nice of you," the girl said. "My name's Jane."

"Pleased to meet you, Jane," Uncle Abbott said, taking her unoffered hand. Jane tried pulling back, but his fingers coiled around her thin wrist like a snake constricting a mouse.

"It sure is nice talking to a girl like you. I just got out of prison, and a man needs to be around women. Don't you think so, Jane?"

"Yes, sir. My daddy said the penitentiary was the loneliest time of his life."

The bartender inspected the money and served the drinks. I downed my moonshine. It burned like hellfire.

"What did you go to jail for?" Jane asked. She didn't sound afraid or particularly curious, just trying to make conversation.

"I held up a liquor store."

Uncle Abbott had probably robbed over thirty liquor stores in his time, but that wasn't what convicted him. He'd been charged with kidnapping. When his dealer hadn't shown up with the agreed-upon product, Uncle Abbott put the man in the trunk of his Volvo with the intention of taking him back to the stash house. The cops pulled him over for a broken taillight and found the bound man stuffed in the space for the spare tire. Uncle Abbott said he was going to toss him out in the state park, but I've always suspected the man would've ended up with a slit throat, his remains weighed down with slabs of sandstone, submerged in the deepest pools of Cow Creek.

"I had a pretty decent job," Uncle Abbott said. "Worked construction. I lost a lot of money on the horses. For a while there, I was crossing the state line into Kentucky every weekend and dropping my whole payday."

I wasn't sure how much of the conversation was true. I knew Uncle Abbott liked to gamble, but my father had never said anything about Kentucky ponies.

"I don't condone gambling," Jane said, and produced a pipe from her purse that looked like something Sherlock Holmes might smoke. The scent of cherry tobacco filled the air as she lit it. "But I love horses. My foster uncle owned a farm upstate. He had this gray mare and an Appaloosa, and this one beautiful stallion that he let me ride. Its name was Chester, and he was wild."

"Are we talking about riding the horse or the old man?" Uncle Abbott asked, and let loose with a pleased chuckle. Jane deflated with the remark but didn't let it deter her from offering a scripted smile. She'd seen our money and played the game long enough to understand superiority and insults came with the territory. For some men, unkindness was a sort of foreplay.

"I rode a horse once, but it busted my balls," Uncle Abbott said. "Besides, you aren't in control."

"That's the point," Jane said.

Down by the jukebox, three men watched us. I'd noticed the big one in the middle glaring when my uncle flashed the cash and started chatting up Jane. Now the man was staring over his beer mug. He'd taken off his gray Stetson and laid it on the bar in front of him. I imagined a snub nose .38 under the hat, waiting for the man to build up enough liquid courage to use it.

While I was looking for the bartender, the door behind us opened, and a man came in carrying a mallard. He ordered a beer and set the duck down on the floor, where it waddled about underfoot. No surprise registered from the other patrons, so I decided the man and his pet must be regulars. After taking a long swallow of his beer, the man poured a drink down the duck's beak. The bird tossed back its emerald-green head, casting drops of beer onto the floor as it swallowed. Those seated around the bar laughed and applauded. The man, eyes hidden behind cheap plastic sunglasses, gave a deep bow.

"What's this, the circus?" Uncle Abbott said.

Once the novelty of the duck expired, Uncle Abbott rolled up his sleeves and pointed out his sun-bleached tattoos. He showed Jane the crooked barbed wire that circled his wrist and a bucktoothed rattlesnake curled around a misshapen skull. Jane encouraged him by rubbing the faded ink.

The big man down the bar put on his Stetson and came walking over. When standing, it looked like he wore football pads under his Western shirt. The thick cords of muscle around his neck didn't come from working out alone but from the kind of scrotum-shrinking steroids used on racehorses.

"This dude bothering you, Jane?" the man asked.

She shook her head. "No, Gary. He's a decent-enough guy."

"I just didn't want some lowlife hassling you," the man said.

"That's Gary," Jane whispered to Uncle Abbott. "He's crazy about me, but there's nothing going on between us."

I immediately understood that Jane had once fucked Gary. Probably a one-time mistake for her but clearly a night of transcendent ecstasy for Gary.

"Thanks for keeping the neighborhood safe, shit kicker," Uncle Abbott yelled over the music.

Gary came back down the bar, clenched fists swinging by his side. As a boy, I had thought of all violence as sudden chaos, a ritual-less debasement that robbed us of our better nature. Now I realized that fighting was a lot like fucking: There is the impulse. The fixation for flesh to meet flesh. Next comes the courage, the bravery to convince yourself to initiate the act. Often, it's a small gesture. An insult rather than a flirtatious remark. A push rather than a caress. As Gary retreated like a shy lover, my uncle called him back with a sharp tongue. A simpler seduction I'd never seen.

I might have intervened, stopped things before it got out of hand. Only I didn't want to stop it. Like any other voyeur, I wanted to see how far the two would take it.

Gary leaned close until his face was inches from Uncle Abbott's. "Awful big talk for such a scrawny old shit."

"I've broken the arm of a boy twice your size," Uncle Abbott said.

Gary rolled up his sleeve, exposing more bulging chemical muscle. He put his elbow on the bar and reached out his hand. Uncle Abbott began laughing, even gave his knee an exaggerated slap.

"What is this?" he said. "*Over the Top*?"

"I bet I break your arm clean off," Gary said, thrusting his hand forward.

Jane took a swig of beer. Her back bowed as she sagged on the stool and rested her elbows on the bar.

"I'll judge," she said, spinning the empty bottle.

The forgotten duck pecked at the hem of my pants. I shooed it away with the toe of my boot as the two men locked hands and waited for Jane's signal. She said, "Now," and both began to push. Gary's massive bicep swelled to twice its original size, but his sunburned face was only a little reddened from the effort. Uncle Abbott's cheeks puffed as he sucked in air. He strained hard, gritting his teeth until I thought the enamel might crack. Spittle ran down the side of his lower lip.

The duck tromped over my feet and slipped between Uncle Abbott's legs, where it began eating his shoelaces. My uncle tried edging it away with his other foot, but the duck wouldn't be moved.

Uncle Abbott's resolve weakened. Gary pinned his hand against the bar top.

"Damned duck," Uncle Abbott said and kicked the bird. The mallard tried taking flight, but its wounded wings were unable to spread before it crashed into the far corner, a small plume of talc emitting from the cracked drywall. Blood dulled the worn leather on my uncle's shoe. The bar went silent.

Gary punched Uncle Abbott in the face. The unexpected blow carried the full force of the man's weight behind it. I'm surprised it didn't decapitate my uncle, whose nose exploded, blood spraying out of his nostrils as Gary hit him again in the stomach with his left hand. Uncle Abbott fell and tried scrambling behind the bar, away from the kicks Gary administered, but a good shot in the ribs rolled him over onto his back. Across the room, the man in the sunglasses ran for his wounded duck. The bartender—who had been kneeling behind the bar, loading a sawed-off 12-gauge—stood and leveled the weapon at my uncle.

"You'd better fuck off while you're still able," he said. When I noticed the man's finger rested outside the trigger guard, I grabbed a can of creamed corn off the bar top and tossed it at the bartender's head. The gun clattered across the floorboards as he dodged the sailing can. Uncle Abbott scooped up the weapon. He managed to stand and rest against the bar.

"None of you move," he said, gesturing with the gun as he bled. "Where's the money?"

"I'm being paid in cans here," the bartender said.

Uncle Abbott pressed the barrel into the man's sternum. "All you've got. The same with the rest of you."

Patrons presented their wallets or purses. A few opened their pouches, revealing the empty contents. Meager wads of sweaty bills emerged from pockets. Uncle Abbott grabbed them with his free hand while I hopped the bar and searched underneath. Nothing but stacks of canned food, milk jugs full of moonshine, and two leaking coolers with beer bottles floating in tepid water. I didn't understand why my body was performing these tasks—I just moved fast, wanting the situation over with.

"There's no money here," I said.

"Grab one of those jugs," Uncle Abbott told me.

I retrieved two jugs from the mirrored shelf behind the bar. As I was clambering over, Uncle Abbott shot Gary in the left leg. The buckshot decimated his shin, collapsing the man like a felled pine. He lay on the floor, screaming, trying to hold the missing piece of his calf in place as his leg threatened to come apart. We ran for the Mustang.

In the car, Uncle Abbott chugged the stolen moonshine and tried stanching the flow of blood by shoving a bandanna from the glove box up his left nostril. I floored the gas, waiting for the empty rearview mirror to fill with the beaten trucks from the bar. Uncle Abbott fish-hooked his cheek and pulled it back to see if the kicks had loosened any of his molars. I watched as the white fabric and black paisleys on the bandanna were swallowed up in a red tide.

"What the fuck?" I asked, holding out a fistful of bills. I counted around fifty dollars total. Meager riches, considering an armed-robbery sentence could last a decade. Not to mention the man he might've murdered.

"I'm bleeding all over. We might as well have a little payback."

I looked over his wounds: what was soon to be a black eye and a bottom lip swelled to twice its normal size. I couldn't believe the way I'd jumped the bar. My mind had simply shut off, my body responding as if possessed.

"You are the stupidest man I've ever met. Half a dozen witnesses and your blood all over the scene. You're going right back inside, and I'll end up there with you."

Uncle Abbott pinched one nostril closed with his thumb and blew a clot of blood onto the dashboard. Afterward, he wiped his face with the back of his hand and used the only clean section of the bandanna to mop up the dash.

"Think anyone cares about a place where people pay with canned food? If you do, you haven't been paying attention. It's Wild West rules out here."

For a moment it looked as if my uncle had more to say, but he just winced while probing his fat lip. Uncle Abbott poured liquor over the bandanna until it was soaked, then dabbed the cut where his teeth pierced the flesh.

"You probably should've sold this thing," he said, rubbing the Mustang's leather interior. "But it sure does feel good to hear you turn the engine out."

CHAPTER FOUR

In the pulp novels I loved as a boy, the detective was always two steps behind. Our whiskey-dicked, burned-out protagonist rambled from one scene to the next, conning and charming his way past criminals and beautiful women who all lie. This went on until some falsehood revealed a half truth, and a large piece of the puzzle materialized, making itself so apparent that it couldn't be ignored even through the drunken haze we'd endured for the better part of the story. Eventually, fate would intervene. Some hired killer with a switchblade would show up to gut the protagonist, or a woman would fall into his bed with the whole story. She would spin it while smoking a cigarette, her naked curves hidden within his sheets. The formulaic plot was half the point; there's comfort in such familiarity. Since plot was constructed to lack all the absurd indignities found in life, things were certain to conclude nicely. In real life, no gorgeous woman gives you the answers while you lie satisfied next to the wet spot. In real life, no assassin comes to finish you off in your disheveled studio apartment. Endings come with boredom. You die a little with each concession.

Everything I knew about detective work was confined to those stories. I understood interviews and stakeouts, deductions made from clues, but where to begin my investigation? I had no clues to set me on a path, and no one from The Lighthouse would be answering my questions. I considered this dilemma while leading a semiconscious Uncle Abbott into the basement. My fear of returning to those rooms was overcome by the desire to leave him downstairs. I didn't want him near me, and the spare guest room and my father's untouched bedroom were both too close. I wanted an entire floor between us. Besides, I couldn't spend the rest of my life avoiding the basement because something bad had happened there. Each room of the house had carried ghosts long before I thought I'd seen Brandon. The times at the kitchen table when my father washed my cuts from fights at school, or the days when Uncle Abbott lay in his drunken stupor on the living-room carpet, the .38 snub nose he carried resting on the end table beside the couch. Those memories remained as vivid as if they'd happened moments ago. I didn't let them keep me from meals in the kitchen, and I still rested my morning coffee mug on the same spot of the end table where Uncle Abbott always put his gun. Why let one more occurrence keep me from going where I pleased in my own house? Better to remind myself it was just a room.

Uncle Abbott finally stopped dripping blood by the time we reached the bottom step. I placed him on the sofa, where he continued snoring, head lolling and dirty shoes grinding mud into my carpet. I fired up a hand-rolled smoke while watching him sleep. Things in the bar had escalated quickly, and I didn't like the way I'd slipped back into the role of loyal soldier. I didn't want to be like I was before—not just quick to violence but hungry for it. Of course, that's why the twins had hired me. Even if I was totally inept at finding their lost brother, they knew I was game for whatever might be necessary.

I draped a blanket over Uncle Abbott and went upstairs.

The lock lay where I left it on the kitchen table, only now it floated like an island in a pool of blood. The rest of the room looked pristine. No bright droplets dotted the floor. No arterial spray dripped down the walls. The fresh gallons should've flooded the cracks between the boards of the tabletop, irrigating the far corners before cascading little waterfalls down the table legs, but the blood remained in a perfect circle as if collected inside an invisible reservoir. Ripples spread across the surface like a placid pond disturbed by something breaking in the shallows. Rather than sink in these unexplained depths, the lock bobbed, the stainless steel gleaming as it floated.

When I'd left that morning, the dried smears of blood had flaked off the metal like old scabs. I closed my eyes and told myself all this would be gone when I opened them. There'd be no blood, no lock—nothing but the scarred wooden tabletop. When I opened my eyes, the blood was still there, but the lock sank.

Without thinking, I reached out, grasped the lock, and watched as my hand submerged to the wrist in the warm blood. Nothing solid met me on the other side. I didn't know how deep the pool went but felt a tug like the undertow of the ocean instead of the hard reality of my kitchen table. All of this was impossible. My fingertips should've scraped the polished wood as I plucked up the lock. Instead, my hand disappeared through the table, gone somewhere beyond the kitchen. There was only one certainty: if I let the lock go, it would sink and vanish forever. I should've welcomed the loss but held fast.

Something touched my skin. I tried to pull my hand out, but my wrist was snared, a current dragging my arm deeper until I was submerged to the elbow. When I glanced at my reflection in the pool, I imagined the visage of the scarred beast from Franklin's portrait. The same bald head and serrated teeth, with two fangs extending from its lipless mouth. I felt it watching from underneath the waves while dragging me deeper.

I braced myself by placing my other hand on the edge of the table, but regardless of how much I struggled, I couldn't break free. In another minute, I'd be shoulder deep, my nose inches from the blood. What would happen if my head broke the surface? What if my entire body spilled through the table?

I let the lock go and fell back on the kitchen floor. Blood spilled through the bottom of the table, splashing across my shoes and depositing the lock close to my feet.

The metal was cool and dry when I picked it up. The dial began to spin, just as it had in the basement. Two full clockwise revelations before it landed on 25, a counterclockwise rotation before stopping on 40, and a cautious tick back to 15. The tentative movement reminded me of a child afraid of messing up and repeating the process. The lock popped open, and I tossed it away.

I sat completely still, my muscles frozen in fear, until each breath felt shallow, my chest tight with panic. The nearby lock lay at my feet like a coiled snake. I waited for the dial to turn again or for Brandon to appear at the head of the table in my father's chair, watching me while that crimson drip leaked from his nostrils.

I closed my eyes and tried willing myself back to reality. I felt the cold wooden floor against my slick palms. My father had installed the flooring himself after salvaging the discarded wood from an abandoned house on Selby Hill. He'd worked all summer, tearing up the prior linoleum and taking extra time to revarnish the wood. It was the hardest I'd seen the man work at anything. My bare feet had traveled over the planks my entire life. I knew it well. Rubbing the wood grain, I believed it might pull me out of the nightmare and back to sanity, but I couldn't discredit the blood staining it. The coagulation had already begun, the slickness of the thick coating drying on my hands.

I didn't know much about hallucinations, but if that's what I was experiencing, it contained a multitude of sensations. I took in all the sensory information: The slaughterhouse smell of the blood. The cold metal and weight of the lock when I picked it up. I suppressed a brief urge to put my finger in my mouth to see if I tasted the blood. I'd almost convinced myself that the scene in the basement had been a waking dream. Now the impossibility of my circumstances was undeniable.

I took the lock and hit it hard against the kitchen wall. It left a tiny dent in the drywall.

What does one do when faced with losing one's mind? In a sense, why do anything? The person I was would soon be gone, lost entirely to a world of fabricated paranoia so deep that I wouldn't recognize myself. The one redeeming factor seemed to be that I was aware I must be going insane. Did that mean I had a chance of saving myself? I didn't know. Fear or doubt or maybe the decline of my rationality wouldn't allow me to clinically analyze the situation.

I wouldn't permit myself to believe I was haunted. A true supernatural experience would break not only my knowledge of the body but also all other natural laws. If ghosts were real, who said that any of the other certainties remained? Gravity might also cease holding us to the earth, or I might spontaneously flower like buds on a tree. Anything—wondrous or horrific—might be possible. Better my mind be broken than the whole world lost in uncertainty.

I thought of the sudden violence in the bar, the way Uncle Abbott blew off Gary's shin with a quick pull of the trigger. Beating Brandon with the lock had required so much effort and energy, a physical labor that left me soaked in sweat the same way I'd been drenched in the bottomless pool of blood moments ago. Disfiguring a man shouldn't be so easy. I hadn't pulled the trigger, but I hadn't stopped my uncle either. The whole way home I'd been worried about retaliation. We'd spent enough time drinking at the bar to be identified, and the Mustang alone made us easy to trace. Perhaps the stress of waiting for vigilantes to hang us from the nearest tree had manifested the blood on my table? Maybe this was shock-induced PTSD? Only it didn't explain the lock.

Just like the buckshot tearing through Gary's flesh and bone, the lock was real.

Hot tears clouded my vision. I hadn't cried in years. Not since I lost Gabrielle. My father had always rewarded tears with pain. "A real reason to cry," he used to say. But looking at the lock, I couldn't stop their flow.

Fear and self-pity gave way to a new wave of panic, and suddenly the kitchen made me nauseous. I climbed to my feet and staggered outside just as I spewed vomit across the front porch. I leaned against the banister, crying until the effort left me exhausted. The night was quiet, all owls and coyote songs silenced by my wailing. I waited awhile, catching my breath and collecting myself before going back inside.

I retrieved a plastic grocery bag, tied the lock up inside, and placed the parcel in the empty sink before I fetched a mop. Halfway through mopping the floor, I wondered if I should go wake Uncle Abbott. If he saw the carnage in the kitchen, would that prove it wasn't madness? I didn't know which I was more afraid of: the idea that all these occurrences might be hallucinations or that something unexplained was happening in my house. I wouldn't sleep that night. Not with only five hours till dawn. I finished mopping and retrieved a canvas bag for the lock. Even wrapped in the plastic, I didn't want it traveling inside my coat pocket.

—

The Sergeant William H. Campbell Bridge was one of two bridges that connected downtown Coopersville to what locals called the Island, an isolated little patch of land just big enough for Coopersville High School, our football field, and the baseball diamond, whose lack of a proper left field kept it from reaching regulation size. Not only was the bridge named after the sergeant but Campbell had been further immortalized as the face of the doughboy statue on Coopersville High's front lawn. Locals old enough to remember their parents' stories said the sergeant was a great war hero. He'd charged across no-man's-land and attacked a German machine-gun position that had been massacring his platoon for days. The sergeant eliminated most of the enemy forces with sniping techniques acquired during a boyhood spent hunting squirrels in the Coopersville mountains, but he eventually succumbed to shrapnel wounds from a grenade.

After the Second World War, the city council decided to honor all our veterans and chose Sergeant Campbell's face for the statue. Something about the bronze soldier's stare had frightened me when I was young. Those flat, dead eyes seemed like they wanted to communicate a crucial truth. I wasn't passing the monument that morning, but sleep deprivation and the lock had silent warnings on my mind.

Copper Creek flowed beneath the sergeant's bridge. When I was a kid, it was a popular fishing spot, full of brook trout. Now the previously high surge had been reduced to a shallow trickle that could barely be called a creek. Some areas dried up completely in the summer months, the evaporation exposing the copper-colored bedrock that gave the tributary its name. After the Decline came to Coopersville, migrant drifters erected a small tent city beneath the bridge. On more than one occasion, the local police tried dispersing the squatters, but they only returned in larger numbers.

I descended the steep bank that morning, using a crooked branch to steady myself. Walking the well-worn path closest to the bridge might mean surprising someone and starting my visit off on the wrong tone, so I stuck to the muddy shallows filled with dry rocks, careful to avoid the slick algae-coated stones of the deeper pools. Scraps of cloth, wastepaper, and the occasional discarded syringe sailed by on the water. A distant garbage fire blackened the sky. Just below the charred air, I could smell the accumulated trash and raw sewage from people shitting in the weeds close by.

The tents I came upon were an amalgamation of styles. Store-bought, multi-person structures with sturdy zippers and mesh windows for suburban campers sat beside tiny pup tents preferred by hard-core outdoorsmen. These models at least looked resilient, built to keep out the worst of the rain and relentless sun. The rest could barely be called tents—just random pieces of fabric or curtain hung from string. The first good storm would blow them down like the hungry wolf in a child's fable. Even if the tents lasted the few weeks till winter, they wouldn't keep the occupants from freezing come the first snow.

A few boys sat huddled in a circle, poking something dead with a stick. As I approached, one of them stopped gouging and looked up from the morbid pastime. We made eye contact, but the child didn't seem frightened. Just brushed his bangs back with a dirty hand and watched me. The others stayed focused on what I finally recognized was a bloated possum. I was introducing myself when a man came out from behind one of the tents. He was a tall Black man who wore a long blanket draped over him in the style of a poncho. His eyes were obscured by a baseball cap. The hat was sun-bleached, faded, except for a sweat line of salt that had formed just above the curved bill.

"Inside," he said to the children. They dropped their sticks and scurried into the nearest tent. One boy kept watching me until the man put a hand on his shoulder and pushed him toward the others. The boy followed, glancing back at me as he left.

"What do you want?" the man asked. When his hands disappeared under the blanket, I raised my own in surrender.

"I'm not looking for trouble," I said.

The man removed a large homemade club from his poncho. Its handle consisted of a crooked piece of driftwood reinforced with black electrical tape. I remembered thinking the prehistoric-looking weapon would probably break on the first blow, but it would only take one swing to fracture my skull.

"If you're from The Lighthouse, I'll give you a head start back up the hillside. That's more of a fair chance than your lot gave us."

He was trembling now, voice wavering like a child finally standing up to some long-suffered bully. I knew all about that. I'd played both the bully and the victim in my time.

"I'm not with them," I said.

Behind him, eyes peeked through holes in the tents. A few men, their puffy clothes hanging off bodies gone skeletal from hunger, stood framed in the openings. I stepped forward. Closer, I could see I'd misinterpreted the man's age. Hard days had carved canyons in his cheeks, reducing a young man's thick neck to a sinewy, deep-pitted hollow with a bulging Adam's apple. Desperation had added decades to the fellow.

"I'm Harlan Winter," I said, extending a hand. The man didn't drop the club for a proper handshake. "Maybe we could sit and talk a moment?"

I dug three cans of baked beans from the small duffel slung over my shoulder. It seemed a paltry offering, but the man touched each dented can as if presented with something precious. The obvious hunger made me feel ashamed.

"You'll have to excuse the precaution," he said, raising the club in an embarrassed gesture. "We've had some security problems."

The man, who introduced himself as Arthur, led me through the camp. None of the others came out to greet us, but the sound of hushed conversation buzzed among the maze of tents. The occasional cooing or cry from a small child broke the quiet. I understood that Arthur was the leader of this community. As he guided me to a large firepit constructed on the outskirts, I saw the burden of that responsibility pressing down on him. Arthur sat on one of the large rocks that circled the fire, retrieved a black cauldron that hung above the coals, and opened the first can of beans.

"You know how to start the fire?" he asked.

It had been years since I'd built a campfire, but I figured I could manage. I broke up some kindling and arranged the sticks into a small pyre. There was nothing but dirt under the bridge—no grass, leaves, or straw to use—so I found some trash paper and piled it on top. As I worked, I noticed several blackened humps scattered in the distance beyond me. A circle of stakes lay pounded into the ground around them, and melted wires, curled like dead serpents, branched out from the burned husks.

"What happened?" I asked, pointing to what I assumed were once tents.

Arthur didn't look up from the can he was opening. "We've had some intruders." He frowned at my progress with the fire and took the kindling from me. "Let me do that."

I opened the beans with Arthur's can opener while he tended to the fire.

"A few of the people here have gone missing. Some believed the community watch was involved. When they went to the church, asking about their loved ones, The Lighthouse decided we were a threat. That red-bearded giant burned the tents to scare us."

Arthur didn't have a lighter. Instead, he took two small pieces of flint from a burlap bag in his pocket and struck the stones together, showering orange sparks over the crumpled paper. The combustion happened slowly, the initial reaction nothing more than a smoldering that I thought the wind might extinguish until I saw the faintest flame. Arthur cupped his hands around that infant fire and blew cautious breath from pursed lips. The flame rose with the offered oxygen. Arthur didn't rush. He continued nurturing the fire until the kindling crackled. Watching was like looking into a time forgotten, as if we were sitting in a cave when the first men discovered the power to create precious heat. But we weren't living at the start of something. Instead, it was a reminder of how far we'd been reduced.

Once the flames had grown to a decent size, Arthur reached for the first can of beans. I handed them over, and he dumped the contents into the pot, then hung it back over the fire while I worked on the other cans.

"Why would people think The Lighthouse was involved?" I asked.

Arthur dumped the next can in and stirred the beans with a bent spoon.

"Logan is more highwayman than preacher. That red-bearded bastard has been known to waylay people and steal their goods. Others say they abduct people. I don't know about the fires in town, but they started the ones here."

Arthur tasted a spoonful of beans. He stood from his crouched position over the fire and walked to one of the nearby tents.

"Benjamin, wake up," he called out. Moments later, a young boy emerged, wrapped in a threadbare blanket, sneakers rotting off his feet as he stood, rubbing the sleep from his eyes. The drowsy demeanor vanished once the boy smelled the beans. Arthur came forward with the pot, which was steaming like a priest's censer.

"Take it around to the others," Arthur instructed. "Make sure you share. Even with those you don't like. Promise?"

Benjamin looked sullen but gave a respectful nod. Arthur watched him go, then opened the flap on a large canvas tent nearby. "Let's talk inside," he said, gesturing for me to enter first. "I've got a feeling the others might not need to hear this."

Inside, the tent smelled of split spruce and sycamore. A stack of firewood rested in the far corner, along with a small hatchet. Tree sap had hardened, creating little amber-colored pearls atop the logs. I found myself looking at them to avoid staring at the dirt floor and matted blankets heaped in the opposite corner. Arthur must have slept swaddled in the thick quilts. There were no other personal possessions. No books or photographs. No clothing or trinkets meant to remind the man of days past. Arthur waited at the entrance with his hands on his hips, his posture one of embarrassment over the surroundings.

"It's hardest here for the young ones," he said. "A few days ago, I caught Benjamin fighting another boy over a cigarette. Even if things get back on track, there's a whole generation who will never fit in. A person can't reenter a society he's never been part of."

When I sat down, the dirt floor felt cold through the fabric of my jeans. I imagined sleeping on that ground, bundled in blankets to ward off the chill. Such misery reminded me of my nights in the basement. On evenings when I hadn't fought with the enthusiasm they'd expected, Uncle Abbott and my father would lock me down there in the dark. Sleep had been impossible no matter how tired the exercise had left me, so I'd grope for the heavy bag and spend a few more hours beating it. Whenever my fists connected, I felt braver and more able to defend myself against whatever imagined horror frightened me that night. Sitting in Arthur's tent, my hands ached from the memory.

"The beans were a nice touch," Arthur said, smiling to let me know the coming criticism was friendly. "But I get the feeling this detective stuff is new to you."

"We're all doing odd things for money," I admitted.

"Well, why don't you tell me who you're looking for?"

"A young man named Franklin and maybe his girlfriend, Alice. They might not be together, and they might be using different names."

Arthur nodded. "We get a lot of drifters. Some are loners, others have families. Not too many young lovers. Got a picture?"

I showed him the copy of Melvin's Polaroid I'd snapped with my phone.

"Yeah, those two were here."

Were here. The past tense made me want to spit curses, but at least I'd established a trail.

"How long ago?" I asked.

"A few weeks. They only stayed a couple days." Arthur took a tiny log from the stack and ran his hands over the knots in the wood. His calloused thumbs picked at the bark while he contemplated the details. "Things were bad for those two."

"What do you mean?" I asked.

"There's only one kind of bad between two young people like that. They were falling out of love. Or at least, she was falling out of love with him."

"Tell me what happened."

"The man arrived first. I could tell he was on the run from something, but that's not new. Not these days. He kept to himself. Stayed in a tent we loaned him and painted. Didn't bother anybody. The girl showed up a day or so later. I don't know how she found him. She was deep into a bender. When you've seen it as much as I have, you can tell with a glance. I'm a drunk. Spent maybe a solid decade drinking."

"What about the man?" I asked.

"Sober as a judge. He spent the night just trying to take care of her, but you can't manage someone that far gone." Arthur grinned. It was the shy smile of a man who'd once been a burden and was glad he survived it.

"I got the feeling it was a reunion," Arthur continued. "Like they'd been separated for a while. Neither one of them left the tent during the day. I heard them talking a bit. Loud whisperers, you know. Arguing under their breath. They didn't come outside until late the next night while everyone else was asleep."

Arthur kept peeling long strips of bark off the log until the scraps collected in his lap like fallen confetti.

"How much of this you need to hear?" he asked. "I mean, aren't they entitled to a little privacy?"

"Nothing you say leaves this tent. You've got my word."

"I'm not a snoop. I want you to know that. I leave people be, but she looked so sick I decided to be close to their tent that night. When they started fighting again, it was over the paintings. She wanted him to stop. You could tell she'd tried everything. One of those nights where you beg, threaten, and scream. Anyway, I was just about to leave them alone when I heard the slap. Loud as a tree branch breaking. She came out of the tent carrying some of the canvases and tossed them on the coals of the cook fire."

I imagined Alice in the firelight, shadows dappling her bare arms as she held the canvases against her chest, tears running and hair lashing.

Franklin reaching for the artwork the way a man might grasp for a stolen child. The whole camp would be watching.

"He tried to save the paintings. Reached right into the flame and pulled them out, but it didn't do much good. They went up fast, and she was still pulling at him, trying to keep the fool from burning himself." Arthur paused again. "I'm a little ashamed to go into the next part."

"You're doing fine."

"He hit her. A couple of us held him down while he cursed her. It took three of us to restrain him. You know that story in the Bible where the guy wrestles the angel? That's how he fought. Like he wasn't even human."

"What was Alice doing during all this?"

"She wandered off. I never saw her again."

"You didn't send anyone after her?"

Arthur shrugged. "I just assumed she needed a minute to herself. I didn't know she wouldn't be back."

"Are you sure she didn't circle back around?"

"I spent the next few hours sitting in the tent with him. Something must have happened to her."

"Why do you say that?"

"Anyone could see she really loved him. Even after the slap."

Hearing the story, I felt a brokenhearted camaraderie with Franklin. I hoped that Alice didn't really love him. Finding out he'd pushed the woman away would be more painful for him than any lost art.

"Did they leave anything behind?" I asked.

"Just some clothes and food. I redistributed it among the people here."

"Is there anything else you can think of that might help?" I asked.

"There was one other thing. He was talking crazy, so I didn't think much of it . . ."

Arthur faltered.

"Go on," I said. "You're doing good."

"Franklin said she couldn't burn them all. It struck me as an odd thing to say. There weren't any more paintings here."

Since I'd brought along my medical bag, I spent over an hour making my rounds in the camp. I treated some old folks with ragged coughs and slathered one young boy's poison ivy with cortisol cream. There were others too sick to be helped, those in need of antibiotics or medicines I couldn't acquire without a license. I did my best with home-brewed remedies before explaining to the families that proper treatment meant a hospital, but I could tell they wouldn't comply by their vacant looks as I gave my instructions. I didn't blame them. It was news they didn't want to hear. Just another tragedy they couldn't prevent.

I strolled past the burned tents on the far edge of the camp, crossed the shallows of Copper Creek, and climbed up the side of the mountain. Without one of the many hiking trails that crisscross through the Coopersville woods, my progress was a slow ascent, anchoring myself on nearby trees as my feet slipped on the generations of fallen leaves that carpeted the forest floor. I found a well-trodden path near the crest of the mountain and followed it deeper into the woods. By the time I stopped to rest, I was lost, just like I'd intended. No landmarks gave any clue as to my location, but I wasn't worried. All I needed to do was walk downhill. Once I reached flat land, I'd find some semblance of civilization.

I rested against a rotten maple tree and took the plastic-wrapped lock from my doctor's bag. The metal felt cool through the thin plastic, but I was still afraid to open it.

School had trained me to look for the most logical explanation in a crisis and use evidence to eliminate possible illnesses. If I followed that rationale, there was no way the padlock was anything other than a piece of metal, and all the strange occurrences surrounding it were hallucinations brought on by the continued stress of the economic collapse, my uncle's return home, or residual guilt for the atrocity I committed when I left Brandon bedridden. Only I didn't know if I still believed that. The man of medicine I'd nearly become was still concerned about schizophrenia or masses growing inside my brain, but I couldn't shake the worry of an inevitable reckoning. A trial like those the prophets in Pastor Logan's holy books might be made to endure. This cold piece of metal could be my burning bush.

I tore open the plastic. No blood poured from the combination lock. The dial didn't spin. The lock remained inanimate, no matter how hard I willed it to show me its true nature. In the end, I fetched the garden trowel from my doctor's bag and buried it in a shallow hole beneath the birch tree.

And then, just to be safe, I paused on the way out and washed my hands in Copper Creek.

CHAPTER FIVE

Looking through the wrought iron gates separating visitors from the dirt trail leading up to the sanctuary, I could see The Lighthouse hugging the mountainside like a castle ready to withstand a long siege. I'd expected something more provincial. A little church house with whitewashed paneling and a few stained glass windows. Absent the steepled roof and missing all the ornamentation of other holy places, the three-story brick structure reminded me of barracks—something sturdy, thrown up fast out of necessity rather than labored over like most modern shrines. The only adornments were a pair of large crosses. One hanging on each side of the double doors.

I'd spent my life avoiding religion but assumed most congregations conducted services with handshakes and hymns, passing casseroles around in the fellowship hall once the prophesizing had concluded. Even without my confrontation with Logan, there'd be no such hospitality from The Lighthouse. Everything—from the locked gate all the way to the barred double doors—felt like a deterrent.

Eventually, a man came walking down the path. He carried a rifle slung over his shoulder. I'd expected something with a scope and bolt-action breech used for hunting, but this was a military weapon with a tactical sight. The curved magazine clacked against his elbow as he stumbled toward the gate.

"Can I help you?" he called out. He didn't come close, just stood watching me from a distance.

"My name is Harlan Winter. I'm here to speak to your pastor."

I was searching for Logan's card when the man unlocked the gate. He followed behind me as we walked up the path flanked by oak trees. Two more men waited in front of the church. The first was Redbeard. Outside of his truck, he was larger than I remembered from our conversation at Dairy Delight—well over six feet, with a barrel-shaped gut like a Prohibition-era boxer and swollen arms covered in red hair that caught the sunlight. Logan stood beside him. He smoked a cigarette, taking long, contemplative drags. His hunched posture made him look tired, but his blue eyes were alert.

"Mr. Winter." Logan smiled, exposing small brown teeth. I would've been ashamed of such a stained grin, but he bared them with pride. "I prayed you'd see reason."

Spice from the man's aftershave merged with the acrid smoke of his cigarette. I decided the pastor's smile was the most unnatural thing I'd ever seen—the sort of smile an alien might offer if attempting a human gesture.

"I don't know where those kids are," I lied. "I'm here because I'm looking for their brother, Franklin."

Redbeard's hands clamped into fists. Logan just shook his head. His previous smile melted away.

"Did those siblings of his put you up to this?"

"Why would they do that?" I asked.

Logan shrugged. "Brothers and sisters often love one another unconditionally. It's a terrible trial, unconditional love—one of God's hardest requirements of us. But He wouldn't ask us to follow a standard He doesn't keep Himself. Our Lord loves every single soul smoldering in hell. Each and every last one. If He can manage that, surely we can love our enemies."

The sermon didn't surprise me. Backwoods preachers traffic in a bizarre mix of conversation laced with anecdote and lesson. There's no other person on earth whom people allow such intrusions as a man of faith. They're given almost infinite leniency for commenting on most privacies, offering unsolicited advice on anything they please.

"Forgive me. Without a congregation, I miss the opportunity to share the Lord's word."

"You consider those kids enemies?" I asked. I didn't want that little slip of the tongue lost in another tangent.

"Anyone who defies God is an enemy. It doesn't mean we aren't supposed to love them. Or try and save them. Like I said, God even loves the condemned. Even though they've turned their back on Him, He didn't want damnation to be their fate."

"I don't think anyone deserves that kind of pain eternally."

Logan nodded. "It's not our place to question. Of course, people feel entitled to answers during days of tribulation. It's something I went through myself after my father died. These are the times when Satan is most powerful, when he can whisper falsehoods in your ear and weaken your resolve. Times of tribulation are when faith matters the most."

Redbeard nodded at these assertions like he might contribute a "hallelujah."

"I'm not concerned about souls," I replied. "I just want to know about Franklin's time at your church."

"I didn't understand everything that was going on with Franklin in those final days," Logan said, and paused to ash his cigarette. "I knew the Lord was testing him, but sometimes my faith is so strong I fear I assume others share the same resolve. It's one of my flaws."

"I understand there was a disagreement about his art."

"That's true. I commissioned a series of paintings to unveil at our revival. I thought it might help rebuild our congregation. Something to get people interested in church again. Those paintings are still in the possession of his siblings."

Logan took a final puff off his cigarette and stubbed it out on the back of his hand. He didn't flinch as the glowing ember extinguished with a hiss and the scent of singed hair filled the air, just brushed away skin and ash as if he'd dirtied himself touching something unpleasant. Redbeard watched this without comment. I suppressed a gag, thinking of the pink blister that would soon bubble up on Logan's flesh. Around this fresh wound lay several similar-shaped scars. Logan offered another alien smile.

"A little reminder I give myself about the pain of hell. It keeps me on the path."

"I write notes," I said.

Logan motioned toward the sanctuary doors. "There is something I can show you that might help. Would you step inside a moment?"

The invitation would be my only chance inside The Lighthouse. I'd be watched closely, only allowed to see what they wanted me to see, but it was better than nothing. There was also the possibility that once inside, I'd never be allowed to leave.

I decided to take my chances.

The sanctuary was a wide room with rows of high-backed pews. Despite the darkness from a lack of electricity, the wood shone, each pew freshly lacquered with a coat of gloss so heavy it might ruin a worshipper's Sunday suit. On the high ceiling, a mural of the heavenly host circled a chandelier. None of the feathered wings were the typical dove white; most were painted the same iridescent shades of purple and green found in an oil slick. The rest were the vibrant reds and oranges found on tropical birds. Instead of carrying harps or horns, the angels were armed with golden spears. I wondered what foes angels would fight. The very suggestion of combat undermined the idea of something as omnipotent as divinity, but soldierly servants of God felt appropriate for The Lighthouse.

"Franklin painted those when my father still ran the church," Logan said, pointing at the angels. "When I asked him about all the colors in the wings, he said he thought angel wings should have all the hues found in the rest of creation. I'm afraid the things I have to show you aren't as beautiful."

The twins hadn't mentioned the mural. It was expansive, covering a large portion of the ceiling. Franklin would've had to work at it daily. He'd spent far more time at The Lighthouse than the twins had let on.

The front of the sanctuary had been raised to accommodate a small stage with an old piano and box for the choir. A pulpit, its front adorned by a carving of a lighthouse that shined its beacon across a tumultuous ocean, sat in the center. Behind this sat a raised fiberglass baptismal pool for washing worshippers clean. The setup must have cost a small fortune, way beyond anything the typical mountain church might accumulate passing the offering plate. Like the ceiling mural, just the quality of the craftsmanship was a reminder that The Lighthouse wasn't like other churches.

Logan ascended the small stage, walked behind the pulpit, and picked up a pair of gloves. He pulled them on, making his fingers into a steeple as he tightened the leather.

"I don't like touching these things," he said.

Logan ducked behind the baptism pool and rummaged through something unseen. When he rose, he held three framed canvases in his arms. He sat on the lowest step of the stage with the paintings in his lap. The pictures were turned away from me so that I couldn't view the images, but the sadness on his face gave me a good indication of what I was about to see.

"Before he left, Franklin robbed our savings. We had $10,000 put away. Enough to keep us self-sustaining and the community watch running until the Lord lifts this blight."

The revelation proved so mundane that I felt a little disappointed. I'd built Franklin up into some sort of a resistance fighter whose weapons were art and resolve. The idea he'd been nothing more than a thief saddened me. Regardless, I felt my stomach twist into knots at the mention of $10,000.

The money was beyond a reward. It represented salvation.

"We'll never retrieve all the money," Logan said. "All I really want is the paintings he's finished and to ask him about these. He left them sitting in the pews when he fled."

Each painting Logan revealed was a slight variation on the same monstrous theme Melvin had shown me, but there were enough inconsistencies to make an argument for individual creatures. The first demon had melting cheeks, curtains of skin falling off their jawbone. Noses were either absent or nothing more than a broiled bump that barely resembled a nose. In one painting, the creature's eyes were gone, leaving cavernous sockets. In the next, the burned beast scraped at his face with fingernails as long as talons. The only consistency lay in the mouths; the lips had all been burned away, revealing protruding rows of shark teeth.

"If you find any more of these wicked pictures, I want you to bring them to me," Logan said as he set aside the paintings. "We can't have these things damaging people's faith."

Despite the pious act, I didn't believe Logan wanted nothing more than to pitch his church tent and save souls. More likely, he'd stick hot coals to Franklin's feet and saw off fingers until the stolen money was retrieved.

"Why so upset over paintings?" I asked. "What do they matter to you?"

Logan pointed at the heavenly host circling above us. "Would you say those are just paint on the ceiling, or would you agree they have the power to persuade?"

"They're beautiful," I admitted. "But that doesn't make me believe."

"Franklin's portraits weaken faith. That's why he left them here in the pews to destroy our church, same as a bomb. It's my duty to stop that."

Logan stood to his full height. For a moment, I imagined the way he looked positioned behind the pulpit on Sunday morning.

"Somewhere, at some time, a piece of art has changed you," he said. "At the very least, changed an opinion, some inherent prejudice you didn't even know you held. Artistic ability is the strongest creative force on earth. Our ability to imagine and shape reality with our work, that's the one power we share with God."

"You'd hurt the man over a painting?"

"We don't traffic in violence, Mr. Winter."

"Don't ask for my help and bullshit me with the same breath. What about the burned tents under the bridge?"

Logan didn't flinch at the accusation. "Any members of my community watch who utilize violence would be punished. I don't discuss our private affairs."

The pastor approached the baptismal pool, stepped into the tub, and descended from my view. The gloves came sailing out overhead. They dropped like wounded birds on the steps. His jacket followed, tossed across the lip of the pool, where it hung like a black shawl. He sank into the waters and floated.

"Bring me those paintings if you find them," Logan called out. "You'll be rewarded."

I waited just a moment before leaving, inspecting the door's lock and finding nothing more than a common dead bolt. Nothing that would keep a man out if they really wanted in.

Driving through downtown Coopersville always made me think of Gabrielle. When I was young, I promised myself that if I ever met a woman like her, I wouldn't risk losing that love by bringing her home to the mountains. In the end, I'd returned alone as a punishment. Brought myself back to face my father and atone for letting lost love keep me from completing school. After I'd quit persecuting myself, I pretended that a man could still make a life in these woods—a meager existence, but a vocation and a family might be possible. Now I couldn't even remember when I'd stopped believing.

The remains of the Fleming building lay scattered in the far lane of Harris Street. The roof had collapsed in the middle of the night two months prior, and now the building sat with the fallen side gaping open like something decimated in a bombing raid. The cave-in killed three men squatting inside the old warehouse. Their bodies had lain in the street among the bricks for a full day before an ambulance and coroner from a neighboring town collected the remains. No one had even bothered pretending the building would be demolished; the county commission wouldn't allocate the money.

The Germans have a word for taking pleasure in the sight of ruins: "ruinenlust." In America, we're left constructing elaborate, false metaphors to explain the sickness creeping inside us while watching hubris crumble our homes. At least there was a name for the epidemic in some language.

I wasn't sure I believed Franklin had stolen the money. The Lighthouse certainly had some cash stashed away, but $10,000 seemed like an absurd amount. Why would Franklin stay in a tent under the bridge with all that cash? Didn't make sense. Did his siblings know about the theft? It seemed a more promising payday than selling his art to an outside collector. Maybe the twins didn't want him back at all? Maybe they just wanted to find the money?

I was too tired to concentrate. Whenever I squeezed my eyes closed, I saw a flash of those monstrous jaws from the paintings or the lock oozing blood. I imagined myself with the same row of crooked fangs as the beasts from Franklin's paintings. This demonic doppelgänger smiled back at me in the rearview until I looked away and rubbed a finger over my flat front teeth.

I remembered the wraith Shannon had mentioned outside Wildcat's. I drove over, parked in the lot, and walked around the building to the side with the graffiti. Not exactly a demon. The hooded wraith smiled a skeleton smile and reached out toward me with bony fingers. An exposed rib cage peeked through tatters in the torn robe, but what drew my attention were the large wings sprouting from the creature's back. Not the scaled wings of a dragon—these were soft, feathered wings rendered in the same colors as the angels in The Lighthouse's chapel. Weren't demons just fallen angels? What was the true separation between the two? I wasn't sure but felt certain this was more of Franklin's work. Even with spray paint used in place of brushstrokes, it seemed like a chapter from the same story.

CHAPTER SIX

At home, I parked in the gravel drive and spent a moment resting in the truck, fortifying myself against whatever waited inside. I imagined the lock on the kitchen table, somehow transported from the mountain grave where I'd buried it, the numbers spinning independent of touch and blood dripping from the tip of the dial like milk from a nipple. All of this had begun after I saw the first of Franklin's paintings. I didn't understand how, but some connection existed between the art and what I begrudgingly thought of as hauntings. It was simply too great a coincidence to ignore. The real test would be Uncle Abbott. He'd been home alone all day. If nothing had occurred in my absence, perhaps that proved I was crazy.

I'd half expected those weary trucks from the bar to be waiting when I crested the hill, the men leaning on fenders, shotguns cradled in their arms, and a beaten Uncle Abbott kneeling in the yard, waiting to be executed alongside me. Perhaps Deputy Smith and that little black notebook she carried, chewing the end of her pen as she came up on the porch to ask us about where we'd been last night. The visit wouldn't have been out of the question. She might stop by just to warn Uncle Abbott that his first slip would land him right back in the penitentiary.

I couldn't find my uncle upstairs, so I descended into the basement. Uncle Abbott stood in the center of the room, shirtless, sweat running down the slope of his bent back as he leaned over a sledgehammer, trying to catch his breath. A large pair of headphones covered his ears. I recognized them as the noise-canceling earpieces my father had worn when blasting a safe. With them on, Uncle Abbott didn't hear my approach.

As I reached for him, I noticed the crater in the corner of the room. The hole was maybe three feet wide, surrounded by pieces of carpet and broken hunks of the flooring underneath. The wood lay in long slivers like stakes for slaying vampires. He'd gone all the way to the dirt underneath the foundation. The dark earth lay in a mound next to a discarded shovel.

I snatched the headphones off his ears. When Uncle Abbott turned, his cold stare seemed like confusion. By the time I recognized the rage, his dirty hands were gripping the lapels of my coat. He pulled me close enough to smell the sour mash on his breath.

"Where is it?" he said.

"Where's what?" I sputtered.

"The fucking money. What'd you do with all my money?"

"I don't know what you're talking about," I said. I grabbed his wrists and tried prying free but couldn't hold on to his mud-slick arms. A push sent me stumbling back until I collided with the wall. Uncle Abbott picked up the sledge. I thought he'd swing, exploding my teeth through the back of my head, but he just gripped the hammer.

"Before I went away, your father and I buried my cash under the floor. Right over there, in a length of plastic pipe. What happened to it?"

My father had replaced the basement flooring to make some foundational repairs two years before he died. Now I knew that was just bullshit to cover up his theft. I wondered what he'd done with the cash. There'd been no extravagant spending and no stocking up on essentials as the economy tanked. Probably just burned through it. A final self-serving act he wouldn't live to atone.

Uncle Abbott collapsed onto the nearby couch.

"I shouldn't be surprised," he said. "My brother always was a selfish shit."

"And you're not?" I can't explain why I defended my father. Maybe a perverse love remained. The kind of insidious loyalty that makes us delude ourselves.

"You think you remember the worst, but you don't know the half of it."

I remembered enough. Beatings from both of them in that very basement. Smacks across my mouth whenever my footwork had weakened as I circled the heavy bag. I recalled punching and punching until the muscles in my arms felt as heavy as stones. One look at Uncle Abbott let me know similar memories bubbled to the surface of his mind. I knew if I stayed quiet, he'd speak first. As much as I wanted to remain apathetic, I felt myself needing the coming story. I wanted just a hint of truth about my father. Something not grown from local legend or lies.

"When we were boys, your father always did well with the girls. So well that it became a kind of game. Less about liking pussy than stacking numbers. Eventually, I guess knowing he'd had the girls wasn't enough. He started keeping souvenirs."

Uncle Abbott paused and removed a hand-rolled cigarette from his sodden jeans. He waited to see if I wanted the story to continue. Whatever he was about to say couldn't be called back. Afterward, my father would be known. If I wanted the rest, my participation would be necessary.

"What kind of souvenirs?"

"Nothing scandalous. Mom would've beat the hell out of him if she found a drawer full of panties. He had this little cigar box that belonged to your grandfather. After a date, he'd get it out from under the bed, hide something away inside, and then slip it back under the mattress. He caught me watching one day. Told me he'd beat my ass bloody if I ever opened the box. I waited awhile, but you know that feeling when you're sure to fuck up and just can't stop yourself?"

I'd had those feelings before every fight. Certainly before beating Brandon with the combination lock. During the worst fights, my scrotum often tightened along with my fists, as if my testicles were trying to protect themselves from coming kicks. We sense our own violent impulses as clearly as sharks sense blood in the water.

"One day when he was gone, I opened the box. It was full of earrings. Not full sets but a single one taken from each girl. Maybe close to thirty. An unthinkable number for a boy our age. Especially in a small town where people talk. I still wonder how many of the girls knew about each other. Maybe some wanted him more because of what they'd been told. I spent nearly an hour looking through those earrings. Recognized the little fake diamond stud from Elizabeth Bowen, the head cheerleader. The gold hoop that belonged to Jessica Clark, this gorgeous girl I sat near in English. I tried imagining his time with the girls. Not just who did what to who but how he'd seduced them when people knew his reputation. We were country trash from generations back, yet here were the earrings of girls from town, girls whose fathers our old man did odd jobs for, and still they refused to speak to us in public. If I'm being honest, it felt like a sort of victory. I was proud of him for taking something from those who had more than us."

Uncle Abbott flicked the ash from his cigarette. As the smoke banished the stink of his body from the room, I saw him struggling not to cry.

"At the bottom, I found a little hummingbird earring that belonged to Jenny Long. I'd loved Jenny for as far back as I could remember. She was this skinny blonde girl, freckled and lanky like a fawn. So tall. Nearly a full head taller than me. I didn't grow until a year after school."

Uncle Abbott sucked the cigarette down toward his scabbed knuckles. He pinched the butt between two fingers, then extinguished it on the bottom of his boot. The story wasn't finished, but he couldn't say more unless I prompted the conclusion from him.

"What did you do?" I asked.

"I sulked for a while. I hid Jenny's earring and had myself a nice little cry. One day my brother came home drunk, went into the box to make a deposit, and noticed I'd taken Jenny's hummingbird. I let him have the first few hits. Just cried while he bitch-smacked me around the bedroom. I didn't give the earring up without a fight, but your father was always the better scrapper. He knocked out one of my teeth before it was over. After that, he tossed the hummingbird in the creek."

I remembered my father hurling the paltry engagement ring Gabrielle had rejected out our back door. The stone disappeared in the wet grass, where its shine was indistinguishable from the morning dew. Most of my father's cruelty was hidden in the pretense of making me stronger, but occasionally a true sadistic streak surfaced. Once, I'd come home and found fresh biscuits warming on the stove top. My father sat at the kitchen table, slathering jelly onto the fluffiest of the batch, and told me not to touch them. Rewards, he said, weren't for little pussies who lost fights. He ate his fill and trashed the rest. Afterward, we went down into the basement and worked the bag until I puked up the bile from my empty stomach.

It wasn't hard imagining my father standing on the creek bank, my bloodied uncle pleading as his brother tossed the hummingbird earring into the water with a similar disregard for pity. Despite Uncle Abbott's propensity for lies, the story was probably true.

"I blamed him for Jenny," he said. "But I can't anymore. It's not his fault he was so greedy. If we'd had a bit more, your father wouldn't have needed to take so much." Uncle Abbott raked dirty fingers through his hair. "We need money," he said, looking in the hole. "I need to find a buyer for the Mustang."

"Not just yet," I said, but only out of obligation.

"You got a line on some cash? Something to do with this painter?"

"How do you know about that?"

"A girl stopped by earlier today to see you. We talked a little. Look, if you don't have any scores lined up, I don't see any choice but to sell the car. So why don't you let me in on it?"

I still needed an unsupervised look around The Lighthouse before I could move on with my search. Everything else was a dead end. My only hope was finding some piece of the puzzle inside the church. Uncle Abbott would enlist with the promise of cash. The Lighthouse would have plenty of valuables, but I still didn't trust the veteran liar. The sad story about the earring might be another fabrication to lower my defenses. On the other hand, who was better schooled in the art of trespass?

"Go upstairs and brew the last of the coffee," I said. "I'll be up, and we'll go over it."

It took maybe thirty minutes to fill Uncle Abbott in. We sat at the kitchen table and I laid it all out. I knew from the first he was hooked. While I took my time, enjoying the luxury of the last of our coffee, Uncle Abbott never touched his steaming mug. He stared into the dark liquid as I spoke, contemplating the joy of ill-gotten gains.

I left out a few details, like Logan's claim that Franklin had stolen The Lighthouse's savings and the fragile state of the painter's relationship with Alice. These omissions were more than just keeping secrets. Uncle Abbott wasn't a confidant. All I needed from him were the skills of a good thief.

"It needs to get darker," he said after I'd finished.

"I've got a few errands to run," I replied. "I'll be back to get you."

I left my uncle sitting at the kitchen table, went into the bedroom, and changed clothes. I selected a gray flannel shirt, fresh jeans, and a light jacket. Dark shades, but not the conspicuous all-black of a burglar.

The heavy clouds outside looked like rain, so I decided to retrieve a ballcap from my father's room. I didn't like how the scent of his sandalwood cologne remained—the smell sparked memories—but I needed a lid. I snatched a dark-blue one hanging from the bedpost, rolled the bill, and stuck it into my back pocket the way I used to as a boy.

I'd drive down to Wildcat's before meeting with Melvin. Slipping Shannon a few bucks from my advance might square things after I'd run out early the other day. She wouldn't want to accept the gift, but I knew she needed the money. Looking back, I might've actually believed that excuse. The truth was, I just needed someone who'd be happy to see me.

—

I smelled smoke before I spotted the flames. Nothing on earth smells like a house fire. It's the smell of burned hair, melting plastic, and torched carpet. Something that could never be confused with a celebratory bonfire. I turned onto the street, whispering a silent prayer.

The empty parking lot was bathed in a glow from the tall columns of flame as Wildcat's burned. Smoke erupted from the broken windows, the heat climbing up and scorching the shingles on the roof, which curled and twisted. There were no cars in the lot, but I worried about Shannon. I couldn't see inside for the haze. The intense heat evaporated the moisture in my eyes before I reached the front door, and I dismissed the idea of running in to make certain she wasn't trapped inside.

Something scuttled behind me. Bootheels crunched, twisting over gravel, and a tinny ping sounded as something metal dropped onto the asphalt. A hooded figure ran across the parking lot. I chased after them. They were smaller but much faster, moving with speed I couldn't match. I lost sight of them as we left the glow from the firelight but pursued the sound of boots slapping pavement through the darkness. Their short legs pumped hard, their compact body cutting the night air.

"Stop!" I shouted. Each breath burned. My chest tightened, and pain stabbed into my side like a spear. I wouldn't make it much farther.

The parking lot ended. My shoes squished, slipping in the muddy grass leading toward the mountainside. Everything built in Coopersville was threaded through the narrow valley; follow any direction long enough, you come to a steep hillside. The arsonist didn't hesitate. They hit the brush and moved deeper into the woods. I kept up for a bit, stomping over tree roots and tripping over unseen rocks. Eventually, I lost track of the figure weaving through the trees. I hugged a nearby trunk while I caught my breath. The night was quiet. No nocturnal animals stirred after my chase through the woods.

Back in the parking lot, I turned on my phone's flashlight app and searched for whatever the arsonist had dropped. I found a circular medallion with the same design as the medallion Pastor Logan had worn that first morning when he came to my house. I snapped a picture of it with my phone and dropped it in my coat pocket.

I dialed Shannon's number. The phone rang until it went to voice mail. I don't really recall what I said. Some rambling explanation of the fire, followed by a desperate plea that she call me back. I didn't realize I was crying until I hung up the phone.

I sat in the car and watched. There was nothing else to do. No fire department remained in Coopersville, and their efforts wouldn't have saved much anyway. I prayed that Shannon wasn't inside. If she was, I was too late to help. The roof finally fell in, releasing a high plume of flame that licked at the night sky. Now I knew that The Lighthouse was involved in the arsons. Only a member of the church would be wearing the same strange medallion as Pastor Logan. All the other fires had been residential. Wildcat's was the first business to burn. Was this some sort of puritanical stance against a place serving liquor, or perhaps revenge against Shannon for some unknown transgression? As far as I knew, she didn't have any grievances with anyone in the church.

The first few onlookers came outside. They stood across the road, watching the fire in a tight little huddle. One man removed his hat and wiped at his brow like he could feel the heat. The longer I stayed parked, the more likely one of the men would notice my truck. They might even come speak with me. I pulled back onto the road. The fire was burning itself out. The collapsed roof smoldered, more smoke and heat than actual flame. I allowed myself a moment to mourn the loss of all those old records on the jukebox. The crooners were already ghosts. Now the vinyl could join them.

I found Miranda Hill sitting on the front steps of Wyatt Grade School. She wore a man's denim work shirt and ripped jeans with her signature cowboy boots, the rattlesnake hide peeling from too many miles. Miranda didn't greet me when I climbed out of my truck, just concentrated on digging the last bit of dirt from underneath her unpainted nails with a stiletto switchblade. I liked the idea of her keeping the knife hidden in her boot, but she probably just stuck it in the back pocket of her jeans, unconcerned that someone might notice the protruding hilt.

"Melvin ain't here," she said. "He's been gone a few hours."

"Care if I sit?" I asked, pointing at the space beside her.

Miranda shrugged and closed the knife. Sitting on the steps with her made me jealous in a nostalgic sort of way. Most of Miranda's coming years were destined to be disappointments, but youth maintains a shred of optimism regardless of circumstance. It had been almost a decade since I'd felt anything like that.

I didn't bother mentioning the fire at Wildcat's. She'd find out soon enough, and I didn't want to distract from my intended conversation.

"Can I wait with you?"

Miranda shrugged. "You'll be waiting all night. He's gone off to meet that art dealer."

I'd decided their story about the New York buyer and his role-playing game was bullshit. I didn't know how exactly such transactions occurred, but a collector wouldn't come all the way to Coopersville in person just to acquire the paintings. Not when he could transfer the funds and receive the packages in the mail. The whole thing was nothing more than a fabricated incentive for finding Franklin and the stolen money, but I didn't say this to Miranda. Better to wait and see how much she committed to the lie.

"I went by the house looking for you," Miranda said. "Your uncle seems like the kind who can get things done. Maybe we should've hired him."

"I'm happy to walk away if you cover my remaining fees."

"As far as I'm concerned, you've already been paid too much." Miranda ground her bootheel into the step as if squashing an unseen insect. "Franklin's dead," she said. "Sunk in the deepest pool of Cow Creek or buried somewhere on the hillside. Melvin and I will be, too, if we don't get out of here."

"You really believe so?"

For just a second, I saw the scared young woman underneath the hardened exterior. The glimpse didn't last long. The blade flashed out of the stiletto as Miranda went back to digging under her nails. The knife reassured her. Only a moment had passed, but she was already back to being hard as a peach pit. I wondered what Melvin would say if he heard his sister talking that way. Probably nothing. I got the impression she was the leader. Not the type to emasculate him in a place where he needed to be perceived as in control but definitely calling the shots behind closed doors. I tried not to be too judgmental of her callous comment. Hunger hardens people.

"Logan said he'd pay me if I found Franklin," I told her.

"He's saying that to throw you off his scent."

"You've got it all figured out," I said, rising off the step. "I need to see the paintings again. Do you mind?"

Miranda just shrugged and concentrated on her nails.

I traveled down the hallway toward the art room. I wanted to compare the first portraits with the paintings Logan had shown me while they were fresh in my mind. Answers to Franklin's obsession were somewhere on the canvas. With enough time, I might uncover the mystery. I stepped over an oboe case and looked through the stack.

Most of the demons were nearly identical: lipless mouths; tears in the cheeks that exposed their fangs; and pitted, hairless heads dotted with scar tissue. The eyes alternated between solid-white fields absent irises or no eyes at all. Others had lantern-handle jaws or the pointy chins of Halloween witches. I stared into the empty sockets of one eyeless ghoul until I felt someone behind me.

I didn't smell Miranda's flowery perfume, the one feminine indulgence she allowed herself, and I hadn't heard the clacking of bootheels coming down the corridor. No shadows cast around me in the candlelight. I simply felt someone watching me.

Brandon Flanders's ghost brought none of the campfire-tale clichés. The room didn't chill and turn my breath to mist. No cold current swam up my spine, and phantom fingers didn't caress my skin. Despite being a dead man, Brandon had a physical presence. I smelled his body—not unpleasant rot and grave dirt, but the simple sweat of a man who needed a shower after a day's labor. He didn't float like a specter. He possessed a swaying physicality that only ended when he bumped against the doorframe.

Brandon stepped forward, and whatever spell rooted me in place broke. I backtracked, knocking several portraits over as he came toward me. I couldn't let him place his hands on me. It was enough to see him and withstand it, but I didn't know what would happen if he touched me. I tripped and put my foot through one of the paintings. When the canvas ripped, Brandon stopped his advance. His mouth opened, shoulders shuddering as he tried words after years of silence. I didn't want to hear his voice. Didn't want to imagine what message he might be bringing me from beyond death. Instead, Brandon raised his arm. In his outstretched hand, he held the combination lock. Blood poured from every seam in the metal. Slowly, the dial began to turn.

"Just tell me," I said as anger rushed up and swallowed my fear. "Just tell me what you want me to know, you undead fuck."

Brandon grabbed my arm with his free hand. There was tremendous strength in his grip, the cold skin more powerful than my father's grasp down in the basement. Brandon opened my hand and dropped the bleeding lock into my palm. Pain jolted through my head, and for a dazed moment, I thought I must be feeling the same pain as Brandon when I'd dashed his temple. I dropped the lock between my feet. It clattered against the paintings as I pushed past the revenant. I ran down the corridor and outside. Only alone in the approaching dusk, without Miranda on the steps to greet me, did I turn around and look down the hallway.

It was empty. No Brandon, no Miranda, and no blood on my hands from the lock.

CHAPTER SEVEN

When I returned home, Uncle Abbott was waiting at the end of the gravel drive with his coat zipped to his throat and a canvas bag resting between his feet. Rain had started falling after I left the school. The showers had drenched Uncle Abbott until his hair hung lank across his forehead, but he didn't seem to mind. He tossed the bag into the truck bed and came around to the passenger side without complaint.

The truck's interior stank of smoke from Wildcat's. I rolled down my window to let in some air, but the fire's essence clung to me the way a man clings to his regrets. I couldn't shake the feeling of Brandon Flanders's dead fingers on my arm. An intrusion on reality like that wouldn't have seemed possible just days before my hallucinations—or maybe now I had to admit they were actual hauntings—but I'd learned that expectations change drastically based on one's situation. Not long ago, I'd imagined a quiet family practice on the plains, where I cautioned old farmers about their blood pressure and spent evenings at home with Gabrielle. Somewhere along the way, I'd diverged so far from my preferred path that I discovered no paths are chosen. We just keep moving through life to avoid admitting how lost we are.

Uncle Abbott drummed on the dashboard and ended my meditation.

"Let's go," he said, urging me to put the truck in gear.

—

The nearly moonless night left The Lighthouse shrouded in darkness, but I still parked the truck down the hill, hiding us in the deep foliage of the mountainside. Uncle Abbott stood with his hands in his pockets, assessing the high fence in the distance.

"It'd be a bitch to climb," he said. "I think we can cut through the chain link on the side."

Uncle Abbott slung the canvas bag over his shoulder, produced a small flashlight from his coat pocket, and disappeared into the woods. I followed at a distance, impressed with the skillful way he moved through the trees. Each footstep came down softly on his heel, the toe of his boot making minimal sound as it crunched the fallen leaves.

After cutting the fence and stalking over the gravel path, Uncle Abbott worked on the front door's bolt while I kept watch. Inside, the sanctuary was empty. The previously bright wings of the angels on the ceiling were only shapes in the darkness, but the host still caught Uncle Abbott's attention. I walked past him toward the altar, peeking down each row along the way to make sure no one slept in any of the pews. There were no signs of a congregation at all. If members resided on the compound, where were they?

Uncle Abbott opened the door on the far side of the room, and I followed him down a long hallway flanked by doors on either side. There was nothing of interest in the first three rooms I checked—all identical in their scant layout, with only a round table, a few bookcases, and a whiteboard hanging on the far wall with partially erased Bible-study notes. Uncle Abbott shook open books and looked behind shelves for anything of value. Eventually, we split up. He continued searching the classrooms while I traveled down the hallway until I reached a large kitchen with black obsidian countertops.

I opened the pantry, expecting more food than I'd seen for months. Rows of canned fruits and vegetables, sauces and soups, stacks of hot and cold cereal, even canned meat and fish. Perhaps a stock of fresh produce: squash; zucchini; carrots; potatoes of the red, russet, purple, and golden varieties. I fantasized about lifting a head of iceberg lettuce with no wilt, of biting into an apple and leaving it between my teeth as I dug through a bin overflowing with plump grapes, but there was nothing inside the pantry. Not even a single dusty can remained. Where was the food, and where were the other members of the church? I leaned against the island and contemplated this until Uncle Abbott came into the kitchen.

"You need to see something," he said.

"All the food's gone," I replied.

"Come on," he said. "This is big."

I followed, wondering what could be more important than food in a time of famine.

Uncle Abbott led me back to the end of the long hallway and through the last door on the right. It was another typical classroom with rows of child-size desks salvaged from the elementary school. The names of prior students scarred the wood. A chalk-stained blackboard hung on the far wall beside a bookshelf covered with hymnals and illustrated children's Bibles. Uncle Abbott had slid one of the bookshelves to the side, revealing a door hidden behind it. A padlock dangled on the upper latch, already unlocked.

Uncle Abbott opened the door. On the other side, a set of wooden steps led down into darkness. The pungent scent of mildew and wet earth rose to greet us, but there was another unidentifiable odor underneath. I put a hand on the wall, steadying myself. The steps looked steep. The kind ready to break spines if you slipped.

"I wasn't going down any hidden passages alone," Uncle Abbott said.

As the flashlight's beam traced over the steps, it occurred to me that we didn't have to do this. We could simply leave and never tell the twins we'd found any secret door. But that option carried too much cowardice. If nothing else, my imagination would never accept not knowing. I told myself the tightness in my throat was only residual fear from my encounter with Brandon, and even that could be attributed to some subliminal property in Franklin's paintings. An optical illusion or some other type of trickery that made you see things after looking at them too long. I swallowed these lies, assuring myself the fear would dissipate as soon as we found whatever was stored below.

The steps proved even more treacherous than I'd anticipated. There was little room for my feet on each plank, my heel almost sliding off more than once on our descent. When we reached the bottom, Uncle Abbott shined the dull flashlight beam over the cinder block walls and dirt floor.

On the other side of the room, two boxes lay spread across the ground. Each maybe seven feet long, shaped like the antiquated coffins that might populate Boot Hill in a dime Western. Tiny holes had been drilled into the lids, and a chain was wrapped around each one, securing it closed.

A pounding sounded in the darkness.

"What the fuck?" Uncle Abbott said. The pounding reached a frantic pitch at the sound of his voice. The knock fell into a rhythm—a deliberate beat, beat, pause—that sounded almost musical. The nearest box rocked, and a waterless scream emerged, the voice reduced to a whisper by the heavy wooden lid. I dropped on my knees beside the heaving box and inspected the lock.

Of all the things already endured in the last few days, the lock was the hardest strain on my sanity. I'd expected a heavy padlock cinching the chains together but found the same model combination lock I'd used to ruin Brandon Flanders, the same lock he'd been haunting me with for days. I had no doubt those rehearsed numbers the ghost showed me would be the correct sequence to open the lid. When I touched the lock's cold metal, it seemed not just a replica but the same bloody weapon I'd hidden in the trash years ago.

Whimpers like those from a whipped dog came spilling through the air holes as I dialed in the first number and heard the click. I turned the dial counterclockwise, moving to the next in the sequence Brandon had shown me. After I popped the lock, Uncle Abbott and I pried the lid off together.

The man inside resembled a corpse. Matted locks of hair fell over his eyes and hollow cheeks, nearly coupling with the long beard grown during captivity. He was entirely nude, smeared in his own dried filth, with bits of crusted vomit clinging to his beard, no doubt sick from being trapped inside with his own stench.

Uncle Abbott stepped back, clasping his hands over his mouth and nose. I barely noticed the stink. I was too busy staring at the man's fingernails. I'd expected the claws of some creature from old-world legends, maybe even worn to a point from scratching inside the box, but the nails were immaculate. Free of any dirt, filed and lacquered. The hands themselves appeared recently washed—everything above his wrists in pristine condition; everything below slathered in layers of ancient dirt.

We were both afraid to touch him. I couldn't have articulated why at the time, but now I think merely looking allowed us the possibility that none of this was real. Our eyes might deceive us, turning shock and darkness into illusions more drastic than they really were, but once we touched him, I knew that broken logic would no longer hold.

I didn't have to make the decision. The man grabbed my shirtsleeve. His mouth opened and he muttered, trying to force an explanation through a throat gone dry with screams. In the end, he only choked out a little sob.

"Help me stand him up," I told Uncle Abbott.

We took hold under the man's arms and lifted. The load felt nearly weightless. My fingers poked through the coarse hair of his armpit and into his flesh. It reminded me of fragile things: infants, kittens, a baby bird fallen from a tree in the backyard I'd plucked up in my baseball cap one summer. Uncle Abbott tried standing the man up as we reached the stairs, but his legs remained too weak for use. My grasp slipped until I thought we'd never make it to the top.

Slowly, the man rolled his head. I couldn't gauge his awareness. At the time, he seemed more zombie than person. I stroked his back, soothing like a mother as we climbed the stairs. Freedom forced the atrophy from the captive man's legs. He took tentative steps, careful his feet didn't betray him.

The door at the top of the stairs swung open, and a silhouette eclipsed the upstairs light. I heard the pounding of boots coming toward us. It wasn't until the shadow grasped my shirt that I saw his red beard.

I anticipated the punch before I felt it—not the best shot for a man of such size, but a solid jab that burst my bottom lip against my teeth. My neck snapped back with the kind of jerk that severs consciousness as the brain rattles inside your skull. I raised my hands in defense, blocking the next blow with my forearms. A third punch plowed into my stomach, forcing a hot plume of acid up my esophagus. I was losing a fight I couldn't afford to lose. If Redbeard knocked me out, I'd end up locked in one of those boxes.

I pushed Uncle Abbott and the man from the box flat against the banister behind me and swung an elbow that connected with Redbeard's neck. The strike ached through the already sore muscle, but it was a pleasant pain. I'd almost forgotten the pleasure of throwing your bones at someone else, that violent connection of flesh on flesh. Redbeard tried wrapping me up into a bear hug, but I slammed my forehead into his face and felt something break against my hairline. Warm blood ran onto my cheeks. I grabbed a handful of the red curtain hanging from his chin and used his staggered momentum to jerk him past me, sticking out a tripping leg for good measure. Redbeard sailed downstairs past Uncle Abbott, who still clung to the banister alongside the man from the box. I worried Redbeard's girth might drag them down with him, but he missed both entirely, his right shoulder splintering the handrail as he rolled down the steps.

I grabbed Uncle Abbott with one hand and the man from the box with the other, and we ran toward the top of the staircase without looking back.

The smell couldn't be endured inside the closed cab, so we drove with the windows down despite the night's chill. The man sat in the middle of the back seat, swaddled in a large quilt Uncle Abbott had found in the truck. There'd been some debate on what to do with him once we started driving. Uncle Abbott suggested leaving him somewhere by the side of the road. He argued it wasn't our responsibility. We'd only created a witness to our illegal endeavors, and it was best we sever any further involvement. I needed to know why the man had been kept in that box. Uncle Abbott pointed to the nearly catatonic soul resting naked in the back seat and reminded me that we were talking about the man as if he weren't present, discussing options without any protest from this stranger regarding his fate. That, he said, told you everything you needed to know about the man's capacity for communication. In the end, I won the argument because I was driving and refused to pull over and put the man out.

My mind continually replayed Redbeard's tumble down the stairs. Just like all the fights from my youth, I'd taken things too far. Tripping him hadn't been necessary. Once I'd regained my composure and gotten ahold of the man's beard, I could've found a nonlethal way to subdue him. Now he was probably dead, and just like with Brandon Flanders, I had another stolen life on my conscience. Worse, the adrenaline still coursed through me. The pleasurable chemicals of victory flooded my brain until every aspect of the night drive felt beautiful. Everything was rendered glorious because my body wasn't only thankful to be alive—it was thrilled at having snatched life from another. No matter how much I wanted to resist it, the primitive parts of my brain reminded me there was reward in violence.

I waited in the living room with the man while Uncle Abbott went into my father's bedroom to find some clothes. We'd wrapped him in an old terry cloth robe with a tear under the left arm. I wasn't confident about getting the smell out of the furniture, as I figured the funk would seep down into the fibers.

The man had calmed considerably since we'd taken him inside, but he wouldn't look at me. His eyes stayed on his dirty feet and their long toenails.

"Are you hungry?" I asked.

He still didn't speak, but his eyes brightened with recognition when I brought food. I popped open a can of peaches and passed it. The man dug into the can with those perfect fingers. I thought about taking the can from him to put the fruit in a bowl, but he ate so ravenously I didn't reach for it. After the last of the peaches was gone, he tilted the can and drank the juice.

"Would you like a bath?" I asked him. "We could warm you up some water."

"No point in putting these on the way you are now," Uncle Abbott said. He stood behind me, a pair of corduroy slacks and an old flannel shirt folded in his arms. When the man didn't respond, Uncle Abbott lost his patience. "You gotta use your words, asshole."

Uncle Abbott left for the kitchen while I sat with the man. Once we were alone, he spoke, his voice soft, raw from his screams and otherwise lack of use.

II

Carson's Story

CHAPTER EIGHT

His name was Carson Mendez, and he'd been a musician before things went to shit. Nobody famous that you'd remember, just one of those singers who haunted local bars, playing a peculiar blend of folk, rock, and country miles from any city circuit where the larger acts appear. That didn't mean he'd never tasted success. He'd released three LPs on an independent label and sold one song to a famous up-and-comer, but that song remained a deep cut on an otherwise well-received album. The song got his foot in the door with some of the Nashville producers and began his career in songwriting, but the producers' consensus was that Carson wasn't radio friendly. Not only were the lyrics about rural poverty (something the producers in the still-lucrative cities didn't understand before the depression), drugs, and violence, but the songs he wrote lacked cohesion. Most were strings of rambling verses without a bridge or chorus. Because of this, the unaccompanied guitar ballads with finger-picked melodies had never found any radio-approved structure. The Nashville producers tried persuading him into attempting a more marketable sound, and it wasn't as if Carson were unwilling to compromise. The songs simply came out of his head a certain way. When he tried revising the tunes into something else, they disintegrated like sand poured into a river. Others might have grown bitter over this, but not Carson. His one well-known song, "Lonely Weekend," had left him with enough clout to tour locally. He didn't complain. In artistic pursuits, every little accomplishment was its own miracle.

The problem that had plagued him was the same as so many other musicians: he got saddled with a habit. The trouble had started in a Pikeville bar called the Barnyard when his bassist, Randy Court, offered him a toot of coke in the bathroom to keep playing till dawn. Carson had been a hard drinker before, preferring the numb disassociation of a good stone-drunk. It had been a way to clear his head after the buzz of the amplifiers died. Drinking made the road tolerable, the strangers he met more interesting. Considering this preference, Carson had been a little surprised by how well he took to the speedy white powder. Still, he'd kept it in check. Used it to stay up writing or keep going when they had miles of night driving before the next gig. If coke was a habit, it was one he'd thought he controlled fairly well. He had acknowledged that false sense of security as something most addicts told themselves. He'd been a drunk for years and certainly bragged that he could imbibe enough bourbon to kill a mortal man. If asked to look back on the moment when things inevitably went off the rails, Carson would recall the time a pretty little blonde offered him a bump off the bar and he snorted heroin by accident.

Carson had long believed that there was a difference between using and experimenting. There was also a difference between experimenting and an honest mistake. So, despite the pure, unbridled euphoria of the heroin, he told himself he'd made one of those rare honest mistakes and that would be the end of it. The high had been the best feeling of his life—better than love, money, or his most fulfilling musical accomplishment—but it would be chalked up as a one-time crazy story to be looked back on fondly. Like the time in Colorado when two brunettes sucked his dick at the same time after he finished a set, the first undoing his rodeo belt buckle before surprising him by pushing her friend down onto her knees with a smile. One of those unexpected once-in-a-lifetime experiences that he'd never see again. That belief was shattered by the time they were playing the next show and Carson found himself in the bathroom, snorting a fat line off the toilet lid with some skinny old man wearing a varsity letterman jacket. Within three months, the rest of the band had split, and he began thinking of himself as a junkie. That had been three years before the economy collapsed.

On the night he was placed in the box, Carson played for a group of disheveled men and women in downtown Coopersville. After busking on the street for hours, Carson left the guitar at his squat and went walking in the predatory circles of a man who needs food but is only focused on his next high. He'd completed his second round of downtown Coopersville when a poorly tuned guitar echoed from the balcony of a nearby apartment complex. A girl sat up there in a folding lawn chair. She strummed a Taylor with a tobacco sunburst erupting from the sound hole. The combination of instrument and woman was just about the most beautiful thing that Carson had ever seen.

"Hey," he called out. "Can I come up there and show you how to play that thing?"

The girl leaned over the rail. She had the sort of black hair that could have only come from a bottle, her skin pale and eyelids slathered in dark makeup that left her green eyes looking eerily like a cat's. She wore no coat against the cold from the evening's rain, but she didn't shiver as she stared down at Carson.

"I'm cold out here," Carson said. He didn't include "dope sick," but something about the girl told him she might be able to help with that. Skinny little goth beauties seemed like just the type who'd be able to secure some powder.

"If I let you up, will you really teach me to play something?" she asked.

Carson wondered what she was doing with such an expensive guitar if she couldn't play, but he didn't complain. He'd teach her the whole fucking Hank Williams discography if that's what she wanted. She'd probably prefer The Cure, from the looks of her, but roadhouse country was the best he could offer.

"I promise," he said.

"Come on up," she called out, and she tossed a key ring down to Carson. "The gold one. I'm on the fourth floor."

All this should've been alarming. What woman would toss her key to an unknown, unwashed man catcalling her from the street? If he hadn't been stupid sick, Carson would've felt the oncoming danger.

Carson found the gold key hidden in the mess of others and unlocked the downstairs door. The apartment building's lobby carried the odor of spilled alcohol. Urine and vomit hung about like loiterers on the staircase—the same smells that used to greet him on the road. Carson climbed the steps, realizing he didn't know which door to knock on. Not that it mattered much; he'd try them at random, if necessary. He was almost at the top of the landing when the girl stepped into the hallway from the first door on the right. She stopped his approach by placing a hand on his chest. Her tiny palm felt icy even through his T-shirt. Carson wondered how a living woman could be so cold.

"I'm not going to regret this, am I?" she asked. Carson thought he detected a flirtatious lilt in her voice. Her eyes, however, were dead serious. "I mean, you're not dangerous?"

"I'm a teddy bear," Carson replied. He knew he certainly didn't look it. He'd been sweating oily ice water, and his clothes were several days dirty. He smiled tight-lipped to avoid exposing his plaque-stained teeth. Nothing much could be done about his breath or other bodily odors; Carson wasn't overly concerned about them anyway. Most of his vanity had been lost, along with other carnal proclivities. Years ago, he'd have noticed a pretty girl with a guitar, and seduction would have been of paramount importance. Now he was too excited about the prospect of dope.

The place certainly had the appearance of a junkie's squat. The white walls and ceilings were stained a pale yellow from all the cigarettes smoked indoors despite a perfectly good-looking balcony. The furniture, what little was present, looked secondhand. The tattered couch cushions had been covered by quilts, the carpet the same stain-masking brown installed in every rented room in existence. Carson knew it would come a little more unraveled each time a vacuum cleaner passed over it—not that a vacuum had touched this floor recently.

He'd been high in so many rooms like this that, for years now, they'd felt almost indiscernible from one another, all the people and places melding together the same way junk melted down in a spoon. He'd spend the night playing tunes, get high, and leave in the morning. It was both sad and a great comfort to be so sure how things would transpire. You didn't have that on the road with shows. Sure, the bars, songs, and crowds might all be the same, but you had the unpredictability of drunks and the egos of other musicians. Addiction at least simplified things down to the essentials.

As Carson passed the apartment's kitchenette, he noticed a large mural painted on the far wall. The woman sat cross-legged on the floor in front of it, her back resting against the image while she tried tuning the guitar. The wall depicted a lush Edenic garden. All manner of vibrant green plants bloomed in fields of multicolored flowers; a menagerie of beasts grazed among them. As Carson traced his eyes across the painting, he noticed that the landscapes changed, reflecting all sorts of earthly geography. Snowcapped mountains rose in the background, while the foreground transformed from tropical jungle on the right to woodlands on the left. The leaves on the oak and sycamore trees faded gold, orange, and crimson in an eternal fall. A nude woman, who must've been Eve, sat alone under the trees. There was no sign of Adam or the serpent. Carson was still searching for both when the girl with the guitar spoke.

"Pretty good, right?" An unlit cigarette hung from the corner of her lip. It rose as her mouth curled into a smile.

"Stunning," he said, and meant it. Even the woman's beauty seemed elevated as she sat in front of the mural. Carson noticed she shared a resemblance with the artist's Eve. The same dark hair and pale skin. Similar heart-shaped face and heavy eyebrows.

"My boyfriend painted it," the woman said. "This is back when he still painted beautiful things."

Carson sat down on the carpet across from her. The woman lit her cigarette and passed him the guitar. "Tune this damned thing," she said.

The guitar was miserably out of tune, but Carson felt good doing something mindless and familiar. Once the guitar had been tuned, he fingerpicked a random song, just improvising while he sat with the woman and waited on her story. She offered him a puff off the cigarette, and even though he hadn't seen a machine-rolled smoke in weeks, he declined.

"Where'd this boyfriend go?" Carson asked.

"Off sinning somewhere," she said. "He wasn't the man I thought he was."

"A cheater, huh?"

The girl shook her head as if the sad reality were something worse. "Most men are only as faithful as their options, but mine had real loyalty. He could've had any girl he wanted, but he never believed that."

Must've been an ugly bastard, Carson thought, but how a girl so beautiful could wind up with an ugly man confused him. Then again, he wasn't unaware of the power talent played in romance. Carson was handsome enough, but he'd been successful with women far more attractive than he should've, simply because they were enamored with his music. Talent had been getting unworthy men affection since the beginning of time. Perhaps it was the main reason men cultivated something so ethereal. It wasn't until he'd completed this rumination that Carson realized she'd never explained her man's troubles.

"Why didn't he have more confidence? He had a pretty girl like you, didn't he?"

She gave a shy smile. This woman was obviously no stranger to admiration, but she remained coy. Carson found her embarrassment extremely attractive.

"The truth is, I don't think he liked women much. There was a time when I thought all he really loved was me and painting. Then he quit on both."

"How come?" Carson asked, half interested, half knowing that conversation was expected of him.

"He was being tested," the girl said. "God gave him a great gift, but that skill made him vain. I guess I helped with that too."

The girl was talking in riddles. Not the fucked-up snippets of high conversation Carson was used to deciphering but the strange coded speak of religion. His spirit sagged at the idea that she probably wouldn't be holding. What he'd thought was a drug pad was instead the meager home of a disciple.

"I know I'm beautiful," the girl said. "You're not supposed to say things like that. Vanity is sinful. I just know how men look at me. My Franklin wasn't really a handsome man, but I never cared much about that. I cared about this." She reached out and ran her hands over the painted wall, fingers tracing the bony knee of the Eve to whom she bore such a likeness.

"He stopped painting beautiful things that please the Lord and started using his art for blasphemy. That's why I came back here."

"To get a last look?" Carson asked.

The girl shook her head. "To pass my own trial."

Carson had no idea what she was talking about. This whole exchange was too bizarre, almost as if fate were mocking him by putting a gorgeous woman and a quality instrument within reach, then having the girl turn out to be crazy. He began thinking of a way out of the apartment. His only reticence came from the pleasure of the guitar. The Taylor played beautifully, his hands moving across the neck with grace despite the stiffness in his fingers and the clammy wetness of his palms.

"You believe in magic?" the girl asked.

"Like pulling rabbits out of hats and sawing ladies in half?"

"No, I mean real magic. The ability to change reality."

Carson didn't understand the angle, but the question was intriguing—at least more interesting than the girl's sad love life.

"I've always found reality stubbornly unchangeable," Carson said.

"That's only your perception. What if you're wrong?"

"If I'm ever wrong, I guess they'll put me in one of those jackets where the sleeves tie up around the back."

The girl nodded. "Unless you're the only sane one left. Maybe your version of reality is what's real and the world is crazy. It's been that way before, back when they were feeding Christians to the lions. All these people knew God, yet society deemed them heretics."

Carson strummed a solemn A minor configuration. "I think the jury is still deliberating on that one. Some believe they're just stories in a book."

"Why would that make them false?" the girl asked. "I'd argue that's exactly what makes them real."

"Now you've lost me," Carson said. He shifted to another minor chord. Slowly, a melody was building. Maybe the beginning of a song. He hadn't written a new song in three years.

"Being stories is exactly what makes them powerful," the girl said. "Someone wrote the stories down, and they got repeated over and over again, and now those stories are true for millions of people. Art casts a spell over us. Right now, that tune you're playing is making me sad. Isn't that sadness real? Does it matter that it's only coming because of vibrations in the air made from those strings?"

Carson couldn't deny her point. He'd spent countless nights watching the music from his guitar change the crowd. The sad ones made them morose, and the exciting ones riled them up. Onstage, he was a puppeteer—a conductor of people, leading them through the emotions he'd once felt when writing the songs. Even as his abilities had declined with the dope, the power to change a person's feelings with a few notes and a lyric remained.

"This isn't really a painting," the girl said, placing her hand flat against the wall. "This is a spell. It started as nothing but paint, but it changed you the moment you saw it. You went from dope sick to distracted. For a brief moment, it sated your hunger."

Carson wasn't accustomed to others immediately knowing about his addiction. Sure, drugs let you see people in some of their worst moments, but enough time wallowing in addiction would teach you that most of the suffering was hidden. Unless you caught a man in the middle of a blackout drunk or nodding off after just mainlining, the average addict remained the elementary school teacher, the businessman in his three-piece pinstripe, or the local reverend. If the girl knew, Carson was way sicker than he'd ever imagined. He strummed a slow twelve-bar blues to calm his nerves.

"I've been better," he said.

"I've got a remedy for it," the girl said. "My name's Alice, by the way."

Carson didn't stop playing, just nodded his head in greeting. "Nice to meet you, Alice. I'm Carson. So you holding, or are you gonna do a magic trick?"

"You're making fun now," Alice said with a grin. "Only artists can do the sort of thing I'm talking about. As far as the rest is concerned, I think I can hook us up. It's a little bit of a drive."

Suspicion crept in. How did the girl go from some New Age church sermon to talking about resupply? People into junk as deeply as he was didn't even talk about resupply. They went out, found it, and usually spiked that needle into their arm on the spot. Most couldn't wait to get home. Just three weeks ago, a man had overdosed inside his car in the Walmart parking lot.

"Well, I don't have any wheels," Carson said. "But I'll toss in if you drive." He only had a few dollars, but it seemed wise to lie.

"I got one thing left to do first."

Alice stood, walked out of the small room and into the tight hallway behind Carson. He stopped playing, turned, and noticed her pulling a red gas can out of the bathroom. She carried the little plastic container as if it were only a handbag, no consideration for the smoldering butt pinched in her opposite hand. It was a strange sight, but Carson had seen stranger things. Once, while briefly sober, he'd attended a meeting where one of the veterans receiving a chip talked about his love for huffing gas in the old days. The man had huffed so much he'd developed brain damage and swore he was able to tell the difference between premium and regular unleaded just by the smell.

Alice opened her mouth and extinguished the cigarette on her tongue. "Neat trick, huh?" she said. "A little reminder to stay on the path and out of hell."

He was setting the guitar aside when Alice splashed gasoline on the mural. Carson jumped to his feet, the guitar striking the ground with a harsh, unmusical note. Alice didn't seem affected by his distress. She poured a puddle of gasoline onto the carpet and continued dousing the wall with the can.

"Play something somber," she said. "After all, this is a funeral pyre."

Carson picked the guitar up by the neck. If the crazy bitch tossed the gas on him, he'd brain her with the acoustic.

"I told you my man used to paint beautiful things. This is the last of those. Once you've crossed that line, the world needs rid of everything you've contributed. It's all tainted."

Alice stopped pouring the gas and considered Eve on the wall. Carson thought she might've changed her mind, standing there with her hand pressed against the portrait the way lovers in prison press their palms against the visiting-room glass. Whatever she felt, Carson saw it surge through her with a tremble, and then she was fishing inside her jean pocket for a matchbook. He didn't try to stop her. There was a look of total conviction in her eyes that he'd only seen in drunks walking into the barroom for that sobriety-ruining drink, or addicts like himself dialing that memorized number of the pusher they'd never been able to forget. He slid away from the fumes.

Alice dropped the match on the living-room carpet. The fire climbed up the mural, melting the images into rainbow-tinged rivers of greens and blues. She grabbed Carson by the wrist and pulled him out the door. The stairwell was already filling with smoke by the time they reached the bottom floor. Carson expected some alarm, but no warning sounded in the night; it was just the crackling of flames, his rugged cough, and their shoes beating the pavement as they ran. From the street, the windows glowed orange while smoke billowed from the shattered panes. No one followed them out.

Carson dropped the guitar. Alice picked it up, inspected the new chip Carson's mistreatment had put in the neck, and handed it back to him. He took it without thought.

"We can't be here," Alice said. She took him by the hand again, leading him the way a mother might lead a child. They turned a corner and sprinted toward a parked Jeep with bald mud tires. A crowd had gathered by the time Alice started the engine. The old men and women of the neighborhood stood in the street, most still dressed in their nightgowns and robes, their eyes on the flames.

—

Alice wheeled the Jeep across dirt backroads, down mountainside paths that looked too narrow and treacherous for even an ATV. Carson had witnessed all manner of chaos from his time on the road and his fair share of calamity since he'd been on the needle. After a certain point, fights, overdoses, and robberies were, if not expected, at least part of the lifestyle. He'd never imagined being an accessory to arson as a form of art criticism. Was that what he'd seen? He still wasn't sure. All he knew was the girl had loved the mural once, and now that it was gone, she seemed reborn. Fortified in the way that only great loss hardens you. Meanwhile, Carson felt weak. He was scared, sick, and praying their eventual destination would have the cure she implied.

Alice stopped the Jeep at the end of the road. They walked through the woods until the path opened onto a large field. Under the canopy of a few twisted oaks sat a small cabin. Carson had expected something once quiet and cozy gone to ruin. Birds in the eaves and holes in the roof. Roaches and rats prowling the dark rooms. This was pristine, the lumber exterior treated with a dark stain that brought out all the wood's luster. Small flower boxes framed the single front window, and the porch offered a hanging bench that rocked in a lazy sway from its suspended chains.

Too perfect, he thought. A witch's candy cottage in a fairy tale.

"This is my friend's place," Alice said. Carson let himself be led up the path toward the cottage. Despite all he'd seen that night, following was easy. He fell into her stride, trusting, in that childlike way, that even after the bizarre revelations of the last hour, Alice would take him inside, tie off his arm, and slide the needle in gently. The fix was more important than anything else.

The living room was quaint—a small sitting area with rustic high-backed wicker chairs flanking a coffee table, where forgotten mugs created rings on the tabletop. Past this, Carson could see a kitchen area with an old woodstove and what he believed to be an icebox. He collapsed into one of the chairs and sat, hugging the guitar. Exhausted, he took deep breaths, pulling the scent of recent fire into his lungs. Alice walked into the kitchen and returned with a small pitcher of water. The water was lukewarm and tasted metallic. Alice straddled a ladder-back chair. She looked at him with a deep sadness, and Carson realized there were no drugs here. He took another drink.

"That's good," Alice said, her hand reaching out to tip the pitcher until the water rushed into his mouth. "You need to stay hydrated."

Carson wiped his mouth with his sleeve. He swore he could still taste the ash and bubbling paint.

"I'm still sick," Carson said.

Alice only nodded. A sad acknowledgment, as if she were ashamed for having expected better from him.

"What did you think of the sacrifice I made?" she asked.

Carson was too angry for more crazy talk. If this was as good as it was getting, he wanted to play guitar. Let the music silence the constant gnawing of reality until it was only fingers on steel strings, notes bright in the otherwise dull peace. Only the girl wouldn't shut up.

Alice nodded again. "I'd think the same thing from where you're sitting. So tired and beaten down by life. Some paint on a wall isn't sacrifice when you'd rob your own mother for a fix, right?"

Carson recognized the speech. Soon, the higher power, the mantras, and all the other tired tropes of the twelve-steppers would spill out of her, assuring him of salvation on the other side of sober time. All he needed to do was admit his powerless position and come sit in those holy basement rooms, swap sad stories while sipping coffee, breathe in the collected haze of a half dozen cigarettes burned in frustration that the nicotine wasn't something more potent. Receive his little chips and thank the higher power that he'd managed a shit job and some peace of mind. What the twelve-steppers never understood was Carson didn't want that life. He was locked into the ride, ready to burn out in bright chemical ecstasy and be done with the world. A prolonged suicide party was the objective. Better than minimum wage, bridges that couldn't be mended, and bending the knee. He would've told the girl so, but the cabin was comfortable and the guitar a thing of grace. Better to nod through the speech, play a bit, and sleep somewhere warm.

"You don't know how bad things can get," Alice continued. "After walking through hell barefoot, erasing some token of affection a man gave you is no sacrifice at all. It's just breaking an unfair love spell. Have you cast a few love spells in your day, Carson? Pretty songs to enamor pretty girls? I bet you have."

Carson positioned his fingers to strike a chord, but subtle movements behind Alice stopped him. He leaned forward, peering over the girl's shoulder into the kitchen. A gigantic man stood beside the old refrigerator. A thick red beard sprouted across his cheeks, his mouth hidden behind the furrowed whiskers.

"It's not going to be easy," Alice said, her voice soft and reassuring. A nurse trying to convince a sick patient that some bitter medicine would be for their benefit. "There are times when you'll want to die, and if I'm being as honest as I should, there will be parts of it worse than dying. Right now, you've got too much power and no control. We can't have that."

The bearded man came forward, and Carson swung the guitar at Alice's head. She managed to get her arms up, and the solid wooden body rebounded off her elbows. Before Carson could swing again or scurry away, the bearded man grasped him by the shoulders, lifted his thin body, and slammed him down onto the floor. A size-fourteen work boot kicked Carson in the stomach. All his oxygen disappeared. The ability to breathe left him so completely that he suspected his lungs had burst like overfilled balloons. As Carson lay drowning on land, the bearded man rolled him over, grabbed his heels, and dragged him across the floor. Alice followed behind, offering passive orders. Little squeaks like "Don't hurt him too bad," and "Careful of his hands." Carson's head thumped against each floorboard, but he didn't have the strength to lift it.

When they reached one of the spare rooms, the giant released him. The interior was pitch-black, but his other senses were aware of the smell of fresh-washed linen and the sound of something large being dragged out from underneath the nearby bed. Latches snapped open, and Carson heard the unmistakable sound of a metal chain uncoiling. A hinged lid whined open. The bearded man took Carson by the shirt and pulled him into a sitting position. As his eyes adjusted to the darkness,

Carson looked at the box on the floor in front of him: a rectangular casket-shaped container with a few air holes no more than the circumference of his thumb drilled into the lid. The chain lay beside it, and an open combination lock hung off the lid's hinge. Carson understood he was going inside.

He fought hard. Screamed and cried and begged and bit the man's arm through his flannel shirt, but in the end, the bearded man put Carson inside the box. The confines were tight. Carson couldn't lift a leg or bend the arms pinned by his sides. When the lid shut, his nose grazed the surface. Only the tiniest bit of air through the small holes and the muffled sound of Alice's voice crept in as the chain fastened around the box.

—

Time had no definition within the darkness of the box. There was only the hot smell of Carson's breath as it rebounded off the closed lid. The vague sense of motion facilitated by the pinholes of light that dimmed or brightened with the possibility of travel. Occasionally, the box rocked like a ship on a violent sea, crashing his body against the tight wooden sides. Carson thought he heard the growling of an engine and decided he must be in the back of a pickup, the truck traversing some dark country road toward a final destination where he'd be sunk in the river. The idea of cold water seeping in, swelling the wood as the muddy liquid filled his mouth, terrified him, but at least it would be quick, if not painless. Carson's real fear was that they might simply deposit him in the woods, and the world would forget he existed. Like the doomed character in that Edgar Allan Poe story named after the wine he could never properly pronounce, he'd die hungry in the dark, driven mad from the solitude. No one would come looking for him. No mourners would lament his absence. All he'd have left behind were a few mediocre songs that had once played on the radio. Background noise for barroom scenes most of the participants hoped to escape. Taking stock of his lacking legacy, Carson decided he wasn't bothered much by the idea of being so forgotten. He just wanted to hang on to the remaining tatters of his life for a few more minutes. Dope sick, broke, homeless. All these insults were agreeable if he would only be permitted to continue living. Any indignity could be endured so long as he was still present for it.

The sound of the engine expired, and the box suddenly lifted. Even with dampened senses, Carson felt the presence of those who carried him. He could hear their ragged exhalations and the stamping of boots. One of his capturers slipped, and Carson felt the others' strength hold fast until the staggering laborer regained his footing. Something about the human presence made Carson consider begging to be released. He decided against it. Anyone who knew the cargo would be too culpable for sympathy. They ferried him across a great distance with the solemn dedication of pallbearers.

The box pitched forward again. Carson heard muttered instructions and felt the wooden shell descending with a rhythm he recognized as bodies trying to navigate a staircase with a heavy load. Carson tried counting the number of stairs, but the movements were too clouded inside the box. He could only be sure that no one had carried him upstairs to any second floor. He had to be somewhere underground. Eventually, they sat the box down and departed.

Patience had never been a virtue he possessed, and the uncertainty of the box left him fluctuating between meditative serenity and panic. One moment, he was in control of his rambling mind; the next, thoughts stampeded through his consciousness, too fast and slippery to grasp. He began doubting his appraisal of reality. Perhaps he'd expired and this new incalculable state was the beginning of the eternal void. All he had left was the gnawing dope-sick hunger. With time, Carson knew even this would wane.

Carson was stricken blind the first time they took him out of the box. Part of him had grown accustomed to the loss of his vision and learned to substitute hearing for his eyes. He had tried identifying the sounds echoing outside the box—the scraping of tiny clawed feet that suggested darting mice and a muffled flutter when some insect landed on the lid. The moment just before, the lights had felt different. There was a weight to each approaching step. A sound of impatient breath as someone unfastened the lock. When the lid yawned back, Carson threw his arms over his face. The dim light outside felt as if it might fry his retinas.

When Carson's eyes adjusted, he saw an older man holding a tin cup and can with a spoon shoved inside. The man didn't introduce himself. He just placed the can on the dirt floor between his feet and grasped Carson by the back of the neck. Carson went rigid with resistance, ready for some violence, but the man only pressed the tin cup to Carson's chapped lips and poured warm water into his mouth. Carson sputtered and spit. The man barely noticed. He wiped the corners of Carson's mouth with a rag taken from the back pocket of his slacks before clacking a spoonful of cold spinach against Carson's clenched teeth. Carson tried spitting the mess out, but the man squeezed his cheeks, forcing the jaw muscles to chew.

Sometime during this feeding, the bearded giant who'd placed Carson in the box entered the room, carrying two folding chairs. He set both beside Carson's box before retreating to the corner by the door. The old man sat in one of the chairs, crossed his legs, and waited for Carson to stand. His stiff muscles protested the effort, but Carson managed to rise to his full height. He sat in the remaining chair, his mouth still thick with the slimy texture of cold spinach. The stink of his unwashed body embarrassed him, but the man didn't seem to notice.

"Let me see your hands," the old man said, holding out his own. The wrinkled, liver-spotted fingers trembled, ready to receive Carson's touch. The bearded brute by the door watched with hateful eyes, so there seemed no choice in the matter. When they touched, the stranger's warm skin felt foreign after so long without human contact. The man turned Carson's hands over, inspecting the burn scar on his thumb and the way the ring finger on his right hand was crooked, forever jutting left after being dislocated and poorly splinted during a pickup basketball game.

"I told them to be careful of your hands."

After he'd pushed down the fear, Carson decided they weren't going to kill him. At least not right away. If that had been the case, why move him at all? Why drill air holes in the box? Now they were feeding him. All this implied some deeper purpose behind the abduction, but Carson still struggled to expel thoughts of torture-loving sadists and sex cults. If they were only going to take him apart, piece by piece, over the next few days, he'd try his luck fighting. The red-bearded giant would almost certainly kill him, but not before he could strangle this other man.

The man ran his thumb over the ridge of Carson's fingernails. The normally white half moons were blackened with dirt. The man felt the calluses on Carson's fingertips. He lingered here, seeming impressed by the way music and time hardened the skin. It wasn't the comforting touch of a savior; there was a coldness Carson recognized. The old man inspected his hands the way one might a coveted tool.

"I never had proper hands for music," the man said. "Stubby fingers. No poetry in them. I admit I'm a little jealous of people like you. So much ability, yet so many of you squander it on earthly things. How many songs go unsung while you're busy with drugs and whoring?"

The bearded man came forward, carrying the Taylor guitar from Alice's apartment. He placed it on Carson's lap.

"Alice said you showed great promise," the man said. "Play us something."

Carson touched the strings. His fingers automatically formed a G chord, ready to burst into a thousand memorized tunes. Instead, Carson threw the guitar on the ground.

"I'm not doing shit until I know what's going on here," Carson said. "Who are you people?"

The man nodded and tapped the spoon against his knee. "I'm Nathaniel Logan. You're in the basement of The Lighthouse. You're here because you've been chosen to compose a great spell—the sort of work only a powerful artist can craft."

The way the man spoke, as if welcoming a guest and not some prisoner pulled from a pine coffin, told Carson he wouldn't be able to plead with them. Still, his mouth spewed reason they'd ignore.

"I was snatched up off the street."

"That's not true," Logan said. "Alice told us everything. She said you spoke to her first. Afterward, you were invited inside of your own free will."

"What do you want?" Carson asked.

"I want you to use your talent. I want you to cast a spell."

"I don't feel much like playing for people who kidnap me."

"You don't have to play now. You'll have forty days to write a new song. Something that will be unlike anything you've written. Not another derivative honky-tonk anthem, but a true piece of music that will change people. During that time, we'll feed and clothe you and see that you have time to practice. I'll get Alice to trim those nails. We don't want anything to hinder your progress."

Carson didn't know how to respond. If the man had promised to sacrifice him upon an altar, at least that would've been expected. The idea that they'd placed him inside a box and imprisoned him for a song almost made Carson cackle in disbelief.

Logan bent down and retrieved the guitar. "Play us something," he said, handing Carson the instrument. "Please."

Since he'd always thought better with his fingers on the strings, Carson picked a slow melody. Hands moving independently, he thought about how best to improve his situation. He'd written enough songs in his day—perhaps never anything under such bizarre circumstances, but he could have a serviceable tune finished in a few hours. Did he really believe they'd release him after that? The sort of people who burned down apartment complexes because pictures offended them and chained men up in boxes didn't just let people go; however, if the man said that a song was all he wanted, maybe he meant it?

"There's no need for all this," Carson said. "I can have your song finished in a few days."

The smile Logan offered reminded Carson of predatory animals mimicking human emotions for treats. Witnessing it, Carson lost all faith in his ability to control the situation.

"I'm sure you could whip something up fast, but this will be more than a song. It will take days for the vision. The others waited months and never made it to the ceremony. They joined the sacrifice, but I've got a feeling about you."

Before Carson could ask another question, specifically about the alarming term "sacrifice," the bearded man crossed the room and seized him by the shoulder. Carson tried swinging the guitar at him, but he was lifted off the ground and tossed hard onto the floor. The man lifted Carson again and laid him in the box. Logan was shouting, instructing the muscle to mind Carson's hands, when the lid slammed shut.

Like all prisoners, Carson fell into the routine of captivity. He spent days or nights languishing in the box, the endless darkness only interrupted when Pastor Logan or the bearded giant fed him something cold from a can or allowed him to wash with the frigid water from a soapy pail. After he finished, they'd bring the guitar and leave him alone in the room for a few hours. Carson didn't come up with anything during these sessions. He strummed a few chords or played some lost outlaw song from his adolescence, but music no longer provided any solace. If Carson were honest with himself, music had stopped being anything transcendent the day he discovered the needle. The absence of drugs offered a little hope. It sparked the small possibility that maybe with the narcotics gone, his songwriting ability might return. When this didn't happen, the disappointment proved more palpable than Carson expected. He played with frustration. The strings hurt his fingers. Each chord proved a little harder to form, and the accuracy of his strumming became a sloppy, imprecise cadence. The instrument's wood recoiled from his touch like a wounded lover.

Once every few days, whether he needed it or not, Alice tended to his fingernails. These manicures weren't the only visits from Alice. Sometimes, she would lie atop the lid of the box and whisper to him, her long body covering the holes until Carson feared he might suffocate. She promised the music would come drifting back. That after so much time in the box, he'd be blessed with a vision like only the worthiest of prophets. Carson would play music that altered the fabric of reality. Ended wars or won them. Created storms or ceased their violent swells. Killed men or raised the dead. He didn't understand what she meant as she preached and polished his nails, but he understood that if the church worshipped any god, it must be art itself.

On the last morning Alice clipped his nails, she offered no encouragements, just held his hands in a tight grip, clipping the already short nails deep into the quick until they stung and bled. Carson never complained. He was in enough trouble already. After nights of lying in the box with no songs, he'd decided to trick Logan. He only needed to compose one beautiful song, and even though no new material would come to him, an infinite amount of music resided in the world. Unless Logan possessed an encyclopedic knowledge of songs, Carson could simply steal a melody and report it as divinely delivered. Mimicry was available to all levels of mediocrity. What mattered was his ability to sell the lie.

Here, Carson felt more than qualified. He'd been a liar all his life. He'd learned to lie to women about where he'd been, lie to bandmates about the night's profits, and lie to the audience about how honored he felt playing another dive in whatever Buttholeville he found himself that weekend. The strength of his dishonesty only grew since he'd found the needle. In a way, "deceiver" best described his new identity. After deciding on an obscure Hollis Bragg standard that his bandmate Jefferson used to break out on the road during the early-morning hours, Carson hammered on the lid, screaming that he'd received a revelation.

Logan insisted on watching the performance alone. He sat perched on one of the folding chairs next to the box, waiting with the same patience as the day he'd fed Carson the cold spinach. Carson always felt nervous before a performance. There was a tingling in his stomach, a light-headed fear that the booze and pills helped cut through, but none of those fortifiers were available. The minimal concert also robbed him of any scapegoats. No band members to blame mistakes on.

"Go on," Logan urged. "Cast your spell."

Carson cleared his throat and readied his fingers over the strings. Bragg's song was titled "The Way It Is," a ballad about a man who'd lost his lover and was accepting the lonely reality of his new life. Good lyrics that articulated some of the longing after a broken relationship but not exactly appropriate for these purposes. Carson felt he might manipulate a few lines from the chorus. Most pop music relied on a certain ambiguity to make the audience associate it with their own emotional history. The new arrangement turned the song into a hymn.

Carson felt guilty butchering a song he admired but reminded himself theft was part of art. Nobody had any real new ideas. Music was just a constant conversation, each piece a response to those that came before it. One songwriter heard what the last did with a tempo and the key of G, and they responded with their own variation. Why should stealing a few lyrics for freedom be any different?

Carson strummed through the verse without singing any of the words. When he got to the solemn changes in the chorus, he croaked out the bits of lyrics he thought Logan might mistake as religious discovery. Carson watched Logan as he sang, trying to interpret the hard set of the man's eyebrows and immobile mouth. When the last chord rang out, Logan only nodded.

"You said you received this song," Logan said. "You experienced a vision?"

"Yes," Carson lied. He kept all the dishonesty from his posture and lied like a man in total belief of his illusion.

"What did the vision consist of?" Logan asked.

"It's hard to describe," Carson stalled. None of the prophets in the gospels had been asked to prove themselves. He'd figured the song itself would be as convincing as Moses's tablets. "I heard the music and . . . and a voice whispering. I couldn't quite make out all the words."

Logan smiled another of his alien smiles. "And how do you know it wasn't Alice lying atop your box like she does some nights?"

Carson collected his resolve and spoke with the best authority he could muster. "When God speaks, you know it."

"That's true," Logan said. "He spoke to me once. A few simple sentences that changed everything. That's how I know the truth. You haven't been gifted with any divine song. What you played won't rebuild my congregation or reshape our world. That's just some honky-tonk standard, unknown to me but recognizable in its lust and self-deprecation. Did you really think that you could pawn something like that off? All that's good for is some tears in a beer."

Logan left, and the red-bearded man put Carson back in the box.

He wasn't sure how many days ago that had been—not adequate time for the painful trimming Alice administered on his nails. Watching her clip, Carson felt the woman's disappointment with each nail she chopped back.

"Any particular reason why you're torturing me?" he asked.

Alice clipped the nail on Carson's ring finger back so far that the flesh shone an angry red. A trickle of blood oozed out.

"This isn't torture," Alice said.

"You think being locked in a box is just part of the creative process?"

Alice stopped clipping. "Do you remember my painter?" she asked. "The man I told you about on the night we met?"

"Who could forget?" Carson said.

"He'd rather be locked in that box until he starved than have that mural destroyed. The worst thing I could do to him is what I've already done."

"Give him a few days in the dark with only a little water and some cold spinach," Carson said. "I bet he changes from a suffering artist to some poor son of a bitch who just wants to see sunlight."

Alice shook her head. "When we lived together, he used to say that if the house ever caught fire, if it was between dragging him out alive or grabbing a single painting, I had to promise to save the paintings."

"That makes him a fucking nut like the rest of you."

"Maybe just a man who knew his priorities."

Carson saw the serious cast of her eyes. Her cold hands felt certain and steady, holding his bleeding fingers.

"You really believe that if I lie in this box long enough, I'll have some kind of vision?"

"No. I believe that if you're a true artist, you'd either receive a vision or die waiting on one."

Carson couldn't debate away madness. Old ideas of martyrdom would never lead an artistic revolution, and the pain of mysticism melded with old-time religion would write no useful manifestos. The gospels already had their poets, and this was the world they'd made. Carson wasn't the man for this anyway. All the songs he'd ever sung were autobiographical. Anecdotes about life on the road, lost love, and broken promises. They had more to do with his own ego than anything else. The closest he ever came to some universal truth was in the brief moments of specificity. The empty-headedness of a hangover morning, the solemn quiet sitting at a kitchen table on a rainy night with a pad of paper and a guitar. Perhaps he might have something worth saying on the failures he'd encountered while trying to create. Songwriters like Carson didn't even have the luxury of choosing their themes. If they did, he'd have picked something more important than the familiar retread of broken ambitions. Something with a little more dignity than the squalid junkie days he now inhabited. He'd been a pretender. He'd parroted the proper chords and walked in the same fashion of those who'd been chosen. Carson hadn't come near being an artist in a long time. That's why, lying in the darkness of the box, true music wouldn't come to him. He was simply a liar, thief, failure. The sort of man who'd trade his instruments and voice for another fix. Carson had lost faith in music on the day he realized true songs weren't within his reach.

"If you keep making me wait, I'm going to die in that box," Carson told her. "I'm no artist. There's no magic inside of me."

Alice released his hands. She ran fingers through the long tendrils of her dark hair, eyes obscured by heavy lashes as she examined his bleeding finger.

"If you really mean that, I'll help you," she said.

"It's the truest thing I've ever said."

"I'll come down after dark and fetch you. If you promise to do exactly what I say, I'll lead you to a path in the woods. Do you promise?"

"I promise," Carson said. He didn't trust the woman, but it was hard not to hope. He climbed into the box without protest, lay still while the bearded giant came and fastened the lock. He could hear Alice's feet on the floor as she walked away, then waited in the silence, wondering if this was just another cruel trick.

Carson smelled Alice before he heard her. Not the alluring spice of perfume from the first night they met, but unwashed hair, sleep breath, and something else unnamed. Her true scent—the indistinguishable thing he should have noticed in the beginning to save himself from the box. Smelling it now, seeping inside through the tiny air holes, Carson wondered if he could trust her. There didn't seem to be much choice in the matter. If this were some test or another trap, he'd risk it. The music wouldn't come, and without it, he'd languish in the box.

His mouth went dry at the sound of her footsteps, lips glued together by fear as she pried back the lid. Alice wore the same dark clothing as the first night they met. She'd applied heavy eye shadow and piled the curtains of dark hair atop her head, exposing the pale pillar of her long neck. She looked ready to go out and seduce another fool into capture. Carson wasn't sure if the ensemble should be taken as a warning, but seeing it made a brief anger bloom inside him. He promised himself that if presented with the opportunity, he'd strangle the woman before escaping into the brush.

Alice removed a black sleep mask from the pocket of her jeans.

"Put this on," she said. "I can't have you seeing the grounds."

Carson pulled the mask over his forehead and adjusted the strap. He'd grown so accustomed to darkness that relinquishing his sight didn't bother him. As the cloth veiled his eyes, Alice's fingers encircled his wrist.

Alice advised him to step high, and they ascended a staircase. Carson recognized it as the same one he'd been lowered down inside the box. The stairs proved steeper than he imagined, the heels of his bare feet hanging over the edge of each shortened board.

Alice released him at the summit. Carson heard door hinges strain open. They walked across carpet now.

"Not a sound here," Alice said.

Carson did his best to float like a ghost. Alice was even quieter. Had it not been for the cold fingers wrapped around his wrist, Carson would've felt abandoned. They traveled down a long, narrow hall until Alice opened another door. Here the terrain changed from carpet and hardwood to rocky earth that stabbed his bare feet. Carson walked on. If splinters and bugbites were all he endured for freedom, he'd gladly make the sacrifice. What were a few more nicks and cuts on his already battered body?

As they stepped into deeper woods, the sounds of the mountain intensified. Despite growing up in various small towns across rural America, Carson had never spent time in the woods. He imagined the glowing eyes of nocturnal animals watching their strange procession. Had they observed others following the same path? What secrets did they know about this trail?

After a few more minutes of walking and several more injuries to the soles of his feet, Alice stopped him.

"We're here," she said. "You can remove the blindfold now."

Nightmare scenarios tumbled through Carson's mind as he reached for the mask. Anything could be waiting for him. A crooked hanging tree with a braided noose or a coven of hooded figures standing in a ceremonial circle, knives out and goblets ready to collect his blood. Maybe just Logan hoisting a rabbit-eared shotgun, pumpkin-ball slugs loaded into each barrel to blast his unworthy guts out through his spine. Carson willed his eyes open, but nothing greeted him aside from a wide patch of dirt. Alice stood on the margins of this tilled earth. Carson realized the lack of vegetation wasn't some anomaly. Alice pointed to the first unmarked grave.

"This one was a poet," Alice said, and pointed to the unmarked grave on her left. "This one, a sculptor. She made some beautiful busts but nothing you might call extraordinary. The third was a painter. There are more here. When they didn't receive their vision and couldn't cast their spell, they became part of the sacrifice. There's a spot here for you, Carson. Are you ready to claim it, or do you still wish to serve?"

Carson's tongue atrophied inside his mouth. There was no possible answer. No graveside soliloquy explaining that they'd taken the wrong man. If she wanted someone willing to die for art, the only version of him capable of such a fate had evaporated with age and each prick of the needle. Maybe he deserved the unmarked grave. Maybe it was fair punishment after wasted talent, but she couldn't ask him to accept that judgment with grace. Let these other planted failures be messengers for the cause. Let them fertilize the next imprisoned crop with fear.

Carson did the only thing left and ran.

Alice dove for him, but Carson dodged her, his bare feet sliding in the dirt of the painter's grave. She crashed through the underbrush behind him, the sound of her so close that Carson imagined the branches assaulting him were Alice's nails scraping at his back. As he dipped left around a wide oak tree, Carson heard the others—a larger body coming from the left and Alice right on his heels. He might've been able to turn and fight the girl, but the others would catch him before he could deal with her. He bent and grabbed a large rock.

Carson reached the end of the tree line as the bearded giant wrapped him up in a tackle, and they slammed into the trunk of an oak. The tree rained leaves while Carson swung the stone at the giant's head. The blow glanced off the man's shoulder. It only enraged him. He plucked the rock from Carson's fist and hurled the stone deep into the woods. Thick fingers squeezed Carson's neck. His vision faded, the edges obscured into a foggy glare. Carson waited on the encroaching darkness until another man placed a palm on the giant's shoulder.

"That's enough," Logan said. "Bring him back up to the house."

The giant cradled Carson in his arms like a bride, and they trudged back uphill. Alice approached from behind. She'd taken a moment to brush some of the dirt from her face, but the waves of her hair still held traces of the grave.

"I thought the graves might inspire you," she said. "So disappointing."

Carson would've spat in her face if he'd had any spit. Instead, he managed a dry chuckle.

"Why don't you spend some time in the box?" he said.

Alice shook her head. Black tears leaked mascara down her cheeks. "I've been inside every night."

Carson wasn't sure he'd heard correctly. Maybe the strangulation or tree trunk to the head had left him confused, but he received clarification when they came back into the basement. The giant sat him down and removed the sleep mask Logan had replaced over his eyes. Carson was in a different room. It was the same unfurnished four walls and dirt floor, but the coffin-shaped box inside was not his own. This one was smaller, meant to accommodate a shorter stature, and there seemed to be fewer air holes drilled into the lid. Carson couldn't help thinking of it as a child's coffin until he saw Alice standing nude beside the box.

"This is mine. I spend every night inside, waiting on my vision. I'm no great artist. My time's better served collecting others, either for the sacrifice or for the spell, but I long for a vision."

She sank down into the box like a woman descending into a steaming bath. The giant locked her inside. After the latches were secure, the giant dragged Carson into the other room and locked him inside his own box, where Carson's mind played snippets of music. It seemed as if a thousand different melodies, music from each year of his life and perhaps an unknown future, drifted with his consciousness. In better circumstances, Carson might've considered this music some indication that his songwriting ability had returned. It was as if watching Alice's dedication shamed him until the muse finally took pity and slid into the close confines of the box, pouring music into his mind to remember until a guitar was present, but Carson didn't care anymore. He had no desire to document the notes and work the unrefined sounds into something more substantial. Carson's time as a creator was finished. The truth was, he didn't want it anymore. The cost was too great. He'd started out too far behind and was too ill-equipped. Perhaps with enough diligence, he'd produce something Logan found worthy. With years of struggle, he might even remedy those broken aspects of his craft the Nashville producers had pointed out and cut another record. He could force a chorus into the works or continue writing in his own voice until all the weaker songs were spent and the few true pieces of art each writer hoped to find deep within themselves were unearthed, only he knew too much now. The truth of the matter was, he'd never had even an atom-size speck of the resolve these people carried.

III

Haunted House Fires

CHAPTER NINE

The room remained silent for nearly a full minute after Carson finished his story. The whole thing sounded unbelievable, but even if I hadn't freed him myself, a glance at the quivering man would've been enough to make me believe every word.

"I think you should stay here for the night," I told him.

Carson followed me with tentative steps, the robe wrapped around him like a protective shroud. He stopped at the mouth of the hallway.

"There's some candles in the bedroom," I said. "I'll bring one back."

I left him clinging to the wall and moved into the darkest parts of the house by memory. Six steps and a left turn into my father's room. Even sightless, I knew everything's place: The sleigh bed against the far wall. The nightstand on my right beside the large chest of drawers. The vanity, with its oval mirror where my grandmother had applied her makeup for decades.

I felt my way to the closet and opened the sliding door. Flannel shirts and a few suits still preserved in Laundromat plastic hung overhead. Below, stacks of folded jeans sat alongside steel-toed work boots and two decent pairs of loafers—one brown, one black. I tossed the shoes aside and pulled up the carpet. A small lockbox lay hidden underneath in an impression carved into the floor. My father's stash for guns, bail money, and bribes. On the night we celebrated my acceptance into medical school, I kept the drinks flowing until my father passed out, then took $3,000 from the stash before heading west. It was the only thing I'd ever stolen that wasn't time.

I unlocked the box with a tiny silver key, expelling the trapped scent of leather and my father's peppermint aftershave. The way the sharp mint combined with his beer breath had always made my stomach sick.

I moved several items aside, like the small flashlight and gloves my father had carried during robberies. I found his snub nose .38 and put the revolver in my other coat pocket.

In the detective stories I used to read, there's always one ally the hero depends on. Maybe it's an old mentor, disappointed by the way their pupil's life has regressed into day-drinking and snoop jobs, or maybe it's an old flame with enough leftover love for a final favor. Sometimes, it's a former enemy who sees the benefit in a temporary alliance. Did I have anyone like that aside from Uncle Abbott? I certainly couldn't trust him. The Hill twins were out too. The only name that came to mind was Shannon. I tried calling her again, but the call still went to voice mail. Images of Shannon roasting as she tried climbing out the bathroom window or being overcome by smoke inhalation behind the bar filled my mind. I pushed the thoughts away. I'd drive by her place and find her sitting out in the yard, oblivious to the whole affair. The worst part of the night would be delivering the bad news. At least, that's what I hoped. I texted, ARE YOU OKAY? CALL ME, and put the phone away.

I noticed a small, darker square of wood fitted into the center of the cedar planks. A jewelry box no bigger than a paperback novel slid out from the hole. I knew what it was before I opened the lid; Uncle Abbott's story had been true. Inside, a wide array of diamond studs, dangling pearls, and golden hoops glittered in the darkness. I touched each of my father's mementos, both counting and dismissing a number I didn't want to acknowledge. Some of the earrings were expensive, the kind of thing that would aggrieve a young lady if she lost its mate. Why had my father needed these? Wasn't the memory of the women enough? Did he steal them from sleeping ears or request them? And why hadn't he sold any when times got hard? Despite a few obvious pieces of costume jewelry, there had to be several thousand dollars' worth of real jewels and scrap gold.

I didn't know it, but I was looking for the hummingbird that belonged to Uncle Abbott's unrequited love, Jenny Long. I didn't like the idea of the earring discarded like Gabrielle's engagement ring. I wanted the hummingbird safe in this box with the others, not washed away by the creek.

Clumsy footsteps echoed down the hall. I dropped the jewelry box back in place, covered it with the larger stash box, and replaced the carpet. Uncle Abbott barged in just as I closed the closet door.

"Where's Carson?" I asked.

"Standing at the end of the hallway, afraid of the fucking dark."

"He's been locked in a box. Of course he's afraid of the dark."

Uncle Abbott sat on the edge of the bed so we could whisper. "I say we drive him an hour away and put him out of the truck with a few cans of green beans."

"We can't do that."

Uncle Abbott smiled. "So softhearted. I figured you'd never go for it."

"Goddamned right, I wouldn't."

"Junkies are too unreliable," Uncle Abbott said. "He'll go out in public, get picked up or at least seen. They'll know we broke into the church."

"Don't you think they'll figure that out anyway?" I asked.

"If I thought we could just lock him down in the basement, I'd say fine, but you know that's not a real option. Eventually, someone from The Lighthouse is coming with questions. He can't be here when that happens."

It was a good point I wasn't ready to concede. Pulling Carson from the box had made him my responsibility. I'd committed myself to that burden even if I needed help seeing things to the end. I could barely argue. My reasoning was still affected by all we'd been through that night. I'd unlocked the same lock from my childhood with a combination given to me by a ghost. It wasn't something reconcilable with reality, but it had happened.

"Where are you going?" Uncle Abbott asked as I climbed up off the floor.

"I know someone who might be able to help us," I said. "You two sit tight until I get back. Heat him up a bath and put him in the spare room. Make sure he's got a candle. Understand?"

Uncle Abbott rubbed his temples in small, calming circles. "Just hurry up," he said. "I ain't no babysitter."

Shannon lived in a trailer at the end of a crooked hollow called Mills Branch miles from town. The single-wide sat in the perpetual shade of dense chestnut trees that dropped spiked burrs when blooming. A nearby creek provided the only noise. Everything about the place seemed intent on discouraging company. The road's blacktop, compromised by years of frozen puddles forming in the unrepaired ruts, could bust tires and knock a sedan's suspension out of alignment. After braving all this, visitors were greeted with a **No Trespassing** sign sprayed with buckshot. Assuming you made it past these deterrents, there was still the rusty chain-link fence encircling the high grass of Shannon's yard. The gate once bore a padlock, but Shannon removed it after she kept misplacing her key.

I'd only been inside her place once. This was years ago, right after I came home and the only decline was my own. Shannon had been embarrassed for someone to see the state of the trailer. The hallway floor had given out, leaving sunken basins the size of footprints, as if she'd walked across quicksand to reach the bedroom. The bathroom was worse, the cramped shower stall and commode so close together you could sit on the toilet, lean over, and wash your hair under the faucet. Shannon kept the place clean despite these cosmetic flaws. The cheap countertops were always immaculate, surfaces scrubbed with soapy water and smelling of diluted bleach. There was a pride in the place that made me understand why she lived in the trailer instead of above Wildcat's.

The property was in complete disarray when I pulled up that night. The underpinning that skirted around the trailer's bottom was pried back like an opened can. The rusted aluminum gaped so that I suspected several varmints had taken shelter underneath. A few of the cracked cinder blocks that served for steps were missing, giving the place a look of uninhabitable ruin. Still, all this paled in comparison to the heap of trash in the center of the yard. Collections had stopped months ago. Shannon had burned all she could, but the accumulation got away from her. The white and black plastic bags lay atop one another, rolling down to the grass, where they sagged open, spilling out their contents for scavenging opossums and stray dogs. Ragged paper, plastic, and scraps of food lay strewn about the yard. As the Decline wore on, that previous pride in her homestead had been replaced with despair and apathy.

Shannon sat in a lawn chair, legs crossed as she smoked a hand-rolled and looked at the miniature dump. She didn't turn as I approached, just raised a hand with the burning cigarette in greeting. Seeing her alive overwhelmed me until I almost pulled her into an embrace, but I calmed myself. Everything about her posture told me she didn't know about the fire. I'd be delivering bad news.

"How'd you know it was me?" I asked.

"Who else would it be?"

"Somebody out to rob you."

Shannon snorted. "What do I have worth stealing? Take my trash, please."

I crouched in the grass next to her. Shannon passed me the cigarette. I put the damp tip to my lips and puffed. It had always been this way between us—easy sharing created by a sense of desperate comradery. I passed the cigarette back.

"I tried calling and texting you," I said. "I have some bad news."

I spared no details of the fire at Wildcat's, even included my chase of the arsonist through the woods. Shannon took the news relatively well. No tears or outbursts of anger. The bar had always felt like a borrowed life. People like us didn't get to own things we loved, so when the universe corrected course and robbed her of that accomplishment, Shannon accepted it. I only held back one thing. If my suspicions were right and the graffiti outside the bar belonged to Franklin, Alice was the arsonist. Just like the apartment, burning the bar wasn't her main goal. Wildcat's had only been another unfortunate casualty in her crusade against Franklin's art. I didn't have any proof, and I didn't fully understand why, aside from knowing it had something to do with The Lighthouse's obsession over the power found in artistic expression, so I kept the information to myself. It wouldn't have helped Shannon's grief anyway.

"The place was a sinking ship," she said. "If there'd have been some insurance payout, I'd have burned it myself months ago."

Resilience was expected of women like her. Even before the Decline, girls who grew up like Shannon hid any dream they couldn't abandon under a deep front of cynicism. It was another of the many things we shared.

"We had some good times in that bar." Her teeth flashed white as she passed the smoke. I pinched it, sucked until my fingers felt the heat, and tossed it into the garbage pile, where it winked out. Wildcat's had been my watering hole when I first came home. The place where I'd washed away all the pain of fucking up my shot at a better life. In those early days, Shannon let me lounge at the bar, falling asleep in my chair or making a mess in the bathroom whenever I staggered in, spraying piss and puke. The place provided a few laughs, but mostly I remembered how it tried to kill me. Wildcat's let me fill the hole with the same ravenous greed as a piglet at a slop trough. Piglets will eat till they burst if you let them.

There was a time when the two of us might have built something together. If I'd have sobered up and the Decline hadn't descended upon us, we might have made a home above the bar, come downstairs after mornings in bed, and joked with the regulars as we served drinks. It wasn't the life either of us had expected, but it might've sufficed. I tried not to think about that missed opportunity, not only because I refused to act on the possibility of romance after Gabrielle but also because now we both knew there was little point in building anything. When even your cheap dive bar is destined to burn, why lay the first brick?

"I need a favor," I said. "I didn't want to involve you, but . . ."

"You know you can involve me in anything, Harlan."

"If I hesitate, it's because this is trouble you don't want."

"And this isn't the same old trouble, is it?"

"No, it's something worse."

"I figured that when the man came by the other day looking for you."

I'd have preferred imagining Redbeard coming into Wildcat's with a look of disgust hidden underneath his whiskers as he observed the bottles and the few drunks, but my mind conjured the sounds of his bones snapping as he rolled down the stairs.

"What man?" I asked.

"Kinda freaky-looking guy. He was wearing this dark coat with paint on the sleeves."

It didn't sound like Redbeard, but I kept my hope at a minimum. Paint splotches didn't necessarily keep Franklin out of those graves Alice had shown Carson.

"What did he say?"

"Just wanted to know where to find you. He left a phone number."

"Do you still have that number?"

"It's kind of a funny story. I had it pinned up behind the bar, but I decided to take it down for some reason. I put it in my coat."

She left me in the yard and went inside to fetch the number. I considered following her. If I stepped inside, she might kiss me in the kitchen. Push me against the fridge as we struggled with buttons and belts. I'd almost lost her tonight, and the reunion seemed like an opportunity for renewal, a promise that our chance at something better wasn't quite over yet. Instead, I waited. It took some time, but she descended the cinder block steps waving the scrap of paper like a flag.

"This guy, what'd he look like?"

"It's dark in there, and he had a hoodie on. Lots of paint on his sleeves. Different colors, not like he was painting a single room."

"About that favor," I said.

Shannon sat back down in the lawn chair, crossed her arms in an *I'm intrigued* sort of way.

"I need you to give someone a ride out of Coopersville. Go visit your sister and take them along."

"Who?" Shannon asked.

"You don't know him, but he's a friend. I'll give you the keys to the Mustang. Consider it payment. Sell the car and start over."

Shannon chuckled. "That's a shit thing for you to offer. You know I can't take it."

We used to prowl the backroads in the Mustang, sliding into mountaintop curves as if we were invincible. We still had some youth, and the Decline was years away. I could have suggested we leave together. Instead, I begged her to go alone.

"Give this guy a ride and help me out. It'd mean a lot to me."

She couldn't refuse, and I felt like shit exploiting that weakness.

"Promise me?" I asked.

"I promise. I'll come by later and fetch the car."

"I'll bring it here," I said. I hadn't figured out how I'd give the car away with Uncle Abbott home and didn't want Shannon involved in that argument.

"Be careful," she told me.

"I promise," I said, and walked back to the car, knowing she was too smart for my lies.

I got my phone out of the center console and dialed but stopped before calling. It was a disconnected number but a familiar one. Franklin had been hidden in plain sight the whole time.

Since Dalton Hardware was on the opposite end of town, the drive offered time to weigh my expectations. I'd thought my eventual meeting with Franklin would be somewhere more secluded. A clearing hidden deep in the woods after a hike up the mountainside or beneath some culvert near the Island. That he'd been so close for so long surprised me.

The place looked squalid when I arrived. Even the graffiti—two four-foot dicks rendered in an arterial red spray and ejaculating cascading arches of jizz—seemed faded. The few storefronts on the opposite side of Dameron Street were equally empty, their showroom windows either covered with old newspapers or left open, allowing streetlights to shine on bare floors where furniture and dressed mannequins had once enticed shoppers inside. No cars were parked along the sidewalk. Even the bits of trash floating in the gutter were remnants from a time of better commerce.

The front entrance of Dalton Hardware consisted of a large concrete porch covered in handcrafted rocking chairs and hanging gliders. Throughout my childhood, this furniture had been a status symbol for the more prominent residents of Coopersville. Respectable homes either displayed a glider on the front porch or placed a rocking chair in their parlor. New models had arrived by truck every Sunday. Poor shoppers lusted over the fresh stock before retreating home emptyhanded, reminded of their low place in the town's hierarchy. Few were immune to this temptation. Even my father would drive by each Monday morning to scope out the newest arrivals. Dad had often hidden his desires, but he kept finding excuses, things like tying his shoe, to sit in his favorite among the chairs and test its comfort.

Now only a few chairs remained on the store's porch, an unsteady-looking lot hewed out of cheap, young wood. No price tags dangled from their armrests. The fact that no one bothered stealing them said something about our town's destitution.

I peered through the dirty windows. With my hands cupped to cut the glare, I could see the racks of tools on the far wall, a portion of the pale-green linoleum floor, and a display of vacuum cleaners. No signs of life inside. I went around the back of the building. The door was locked but easy enough to pick by sliding my driver's license between the lock. It was dark inside; no overhead fluorescents illuminated the aisles. No electronic bell announced my entry, only my footsteps echoing as I walked down the plumbing aisle.

"You recognized the phone number," Franklin said.

Old man Dalton kept the same number for years. It hadn't been disconnected until a few months ago.

"You've been looking for me. I know you went by the camp underneath the bridge." His voice was harsh yet muffled, as if each word struggled out through sutured lips. "I thought I'd offer you some assistance."

His voice rode the high-ceilinged acoustics until I couldn't pinpoint his location. Franklin could be standing in the next aisle over or at the front of the building by the cash register. I put a hand in my coat pocket, let my thumb rub the hidden pistol for comfort.

"Your siblings have been worried about you," I said. "They asked me to find you and Alice."

"You found me. She isn't any concern of yours."

"She killed people when she burned down your apartment building. She also torched my friend's bar."

Franklin appeared at the end of the aisle. The shadows rendered him more a shape than a person. A dark blot with distinguished shoulders and long legs.

"Those are serious accusations. You have any proof?"

"She dropped this," I said, and held up the medallion. Franklin came close enough to touch the talisman but stopped himself from reaching for it. I slipped the charm back into my coat.

"Come with me," Franklin said.

I followed him down the plumbing section and around the corner display of chain saws toward the back of the store. In the far corner, Franklin opened a steel door and welcomed me into his studio. No bed inside, just blankets on the floor, two chairs, and a table pushed into the opposite corner. Canvases lay scattered among brushes, cups, and a broken easel. Drips of paint dotted the floor.

Franklin stepped over the paintings on the ground and pulled out two chairs. I sat while he lit a few melted candles. In the fresh light, I could see that his demons covered nearly every inch of the walls. None were framed. Most of the canvases were stuck to the wall with duct tape, others nailed into the Sheetrock like a crucifixion. I looked over the many drafts. The same fanged, boiled-skinned monsters with their twisted goblin noses and bald heads. Their eyes—or the empty sockets where their eyes should've been—watched me.

"You sleep here?" I asked.

"It wouldn't matter. I see them when I'm awake. I tend to obsess on projects."

"Where did they come from?"

"They're us. A glimpse of what's hidden beneath the flesh."

"You're speaking metaphorically, I hope?"

"All good art is metaphor, but . . ." He trailed off, looking at the monsters on the walls. "I've seen mine. Just flashes at first. Things out the corner of my eye; then one day I looked in a mirror, and there he was. He smiled at me with those sharp teeth, and I recognized myself."

Something like sadness swept over me. It wasn't pity. I didn't have any sympathy for Franklin, but I recognized the familiarity of his rage. I'd carried my own silent anger, caged it deep inside myself and fed it insecurity and injustice until it was time to release it on some poor boy who hadn't deserved the beating any more than I'd deserved mine. Looking at the demons, I saw the same violence in Franklin's brushstrokes.

"I guess Logan doesn't get the philosophical statement," I said.

"Logan just doesn't like what it says. He loved my art when I was working on commissions."

"Help me understand," I said.

"When Logan's father was pastor, The Lighthouse was a normal church. All tent revivals, creek baptisms, and Sunday suppers. After his father died, Nathaniel started throwing himself into art."

"Logan's an artist?"

Franklin nodded. "Logan wanted to be a poet. Alice and I met him during a reading in Charleston, where I'd gone to sell some prints. He liked my work and commissioned those angels on the ceiling as a memorial to his father. Things were cool at first. We talked while I worked. Mostly about art and revitalizing the church. We got along pretty well. I'd expected the age gap to be a bigger divide."

Even after Carson's story, I had a hard time imagining Franklin perched on a ladder, painting angels while Logan relaxed in a pew, pontificating about stanzas and end rhyme, but failed artistic ambitions might explain the tortures inflicted on Carson in hopes the bound man would receive a vision. Alice had shown Carson the box she slept in on the night he almost escaped. Had Logan also lain waiting in one of those boxes for some true piece of art?

"The crash gave Logan an opportunity," Franklin continued. "People had already started drifting. He took them in, gave them food and a bed for as long as they wanted. The price of admission was listening to Logan preach. Hungry people will endure anything for soup, but he never rebuilt his congregation. When they kept leaving, Logan decided he needed something more powerful than words to save souls. That's when he commissioned more work from me. A series of disasters from the gospels."

"Melvin showed me Lot's wife turning to salt."

Franklin cast his eyes away in embarrassment. "I was afraid he'd ask me to leave if I didn't do it. By then, I'd learned Logan was into stranger things."

"Like what?"

"Do you believe in magic?" Franklin asked.

The very question Alice had asked Carson the night she put him in the box. I thought of the combination lock, the bottomless pool of blood on my kitchen table, and Brandon Flanders showing me the combination that saved Carson. Just days ago, the world had felt known to me. Now I wasn't sure. Incantations and spells might bring forth things unimagined, conjuring as rare but real a thing as space travel.

"After his father died, Logan found a book. *The Conjurer's Guide to the Art of Creation*. It's a grimoire. A book of spells specifically for artists. The book discusses how artistic ability is the dominant force that molds our reality. Create a powerful-enough work of art, follow this with an appropriate sacrifice and incantation, and it doesn't just change people's ideas—it makes that artistic subject physically real. Logan became obsessed with it."

Even after all Carson had told me about his time inside the box and the revelatory song he'd been commanded to write, I couldn't square the strange miasma of occult belief and Christianity. The Lighthouse was filled with Christian iconography, from the angels on the ceiling to the crucifixes hanging on nearly every wall. Hadn't Logan wanted Carson's ballad to serve the same Old Testament God as Franklin's paintings?

"I thought Logan was just another Baptist. Now you're telling me he's some kind of witch."

Franklin shook his head. "I never said Logan didn't believe. According to him, man willed each of the gods from history into existence with our creative powers. We used our collective imagination to tell stories about deities. After we rendered them in enough artistic works, the gods became real."

"People create culture through belief, but there's still reality and fantasy," I countered. "Some once thought the earth was flat. That doesn't make it so."

"That's not how it works," Franklin said. "It takes sufficient artistic skill and effort, along with the other steps of the spell, to render something real. That's why he encouraged artists at The Lighthouse. He needed to concentrate all that creativity and provide a sacrifice. After following the steps outlined in the book, art becomes reality. A painting that can make crops grow without sunlight. A dance that could raise the dead. That's the goal."

I closed my eyes and witnessed fire raining from the skies over Coopersville. Floodwaters rising like an ocean tide from the stagnant pools of Copper Creek. Acts of God called down on command would certainly inspire belief in the faithless.

"When did you decide to leave?" I asked.

"After people went missing," Franklin said. "There were only eight of us that summer, but we were splitting into factions. Some listened to Logan's sermons while the rest of us worked on our projects. Around the end of June, a poet named Justine disappeared. Logan said she'd just moved on. It seemed easy enough to believe. Still, it happened so suddenly, without any explanation or goodbyes."

Alice had shown Carson three graves. A painter, a poet, and a sculptor. Logan's own little garden of artistic promise. *The sacrifices,* she'd called them. The poet might be Justine. Maybe she'd been a convert to the coven, all of them willing participants when they were locked in the boxes down in the basement, or maybe they'd been snatched in the night and forced inside like Carson to wait on their vision. Franklin hadn't mentioned the boxes. Perhaps he was working up to it, or perhaps it was a new part of the ritual, implemented after he left. Either way, I couldn't ask about something I wasn't supposed to know. I didn't know if I could trust Franklin yet. Better to wait and see what he revealed.

"By the time the third person disappeared, I tried convincing Alice to come with me. Logan owned her by then. She'd been reading the book with him."

Franklin held his palm over the candle's flame, collecting its warmth.

"Logan said you left the portraits in the pews. Why?"

"I wanted Logan to recognize himself. We all have a demon, but his was let loose a long time ago. I've been hiding in a hardware store or living under a bridge like some troll ever since."

Franklin dipped a thumb into the hot candle wax, peeled the hardening seal off his fingertip, and let it flutter down to the tabletop like a plucked flower petal. My mind issued an unbidden *She loves me, she loves me not*, as he dipped the other digits and discarded each wax fingerprint.

"If it was over between you and Alice, why did she visit you under the bridge?" I asked.

"That trip was her last try to get me back into the fold," Franklin said. "But we fought over the paintings again. She told me I was an instrument of evil, and she'd destroy each one she found. 'Wipe the stain of them off the earth,' she said."

Franklin licked his fingers and extinguished one of the candles with a pinch. The shadows grew. I thought he might snuff out the others, but he stopped himself.

"Why does she burn them?" I asked.

Franklin pointed a wax-crusted finger at the wall. One of the demons, its maw overflowing with broken teeth like shards of shattered glass, looked back at us with empty eye sockets. "Wouldn't you want to be rid of them if you thought an artist could make his work come to life? They don't understand metaphor. It's all reality to them. They're afraid that something like this could be brought into existence."

You'd still need a sacrifice, I thought, but I felt stupid even considering the logistics of such lunacies. I still didn't want to believe in spells and sorcery. Even after Brandon's ghost had revealed the combination on the lock to Carson's box, I told myself there had to be some logical explanation. Holding on to that certainty grew harder with each haunting and new revelation, but I couldn't rationalize a world where the supernatural not only existed but also superseded so much of our known reality. Thinking like that would lead to the same madness as Logan's.

What I could understand was the danger of fanatics and the lengths a man like Logan might go to in pursuit of miracles. Carson wouldn't be the last person The Lighthouse imprisoned or buried on the hill after their sorcery inevitably failed. I just didn't know how to stop them. Simpler to just collect my money and leave town.

"Logan says you stole their money."

Franklin ran his finger through the fire. "He really knows how to motivate you. There wasn't much money. Wasn't much food, for that matter. If they'd had any cash to steal, I'd already be out of town."

I didn't believe that. The guerilla-art campaign implied a deeper vendetta. If Logan had money stashed, Franklin might've taken it just for spite—another angle of revenge over drawing Alice into the church.

"This shit with Logan is going to get you killed and the rest of the town burned down. Give it up and see the twins. They're worried about you."

"Why don't you help me tonight?" Franklin said. "Afterward, we'll go see the twins, and you can collect whatever payday they've promised."

"What's the job?" I asked.

"Just a little art project," Franklin said, and snuffed out the last candle.

I looked at my watch in the dark. Two in the morning. Longer than I'd wanted to be out, and much longer than I wanted to leave Carson alone with Uncle Abbott. Shannon might already have finished packing. I still needed to deliver the Mustang, but I couldn't pass up the opportunity to get Franklin out of the building. There was more he wasn't telling me, and if there really was any stolen money, it was likely hidden right here in the hardware store. I'd have plenty of time to search for it while he hung another of his paintings and waited for Alice to come burn it down.

CHAPTER TEN

Franklin didn't have any wheels, so we loaded everything into my truck. Without any real knowledge of the tools an artist requires, I'd expected nothing more than an assortment of paint and brushes, but Franklin surprised me by exiting the shop with implements better suited for burglary. A crowbar jutted out from his leather bag, and a coil of rope draped over his shoulder like a dead snake. He deposited these in the truck and rushed back inside.

I wasn't above whatever mischief was planned; I'd spent many nights watching my old man count stolen money. But after the incident in the bar with Uncle Abbott, I'd promised myself I wouldn't be roped into any more outlaw bullshit regardless of reward. Yet here I was, back to the family tradition of night raids and thinking about how I might get my hands on Franklin's cash. I didn't believe he'd left The Lighthouse emptyhanded. I couldn't say when I'd decided to take the money from him. No moral debate plagued me. I wasn't concerned about the right or wrong of it. Whether my father's corruptive influence or my own shit-heel heart, something inside me just knew I needed that money.

Franklin returned, carrying a rolled canvas. It sagged behind him, dragging the ground like a dejected tail as he struggled with the weight. I offered help, but he wouldn't let me lend a hand.

"What's this one?" I asked.

"My masterpiece," Franklin said as he laid the canvas in the truck bed.

I drove slow, protecting our fragile cargo. Franklin leaned back into the headrest and closed his eyes.

"You believe in fate, Winter?"

The question startled me. Asked so fast I answered automatically, without time to consider a lie.

"No. I believe things just happen."

"That's a hard sell for most. Alice believed in destiny. She'd go on about it in bed, smoking her cigarettes until my ceiling turned yellow. I was jealous of her certainty. I could never manage it. I mean, if things are predestined, what about all those people who never do anything? Die young from disease or just work useless jobs and get old? Fate sounds wonderful if you're going to be some big shot. Not so much if it's childhood leukemia.

"And what about all of history's monsters? You think they were destined from birth to be hated for all eternity? Maybe you could argue some accepted their unfortunate fate as necessary? You need a villain for each hero. A Judas for each Christ. Take a left."

This was a tirade about the nature of his art, the provocateur's defense for disturbing the masses. Listening to Franklin blather on, I wondered if revealing your creations, even in these unusual circumstances, brought on the same bout of fear as my childhood fights. Franklin was clearly nervous, but did he feel deep sickness at the thought that something irrevocable and permanent was occurring? Once this latest painting was revealed, it would make an impact on the world. Did he ever fear going too far the same way I feared throwing a fatal punch?

We rolled by the blank marquee of the Capital Theater. The movie house wasn't another victim of the Decline; the doors had shut in the early 2000s, when the multiplex appeared outside town near the new Walmart. Wednesday evenings the Capital showed horror double features, old monster flicks with slimy mutants or knife-wielding maniacs hacking up horny teens. My first kiss, an awkward attempt with a young girl whose mouth tasted of peanut M&M's and Cherry Coke, happened in the back row during a *Friday the 13th* marathon. I searched the glass display boxes out front for old posters but couldn't see any in the darkness.

Following Franklin's directions, I parked behind an overflowing dumpster in an alley near the Prescott Hotel. The Prescott had been a marvel before my birth and maintained a resilient, if downtrodden, elegance throughout my childhood. I remembered coming to the hotel on some business with my father. Men lingered in the barbershop adjacent to the lobby, chatting and reading their newspapers while they waited on haircuts and hot shaves. Jealousy always filled my father's voice whenever he spoke about these men he referred to as "marks." I understood why. We'd be back home, plotting theft in our squalor, while they'd retire upstairs to opulent suites.

The Prescott never hosted any presidents or dignitaries but was still a favorite among travelers of notoriety. Businessmen from out of state and the rich from Charleston had often stayed at the hotel. While their tailored suits and uncalloused hands advertised wealth, there was another element that set these travelers apart from the locals: they almost floated without the burden of bills and labor weighting them down. No mine cave-in or foreclosure could touch them. Money would protect against tragedies I'd assumed all men eventually face.

Some of those men had children with them that morning. I remembered my raw envy as those boys walked through the lobby with dull eyes, immune to the place's beauty. I'd never seen grandeur like the Prescott outside of a movie screen. I hated those other kids immediately for their apathy.

Franklin interrupted these memories by opening the truck door. He grabbed the tool bag, slung it over his shoulder, and hoisted the rolled canvas.

"Keep watch," he said as we approached the back entrance. The doors had been boarded up, but the fortifying planks looked weak after years of swelling in the rain and drying in the sun. Franklin drove his crowbar into the wood, splintering it apart as I watched the empty street. It was my second trespass of the evening.

The door surrendered its hold with a crack. Inside, dust thick as snow covered the floors. I couldn't believe that underneath was the same blond hardwood my childhood eyes had once compared to our kitchen's linoleum that peeled away in flecks with the summer heat. The walls were marred with spray-painted obscenities, crude shapes, and dripping slogans left by derelicts.

Franklin stopped beside the elevators. The green patina of the brass made my reflection appear diseased. There was no electricity, so we took the stairs slow, Franklin stopping at every third or fourth landing, leaning against the banister and panting with the canvas clutched to his chest. I watched him blush from the effort, but he still refused my help. After a final rest on the tenth floor, we traveled down the hall toward the bridal suite. Franklin handed me the crowbar. I cracked the door open. I'm not sure what I expected. Maybe the adult version of those privileged kids from long ago huddled around a dwindling fire, finally reduced to the same status as anyone else.

Nothing that shocking greeted us. The walls were bare and the furniture absent, yet there was no denying the power of the vaulted ceiling, the parquet floors, or bay window, where a small stained glass portion above the larger panes would catch the morning light and cast red, green, and blue shades across the bedroom.

Franklin couldn't get the window open, so he shattered it with his crowbar. Glass fell like rain on the street below. He brushed the shards away with his shoes.

"I started simple," Franklin said. "My papaw used to spin yarns about the bestial nature of the deceiver. Spoke of how his skin tanned from all the time dwelling in fire. The typical bifurcated tail and cloven hooves that belong on a mule. I tried to tap into that, focus on where the humanity ended, but then I thought about how demons were once angels."

Franklin unrolled the painting. The imp he unscrolled carried an insidious beauty underneath the scars. Tall and sculpted like the men I'd always envied. Dark hair and heavy brows furrowed in a constant state of agitation, horns sprouting near the temples through a heavy quilt of scars. Perverse leather wings belonging to a bat folded around his shoulders like a cape.

If Alice had burned both their apartment and Wildcat's just to end Franklin's art, she'd come running when she saw this devil perched in the window. The hotel would smolder like everything else the couple touched. A pang of sadness passed through me as I thought about my hometown's last relic of prosperity burning, but those were the thoughts of a rube. I remembered the sneers of the rich boys. The glares from those substantial men in the barbershop while my father discussed business with the barber, who returned to his shaves with apologies for the interruption. Places like the Prescott would've never opened their doors to a young scrapper like me. I wouldn't have even been permitted to fetch guests their cocktails. The dried bloodstains on one of my holey T-shirts and three-day-dirty jeans would've marked me like Cain.

Those who enjoyed these luxuries had never felt their fathers' belt after losing a fight. Their fights were won with campaign contributions. Better the Prescott burn than the lie continue. Franklin understood that. It's why he'd hung a portrait of the basest parts of himself out the window.

Franklin sat on the floor, his back against the wall, legs spread wide as he plucked up a triangular shard of glass. He tested the sliver's edge against his thumb.

"What will you tell her if she comes?" I asked.

"I'll explain that I needed this. The monsters"—he gestured at the demon billowing in the light breeze—"they saved me."

"Think it'll work?"

"Stick around and find out."

"What am I supposed to tell the twins?"

"Tell them I'll be home after I finish this one last thing."

Franklin took a notepad from his pocket and scribbled fat lines on the paper.

"You wanna know what your demon looks like?" he asked. "I can sketch it for you."

I didn't wait on him to show me. I knew too many things Franklin didn't.

—

Back at Dalton Hardware, I let myself in through the same back door. Dread followed me down the aisles of socket wrenches and power drills. Even following my hunch that the money was hidden in the studio, life had been reduced to survival for so long that imagining a surplus of anything felt like foolish hope.

I entered the studio, dragged Franklin's small pallet of sour-smelling blankets out of the corner, and used the crowbar I'd taken from the Prescott to pry up the floorboards. Each one popped up whole, rusty nails still jutting from their ends. I tossed them away, the last board knocking over some paint cans on the opposite side of the room. A blue puddle like a miniature lake spread across the floor. I ignored the mess and lowered one of Franklin's candles into the hole, illuminating a dingy plastic tarp with a duffel bag hidden underneath it. I lifted the bag out and shook it like a curious kid guessing what lay inside a wrapped Christmas present.

The money was secured into a few tight rolls with rubber bands. I fished one roll out of the bag and fanned the crinkled bills. Multiple denominations, all heavily used. Just one roll represented more money than I'd ever held in my life. Considering the current economy, it was more money than I could've imagined.

I wasn't sure how I knew Franklin was lying about the money. It was some sense inherited from my father, a way of sniffing out scores and seeing the weaknesses in people even when they didn't recognize the faults in themselves. Franklin wanted to hurt Logan and win Alice back, but he'd also grown up in the same poverty as the rest of us. He wanted nice clothes. He wanted new wheels. He wanted to lie down at night and not fret over the stack of bills and termination notices on the kitchen table. He wanted Alice to have what she deserved and to focus on his art rather than waste away in whatever minimum-wage jobs were left in this crumbling economy. This wasn't just money. It was salvation.

Underneath the cash, in the bottom of the bag, lay a small leather journal. It bore no title and was sealed with a strip of leather wrapped in a tight bow. *The Conjurer's Guide*. Franklin must have taken the book with him when he left. The cover felt warm to the touch, as if the leather weren't cold hide but living skin radiating heat.

There were a few options now that I had the cash. I could either break up the reunion at the Prescott and demand a cut of the stolen loot when I brought Franklin to the twins, or go home, load Carson and Shannon up in the Mustang, and leave town. There'd be the obstacle of Uncle Abbott, but I'd sort him out. Even after its long absence, I hadn't forgotten money's ability to lift most burdens.

I wanted to run. There was shame in admitting that. What I'd seen in The Lighthouse basement should've fostered an obligation—a sense of duty that I keep innocent people out of those boxes—but I was more worried about saving myself. Logan would come for me after the break-in. Waging war against fanatics with more resources seemed like a stupid way to die. I decided to go home, pay off Uncle Abbott, and part ways. I'd take Shannon with me. We'd ferry Carson wherever he wanted to go and let those left in the mountains save themselves. I'd been a healer once, but I couldn't fix what was broken here.

I took out my cell and dialed Shannon's number. No answer, just the same full voice mail. I loaded the money and the grimoire back into the bag and left.

CHAPTER ELEVEN

Uncle Abbott sat on the front steps with a cigarette smoldering between his fingers while dawn shined its pale glow over the crest of the mountains. A newfound resilience filled me as I climbed out of the truck with the money bag dangling from my hand. I wouldn't even let him pack. I'd cross the yard, shove a fat roll of cash into his coat pocket, and send him on his way.

"Where you been?" Uncle Abbott asked as he stood from the steps. The cigarette dangled from his lip as he blocked the doorway. He'd changed clothes since I left. New dark jeans, a flannel shirt, and thin jacket. He smelled of fresh soap and tobacco.

I dropped the bag between us and took his share out of my coat.

"Christ," he said. "Where'd you get that?"

"This is your share. It's going to be what you use to leave."

He didn't hear me, just reached for the roll. Closer now, I noticed sweat beading on his forehead, his collar damp and flat, hands shaking a bit, either from the anticipation of the money or some unknown labor. Past the scraggly dogwoods that bloomed white in season, I saw Shannon's little shit box Toyota. Branches obscured some of the vehicle, but the rust above the front wheel and the mismatched red driver-side door made it unmistakable.

"How much is here?" Uncle Abbott asked. I observed his hands. Something dark beneath his fingernails. I pushed past him toward the house, but he grabbed my coat sleeve and pulled me back.

"Wait," he said. I jerked away hard, staggering him until he tripped and fell onto his knees.

I opened the front door, calling for Shannon. The house was still dark, just the faintest morning light visible through the living-room windows. I stumbled along in the shadows, expecting Uncle Abbott to be following at my heels, but my footsteps were the only sound. Bleach vapors invaded my nose. The antiseptic smell set off alarms in my head.

I found Carson on the kitchen floor. Uncle Abbott had laid him out on a large rug with his hands folded across his stomach. The respectful posture was ruined by the blood drying over his right eyebrow. No point assessing injuries. His open, sightless eyes told me all I needed. I left him in the kitchen and crashed through the house, still calling out for Shannon.

It wasn't until I was back in the hallway, leaning next to the deep dent in the paneling, that I noticed the bathroom door slightly ajar. I didn't move right away. I didn't want to see inside. Instead, I laid my head back into the crater documenting my foolish love. I could've stayed like that, just waited until Uncle Abbott came in with his excuses, but I nudged the door open with the toe of my boot.

There was little light. Only a sliver leaked in from the window above the sink, letting me see the shape of Shannon floating in the full tub. My knees weakened, bending me over until I sat down hard on the closed toilet lid. Her face turned away from me, her neck twisted into an unnatural angle. I reached for her. My hand submerged in the cold water, and a sob shook me.

Brushing the hair away from her forehead, I remembered the first night I saw Shannon at Wildcat's. Her dark eyes shining in the green and red Christmas lights. The slow smile offered as she'd poured drinks for the misfits. I was willing myself to move, to do anything useful, when I heard my truck's engine start out in the yard.

I ran out of the bathroom, nearly tearing the door from the hinges as my shoulder collided into it, turned hard at the end of the hallway, and burst outside into bright morning light. The truck disappeared as Uncle Abbott gunned the accelerator. I knew I'd never catch him, but chased anyway, hate pumping through me as I drew the gun from my coat pocket. I kept up until my muscles folded me over in agony, coughing and sputtering in the black cloud of exhaust. I emptied the revolver at the blur in the distance. My uncle just drove on.

I didn't have any idea where he was going. Smart money would never slow until the truck reached the county line. Maybe I could pursue him in Shannon's shit box, but there wasn't much use. I limped home. My legs throbbed and my chest filled with an ache that radiated through me with each breath. The money bag was missing from my lawn. Uncle Abbott had snatched it before fleeing.

I couldn't face Shannon again, so I tended to Carson first. The cramped kitchen appeared smaller with Carson's legs splayed across the floor. I knelt beside him, inspecting the dried blood matted in his hair. The man's hands and pockets were empty. I closed his eyes.

Sitting on the floor, I noticed the dull gleam of something beneath the refrigerator. I reached under and pulled out the small leather fob clasped to the Mustang's keys. The room didn't look like the scene of a struggle. No broken furniture, shattered windows, or displaced appliances. I opened the cabinet under the sink and found a hammer wrapped in bloody rags. It didn't take much of a detective to piece the events together. Carson must've tried sneaking off in the car, and Uncle Abbott ambushed him with the claw hammer—or maybe he'd just killed the man to eliminate a witness to our robbery.

Either way, Shannon strolled right into the scene of carnage in my kitchen, and Uncle Abbott decided he didn't need another witness.

On my way to the bathroom, a brief moment of magical thinking occurred in which I expected to see her sitting up in the water with her bare feet resting on the lip of the tub. In my fantasy, I perched near her toes and chatted awhile, but when I opened the door, it was the same as before. I slid my hand into the cold water. Frozen needles stung my fingers long after I'd carried her to the couch.

Shannon's Toyota had a proper trunk, but I wasn't comfortable driving it. A cracked radiator left it prone to overheating, and the timing belt whined. Even when she watched the gauges and kept it running cool, the car occasionally stalled. Those were the problems I knew about. Shannon basically kept the junker running on hope. The last thing I needed was finding myself stranded on the side of the road with two dead bodies. The Mustang was too flashy, the sort of ride guaranteed to draw unwanted attention. If I wanted the bodies out of my house, I'd have to risk it in Shannon's shit box.

Before committing, I asked myself one last time if I couldn't just call the police. I didn't want the burden of putting Shannon in the ground but knew I had no other choice. With Uncle Abbott gone, I'd be the prime suspect. The combination of evidence and my family name would be enough for a local jury to convict. Aside from worrying over the law, how long would it be before The Lighthouse discovered my break-in? Legitimate options were off the table.

Even if Shannon's long legs would've allowed her to fit, I couldn't stand the idea of her in the trunk. She'd be in the grave soon enough, and I didn't want to condemn her to darkness prematurely. I placed her in the back seat and covered her body with quilts from the living room.

The car might appear normal at a distant glance, but a closer look would reveal everything. I accepted the risk.

There was no way I could carry such a large man, so I ended up dragging Carson, my hands under his armpits and his feet cutting trench lines across the yard. I opened the trunk, laid his upper body on the edge, and pushed until he flopped inside next to the shovel Abbott had used to dig up the basement.

The Toyota's engine strained but started on the first try. My destination was Willow Branch, a back hollow on the outskirts of Coopersville seldom traveled by anyone who didn't live among the trailers and shacks. People there stayed in the hills and drifted to town once every few months. If I remained discreet, I'd be allowed to come and go. The problem was the trip. I'd have to pass through town. Logan would know about the break-in by now. The community watch would be out on patrol and looking for Carson.

When I shifted the car into reverse and looked over my shoulder, Brandon Flanders was sitting in the back seat with Shannon's legs stretched across his lap. His eternal nosebleed dripped on the quilts that covered her body. I closed my eyes and counted to ten, but he was still in the rearview when I opened them. His girth seemed uncomfortably cramped in the tiny back seat. I couldn't see with his head in the way, so I stopped backing up. That detail frightened me most of all. Something more ephemeral, a spectral apparition with the translucent nature of frosted glass, would've been easier to accept.

Brandon opened his mouth. His words leaked out as he cleared decades of the grave from his throat.

"The book," he said.

It took great effort for him to utter the words. Even when he'd shown me the lock, our communication had been restricted to a bizarre game of charades.

"What book?" I asked.

I saw the broken blood vessels mapping the whites of his eyes.

"The book the painter stole," he said. His voice was stronger now, each word creeping into my ear like an uninvited tongue. "You have to get it back."

I remembered *The Conjurer's Guide* had been in the money bag when Uncle Abbott grabbed it.

"It's too late for that," I said. My uncle was long gone. Besides, I had more pressing matters with the bodies tucked away in the back seat and trunk. "There isn't time."

The rearview mirror shattered in response, a long-crooked fracture running the length of it. I turned the mirror away from me, backed out blind, and swung the car toward town with the dead man still watching me from the back seat.

—

A blanket of black smoke hung over downtown. I expected the Prescott to be the source of the dark cloud, but as I turned off the boulevard across Elm Street, the hotel stood as I'd left it. The demon still hung from the broken window, the painting fluttering in the wind like a banner of conquest. I wondered if Franklin still waited inside for Alice. There was no time to check. The dead took precedent.

A few blocks away, Dalton Hardware burned. Around twenty onlookers lined the sidewalk across from the smoldering building. Most wore their coats, while others covered themselves with blankets against the early-morning chill. A lone police cruiser parked near the curb with its lights casting blue waves across the scene. I considered turning the car around. The detour would likely add forty minutes to my trip.

Deputy Laura Smith stood in the street, waving back the gathering crowd. I was preparing to execute an illegal U-turn when the deputy noticed my car and waved me forward. Panic twisted my insides, but I let my foot off the brake and rolled up to the intersection.

Brandon still sat in the middle of my back seat, alternating between looking out the window and watching me with alert yet dead eyes. I wasn't sure what kept him there. Perhaps he'd stay until I heeded his warnings about retrieving *The Conjurer's Guide*. The flow from his nose had increased until blood dripped down and stained the quilt covering his lap.

"Hide," I said. If the deputy saw Brandon bleeding all over the back seat, she'd haul us out and find the bodies. Could others see Brandon? What happened if Deputy Smith tried shackling the ghost's hands? How long before the officer realized none of my passengers were living?

Deputy Smith instructed me to roll down my window. When I didn't respond, she stood by the door, miming the turning of an invisible crank. I stifled a nervous laugh. Even Shannon's shit box had power windows. I rolled mine down.

"Where are you headed?" the deputy asked.

The question caught me off guard. I'd been thinking up an excuse for the hemorrhaging ghost. Why did it matter where I was going? I reminded myself that now wasn't the time to argue about civil liberties. Not when I was busy ferrying the dead in a slightly stolen car. Thoughtless, a lie escaped my lips.

"Down toward Charleston to visit friends."

Friends? Anyone in town surely knew I had few friends, much less friends over fifty miles away. I was headed toward the interstate, so it seemed plausible, but the weakness of the lie embarrassed me. Deputy Smith placed her palms on the doorframe as if holding the window down and glanced into the back seat. Brandon's ghost stared back at the officer. I wanted to stomp the gas.

"Well, this road's closed, Mr. Winter," the deputy said. "I'm afraid you'll have to go the long way around."

Deputy Smith looked through the back window. Her jaw dropped as a hand traveled down, fumbling with the holster on her gun belt.

In the rearview, Shannon's foot peeked out from underneath the folds of blankets, the pink nail polish on her toes attracting attention like a signal fire. Smith unholstered her gun. She raised the weapon and looked ready to demand I exit the car when Brandon reached his arm through the closed window of the back seat. The glass didn't break. Brandon simply passed through the solid pane like a hand submerging in water without creating the slightest ripples and grasped the deputy's forearm. Deputy Smith dropped the gun. It clattered onto the concrete between her small shoes. The deputy rubbed her eyes, blinked, and looked around as if regaining consciousness from some fugue state. She didn't check the back seat again, just turned to me with a fresh look of confusion. Deputy Smith adjusted the clip-on tie of her uniform. She cocked her head as if trying to recall the proper procedure for a routine traffic stop. The gun on the ground seemed entirely forgotten.

"License and registration?" the deputy asked. This wasn't an order. She sounded unsure about whether she already had my documentation.

Behind us, the roof on the hardware store collapsed. The center fell, releasing tall flames that stretched into the open air.

Deputy Smith retrieved her fallen sidearm and turned toward the crowd. "Everyone back." She walked to the scene's perimeter to keep the crowd away from the flames.

I threw the car in reverse and swung around. As I shifted into drive, my eyes caught a flash of black hair. I looked in the broken rearview mirror and saw Alice standing on the curb. She was dressed entirely in black. Tight dark jeans and combat boots. A hooded sweatshirt with long sleeves that fell over her knuckles and swallowed her hands until only her black-painted fingertips emerged. Her hood was down, and her hair sat piled atop her head in an unraveling bun. Inky locks spilled across her ears, caressing her long neck. Ash from the burning building speckled her outfit.

Watching, I understood she couldn't stay away from the flames. It was as if she were not only warmed by the heat but also able to observe the chemical change, witness things unseen to mortal eyes. I immediately understood why Franklin felt lost without her. Women like her rarely materialized in a man's life. I'd been fortunate enough to know two. One had refused my proposal back on the plains, and the other lay dead in my back seat, never knowing exactly how I felt.

In a moment, Deputy Smith would be outside my door again. I gave Alice a final look, then drove on.

CHAPTER TWELVE

Willow Branch offered none of the eponymous trees of its namesake. An early settler must have thought the name sounded refined, the sort of title to conjure images of elegant country estates and entice prospective homeowners. As I followed the twisted creek that ran parallel to the road, the title felt like a cruel joke. The homes I passed were dilapidated coal-company houses or double-wide trailers rusted with age. I didn't see any residents. It was as if something unseen marked me as a death cart. Either out of fear or respect, people kept their distance.

The asphalt eventually ended, and I followed a dirt road until there was no road left at all, only a footpath up into the mountains. I parked the car and waited to make sure I was alone. My task was better suited for night, but I didn't have time to wait for dark.

I'm not sure how much to tell you about the burial. Part of me thinks you don't need all the details. That you'd be better off with a comforting lie. I could tell you I lifted Shannon's body from the back seat with some divinely granted strength, carried her up the hill, and dug a grave beneath the trees even without proper tools, aside from my shovel with the broken handle. I could say that my tongue didn't falter, that I found the words to honor her with the eulogy she deserved. I could tell you there was something noble about the unmarked grave. That I remembered its location and returned often on cold nights, decorating the spot with garlands of flowers. I could tell you that Carson went into another plot. That I had the time, energy, and decency to dig two holes instead of interweaving the bones of strangers for eternity.

I could tell you a lot of things, but we've come too far together. I've been too honest. Let's just say I did what I could for them.

Brandon was waiting when I came down the mountain. He sat on a large stone with his hands clasped together in his lap like a child cupping a trapped insect. No blood leaked from his nose. Were it not for the lack of breathing and unblinking eyes, I could've mistaken him for a living man enjoying the morning sun.

"Why are you still here?" I asked.

"You need the book," Brandon said.

"Enough riddles," I replied. "Things would've been easier from the start if you'd just explained the lock."

"Franklin told you the truth. The writings teach the link between creativity and conjuration. If the art is powerful enough and the sacrifice sufficient, it becomes real."

The idea sounded even more ridiculous from a dead man. Paint on canvas and lovely words might be able to manipulate something as fragile as people, but they weren't splitting an atom. All my days poring over textbooks filled with maladies revealed no work of literature capable of obliterating cancer cells any more than a song might cease the ocean tides. Only cold science changed the world in tangible ways. Art might spark inspiration, but math put men on the moon.

"The box you pulled the man from is the first step in the process," Brandon continued. "A conduit where a seeker may receive a vision."

"What kind of vision?"

"That would depend on what the artist was willing into existence."

I remembered Carson emerging from the box on weak legs, slathered in his own filth and clawing at my clothing. After enough time inside, a man might see anything. It didn't make the hallucinations real.

I wasn't entirely convinced Brandon's ghost existed. This could all be the result of bad chemicals flooding my frontal lobe.

"Why should I believe a hallucination?" I asked him. "You're just my own version of Marley's ghost. A bicycle lock instead of a rattling chain."

Blood leaked from Brandon's nose again. The hospital whites collapsed in on themselves as if his mass diminished and regrew underneath the garments. His eyes, always clouded and unblinking, appeared colorless as he looked at me.

Brandon held his closed hands out to me. "This is all I can offer."

Remembering the lock left me hesitant, but I let Brandon place his hands over mine and drop a small trinket into my waiting palm. It was a tiny hummingbird earring with a garnet for a stomach and delicate silver wings. I rotated the minuscule bird, examining the wings forever frozen in flight. Streaks of green and purple shimmered down its back like a mood ring as it glinted in the sunlight.

Uncle Abbott must've waded out into the shallows and sifted through the rocky creek as if panning for gold. I thought of all the years he'd carried the little bird. Wondered where he'd stashed it during his prison conviction and what his reunion with the totem would've looked like days ago when I was out of the house. Had he thought its return a good omen, or was it simply a small pleasure that helped him weather the days of our decline?

"How is this going to help?" I asked. When I looked up from the earring, Brandon was gone.

It was just past two, but the sky resembled dusk by the time I made it back downtown. The streets were empty. No police sirens like that morning and no pedestrians strolling on the sidewalk. The onlookers from the hardware store had all drifted home once the flames expired.

Grave dirt still covered my neck and filled the grooves of my fingernails. I rolled down the window, hoping the wind might blow away some of the dust clinging to my wet skin, but the hot air wafting inside offered no relief. My eyelids kept closing, each squint a dangerous thing that might steal my consciousness. Even after the worst fights, I'd rarely felt so beaten. All I wanted was a bath, but I knew I'd never sink comfortably into my tub again. Not without thinking of Shannon bobbing in the water.

The demon banner still hung from the window of the Prescott. It flapped in the breeze, the monster undulating in a wicked dance. I parked underneath it and climbed out of the car, carrying the crowbar. Locked doors weren't my concern. Just because the banner still flew didn't mean that Alice or Logan wasn't waiting upstairs. I imagined Franklin with his throat slit. Alice waiting behind the bridal-suite door with the razor ready. I still had the pistol but no ammunition.

The Prescott's lobby appeared empty, but I waited by the door and scanned the room for anything unusual. I climbed the stairs once I was satisfied no one was hiding behind the front desk, ready to shoot me in the back. My muscles still ached from digging the grave.

I found Franklin where I'd left him, the sketch pad in his lap open to a charcoal rendering of a raven-haired young woman. The sharp point of her chin hadn't been shaded in yet, but I recognized Alice. Aside from the sketch and the smeared charcoal on his hands, there was no evidence he'd bothered moving since the night before.

"I saw the smoke," Franklin replied. "I guess she's busy somewhere else."

"She burned down the hardware store."

If the loss of his other works, *The Conjurer's Guide*, or the money wounded him, Franklin didn't show it. I didn't know how that was possible. Perhaps he thought that Alice knew enough to take the cash and book, or perhaps he was too disappointed by her absence to care about money. I sympathized with that. Eventually, the weight of my grief over Shannon would recede enough for me to lament my other losses. I considered confronting him about *The Conjurer's Guide*, only he'd never follow me to the twins if he knew I'd taken the book and cash. Better to let him think the stolen relic burned in the fire.

Franklin noticed my dirty shirt as he set the sketchbook aside but didn't ask questions about my appearance. I squatted on the floor across from him, put my back against the wall, and felt a flood of relief at finally resting. Sleep settled over me, but I pushed it away by squeezing my eyes closed, then stretching them so wide the moisture evaporated. My numb hands still grasped the crowbar.

"Is it still morning?" Franklin asked. Sunlight burned through the smoke outside the broken window. "I've lost some time here."

"More like early afternoon. Let me take you back home," I said. "Let the twins know you're alive, and then you can go wherever you want."

"Are you still after that money they promised?" Franklin asked.

"It's not about the money anymore."

He didn't inquire further. I'm not sure I could've explained it anyway. I've never expressed myself well with words. Gabrielle often complained about that. Mocked the way I'd furrow my brow and glare rather than just say what was on my mind. All my honest moments came from my hands. Whether training my fists to harm or my fingers to heal, my hands remained more articulate than my tongue.

I thought of the things lost to the past. Gabrielle, Shannon, my chance at becoming a doctor. Even my hands, my one asset with a modicum of poetry in them, had been rendered useless by age and abuse. After all that failure, I just wanted to do right by someone.

"You've still got some people who love you. You owe them an explanation. Tell them something, even if it's goodbye."

I thought Franklin might collect the sketchbook or roll up the banner and hide them somewhere until he returned, but we left both behind. The demon's infernal smile filled my cracked rearview as we drove away.

Shannon's shit box struggled the whole way. The needle on the heat gauge peaked early on our drive, burying into the red. This was followed by a grinding noise I recognized as the engine's final protest. I pushed it on regardless. The Toyota responded by expelling a plume of blue smoke through the cracks in the hood. Fearing fire, Franklin jumped out before we came to a complete stop in the school's lot. I placed my hand on the warm hood and patted the car like a sick horse. It had done well and had my permission to die.

We stood silently, debating our next move, when the front door of the school opened. Miranda Hill emerged at the top of the stairs.

Franklin didn't move. I recognized the same sort of cowardice I felt the morning when my father slammed my head into the wall. Out of all the fights in my life, I'd avoided the one that mattered most. Not wanting Franklin to live with similar regrets, I placed my hand against his lower back and gave him a nudge.

Rising on the toes of her boots to accommodate for his height, Miranda wrapped her arms around her brother. Her tough veneer cracked. Even at a distance, I heard her choke back a sob.

"I thought I'd lost you," she said.

Franklin patted her in an awkward, rhythmless way that made me wish I could give them more privacy. Miranda's tears dried as quickly as they came. She expelled a single snort while dabbing her eyes with her shirtsleeve, then was back to being tough.

"Come inside," she said.

I waited in the cafeteria under the gaze of the painted clown while the twins took Franklin into his art room. I resisted the urge to rest my head on the tabletop. By that point, staying awake seemed inevitable. I don't recall how long they spent in the other room. I just waited, feeling the steady ache in my knuckles, until Melvin fetched me. He wore the same denim as before, the clothes so stiff and stinking I smelled each unwashed day accumulating in the fibers. His wispy little mustache had finally grown, but it remained pencil thin.

"We'd like a word with you," he said.

The trepidation in his voice sounded like a child recounting a visit to the principal's office. It was about the money. They were about to tell me they'd never had the promised funds. I should've been angry but felt nothing more than weary. After listening to their excuses and apologies, I'd demand a ride home and be done with all this amateur detective work.

When I entered the art room, Franklin was sitting on the floor with one of his dog portraits. He turned it from side to side, as if each new angle might alter the image, but the Great Dane's white face, the snout speckled with a constellation of black spots, stayed unchanged above the high Victorian collar. Miranda pulled me aside as Melvin closed the door.

"Where'd you find him?" Miranda whispered.

I glanced toward Franklin. His attention was now focused on a Doberman wearing an officer's uniform.

"The Prescott. I helped him hang one of his paintings out the window."

"You broke in?"

"I thought he'd be more likely to come along if indulged."

"How much has he told you?" Miranda asked.

"Just that he was hoping the painting would lure Alice out. He wanted to see her again."

Miranda's next comment was interrupted by a scream. I turned just in time to see Franklin put his fist through the Doberman's muzzle. The shredded canvas caught around his bent elbow, the frame hanging from his arm as he tried retracting it through the hole where the dog's nose had been. Franklin kicked a foot through another of the portraits. He stomped on the stack of frames while ranting in half words and feral grunts. Miranda hugged him from behind, soothing him while resting her head against the hollow of his back. Franklin swung the frame, slamming it into Miranda's ear.

"Grab him," she said.

Melvin tackled Franklin. As the brothers rolled across the floor, Miranda produced a small syringe from her pocket. The sight of the needle made Franklin fight harder. He snapped his teeth inches from Melvin's nose, thrashed, clawed, and scurried away until Melvin got a handful of his hair. Miranda sank the needle in just above Franklin's collar. The medicine worked fast. Franklin kicked and screamed a moment longer before a languor filled his limbs. He flopped effortlessly, a drowning man losing his fight against the current. Seconds later, he was unconscious. I recognized the drug's effects. If my pharmacology still served, Miranda had injected him with around five or ten milligrams of diazepam.

Miranda recapped the needle while Melvin removed several long strips of cloth from his pockets and tied Franklin's hands behind his back. Working together, they propped their brother up in the corner.

"He'll be calm now," Melvin said as he smoothed down the cowlick he'd created pulling Franklin's hair. Either he was crying or the effort from the struggle had left his cheeks crimson. "Let's eat, and I'll fill you in."

The Hills provided a small feast. The lack of electricity left only canned foods available, but the school's pantry offered some variety. Heaping scoops of instant mashed potatoes smothered in brown gravy, fruit cocktail in thick syrup, watery green beans (mostly salt), and a mound of canned tuna that stank up the cafeteria. The Hills skipped the fish, substituting baked beans for their protein. I guess they'd been sustaining on tuna for a long time.

Miranda put considerable effort into making the meal a formal occasion. She draped a linen cloth over our section of the long table and lit several candles, a wasteful gesture that offered optimal light instead of us all huddling around a solitary flame. I should've been hungry, but I just pushed bits of fruit around the school lunch tray with my plastic fork.

"I'm afraid we haven't been entirely honest with you," Miranda said. "Melvin was against lying from the first, but I felt it was necessary. We broke your machines because I wanted to see if your famous anger was just a rumor. After you made Melvin demolish the truck, I needed to see if you were ruled entirely by rage."

The candles cast shadows over Miranda's face. I thought about the prepared syringe. Miranda had administered the dose with the skill of someone accustomed to sedating violent patients, and Melvin tied knots with the proficiency of a veteran sailor. The act was rehearsed. The twins knew Franklin had stolen The Lighthouse's money, and if he wouldn't hand it over, they'd prepared other methods to get it from him.

"Franklin wasn't honest with you either," Miranda said. "He wasn't just commissioned by The Lighthouse. He was a member. Franklin and Logan studied *The Conjurer's Guide* together. Both believed the book's rituals would grant them power through their art, but Franklin was the more skilled of the two. Jealousy grew between them."

I thought Franklin took the book to punish Logan. It never occurred to me he might want it for himself. I'd expected two men at war but stumbled upon something closer to a religious dispute between conflicting denominations.

"I've seen the boxes in the basement. Whose idea was that?" I asked.

"It's all in the book," Miranda said. "Passages with specific instructions for constructing the box, fasting, and waiting inside to receive visions."

"Franklin always meditated," Melvin added. "Different techniques promising connection with muses and other beings of pure inspiration. He prayed and offered sacrifices long before coming to The Lighthouse. 'Paltry offerings,' he called them. Mostly birds, fish, or insects. The occasional dog or cat."

"I understand Logan's desires," I said. "Old Testament wrath born from the commissions Franklin painted. Miracles from the gospels delivered by song. Those would make him a modern-day messiah. But why would Franklin choose the demons? What could that kind of art project hope to bring about?"

"Franklin would say they chose him," Miranda said. "*The Conjurer's Guide* manifests desire from the subconscious into the physical realm. It brings things from one plane to another. Maybe Franklin's demons slipped through some crack between worlds, whispered in his ear to render them in art so they could escape into our world, or maybe they're only in his head. Maybe all the things in our heads are just waiting to be born."

"Franklin wanted power," Melvin said. "Any source would do. Our brother tried selling his soul countless times. Midnight rendezvous out at the crossroads with skinned black cats. Ouija boards and black masses. Endless summoning spells and incantations. Nothing worked. No devils ever came calling. *The Conjurer's Guide* promised the power to make his own devil. Logan wanted to be God. Franklin's tastes were always more malevolent."

I recalled Franklin's sermon about destiny in the truck. The way he said every Jesus needed a Judas. Every hero a villain. If he and Logan were dueling, why not let it be on a cosmic scale? Only it wouldn't be a biblical battle between good and evil. I saw no angels in either man. Logan hid his wickedness behind a veil of holy penance. With his demons, Franklin was just more direct.

"Who decided on the sacrifices?" I asked.

"The book is vague on sacrifices," Miranda explained. "It states you need powerful art and an offering. It was Franklin who'd decided the sacrifice should be the life of another creator. It was something the demons whispered to him while he lay in the box. It didn't take long to sell Logan on the idea. If Franklin stayed, eventually Logan would've added him to the sacrifice."

I thought again of the unmarked graves. How many had Franklin helped bury before Logan decided his pupil might better serve their magic planted in the ground? Was their war really over the demon paintings, or was it just the old fears of succession? Another elderly king refusing to abdicate his throne?

"If Logan was hunting Franklin, why leave all the demon portraits around town?" I asked.

"He still doesn't get it," Melvin said.

Miranda leaned forward in the candlelight. "Alice was going to be Franklin's sacrifice. After the first fire, he used the paintings to draw her out."

I pushed my tray across the table, sick of tales layered with betrayal.

"I wanna hear this from Franklin. And then I want the money I'm owed."

"He'll be out at least a few hours," Melvin said.

"And you know we don't have the money," Miranda said. "I'm sorry to have lied. We just needed our brother back. We can't have him buried on the hillside. Regardless of what he's done, he's our blood."

Just days ago, I'd have bashed the twins with the plastic lunch tray and brandished the empty revolver, but all the recent death had sapped my appetite for vengeance. Without condoning or forgiving, I understood the lies. Besides, I'd lost more money than I'd ever seen hours ago, and it was nothing next to the loss of Shannon. That was just one more reason why I needed to speak with Franklin. I wanted to understand how *The Conjurer's Guide* had become more precious than Alice's love.

"You just pumped your brother full of drugs. Seeing as I'm the only one here with any medical knowledge, I'd better check on him."

The twins debated with a silent glance. Afterward, Melvin took me back into the music room, where Franklin lay bound on the floor next to the trumpets and clarinet cases. I checked his vitals. Strong and steady.

"Satisfied?" Melvin asked.

"I'm not leaving until he's awake. I've seen too much death to walk away and let something else happen."

Melvin gazed down at his big brother. "You know I'd pay you if I had the money," he said. "You're owed it for bringing him home to us."

What kind of bonds make you welcome wolves home? My own monstrous relation had managed to not only steal the only real money I'd ever had but also kill the woman I might've loved. Maybe I should smother Franklin, slay the beast before it woke, but I didn't really want that. All I wanted was some sleep and the devil's side of the story.

"If you really feel indebted to me, you can let me crash for a few hours," I told Melvin.

"Miranda won't like it," he said.

"Convince her," I said. "You two admitted you owe me. At least give me the chance to talk with him."

"So you can find where he hid The Lighthouse's money?"

"That money's long gone. Burned away with Dalton Hardware."

"That's too bad," Melvin said. "But that's not why I needed him back."

Maybe that was true. Maybe there were loves in this world that transcended even the worst betrayals. I didn't know if that was a virtue or tragedy.

"A few hours' sleep and a word with your brother when he wakes. Afterwards, we're cool. Deal?"

Melvin led me out of the band room and down the narrow hallway past several classrooms toward the teachers' lounge. Inside, a leather couch with hide as thin as wax paper sat stuffed in the corner next to an empty vending machine. I lay down, took off my boots, and set them underneath a nearby coffee table covered in yellowed math textbooks.

"I'll fetch you in a few hours," Melvin said.

"As soon as he wakes up," I replied. My consciousness was already ebbing away. I pulled my jacket off and draped it over my chest.

CHAPTER THIRTEEN

I'm not sure how long I slept. One moment, I was deep inside a dream, standing in a frozen cornfield, watching snowflakes glimmer in Gabrielle's hair. Suddenly, I was awake. I wiped the drool from my chin, shrugged into my jacket, and closed my eyes, willing my way back into the dream until a strange echo emitted from down the hall. Resigned to consciousness, I stood and slipped on my boots.

Smoke found me before I reached the door. Black curtains of smog had filled the hallway, and a crackling—as if someone were tearing fistfuls of pages from the forgotten textbooks—grew louder as I approached the cafeteria.

Melvin lay sprawled in the art room with blood leaking down his cheeks like unwiped tears. The dome of his skull shifted beneath my fingertips when I raised his head and checked his absent pulse. I searched his coat pockets, found another prefilled syringe of sedative and the keys for Franklin's demolished truck. I kept both. Even battered, the truck remained a sounder vehicle than Shannon's shit box. I didn't like leaving Melvin, but the fire made me press on. I needed to find Miranda and Franklin before the school became an inferno.

The cafeteria doors were locked. I kicked until the hinges buckled, then charged so hard with my shoulder down that I fell into the room. A burning pyre fueled by stacks of the demon and dog paintings greeted me. Gasoline fumes filled my nostrils and clouded my vision with a shimmering haze, but I made out Miranda, bound in a chair that sat atop two tables stretched over the flaming canvases. The cloth gag in her mouth stifled any screams.

Holding a makeshift table-leg torch aloft, Franklin dipped his fingers into a cup of blood and drew a series of strange symbols on the floor. He chanted in low whispers. I didn't recognize the language but understood it as an invocation necessary for completing the ritual. Franklin drizzled the remaining blood over the canvases. He stopped chanting, and the room fell silent aside from Miranda struggling to breathe through the gag. Her pupils widened, silently pleading for help as Franklin thrust his torch back into the pyre.

If I'd just taken a moment to consider my options, things might've transpired differently. I could've pulled the empty gun, bluffed until Franklin snuffed the fire, and pistol-whipped him before untying Miranda. In the end, I did the foolish thing: I ran into the blaze.

I'd always imagined burning as instantaneous agony, a breathless broiling as the body underwent the process of transforming into ash. I expected time to slow as synapses fired in panic and the oxygen in my lungs ignited. I waited for the fibers of my jacket to catch, for my cheeks to blister as the few days' growth of beard singed away, but I didn't feel any heat as I climbed upon the burning table and grasped the metal chair.

Momentum deposited Miranda and me onto the floor of the cafeteria. I beat my arms against the tiles, snuffing any infant flames, while Miranda lay on her side and fought against the ropes. She seemed unharmed, but her boots steamed like something fresh from the oven. Franklin descended on me, swinging the torch at my face while I crawled backward in retreat. My right palm sang out in protest when it smacked the floor. It was the first indication I'd been burned, but I suppressed the pain and kept putting distance between myself and the torch Franklin thrust at my eyes.

I grabbed a piece of broken frame sticking out of the fire and threw it at him. As Franklin deflected the burning javelin, I tackled him to the ground, retrieved my makeshift spear, and brought the sharp point up. The wood pierced his cheek. Splinters spilled into his eyes as I twisted the shaft, grinding it deeper into the flesh until the smoldering wood touched his tongue. When I pulled the stake free, some of Franklin's cheek came with it. Behind me, I could hear Miranda coughing. She'd spit out the gag, but each breath ended in a choke.

Franklin kneed me in the dick. Punched me in the ear. He rolled on top of me, dragging us closer to the fire. I jabbed with my weakened left, but the nausea traveling through my stomach sapped any real strength from the blows. I considered the syringe, but it was in the back pocket of my jeans, and I needed both hands for protection. I struck him with another jab. Franklin only smiled; through the hole in his cheek, I could see the gaps between his molars fill with blood. My vision blurred as our fight brought us closer to the fire. A few more feet and we'd be atop the flames.

Franklin administered a headbutt that broke my nose. My septum split as it was mashed flat. Blood leaked down my throat. Blackness lapped up in waves. If I didn't find the ability to crawl, I'd be unconscious in a few moments, and Miranda would burn.

I reached into the fire, found another sharp sliver of wooden frame, and lunging with all my strength, drove the point into the center of Franklin's stomach like a harpoon. He tried but couldn't grasp the board. As his bloody fingers slipped, I drove down harder. The force toppled Franklin off me and into the fire. I pressed him there, the long reach of the board protecting me as I listened to his cries. I would've held him against the flames all night had it not been for Miranda. I grabbed her by her smoking boots and pulled her away from the fire.

—

The nurses' station where we took refuge was a former maintenance closet. Once the home for mops, buckets, and bags of sawdust to sop up vomit, the administration had cleared it out, installing a child-size exam table and a mirrored medicine cabinet. I looked at my reflection: neck smeared with ash, nose sideways, and the rest of my face pale under streaks of blood. Miranda's left leg was burned, the jeans eaten away until I could see red blisters on her calf. Otherwise, she seemed unharmed.

No smoke billowed under the door. The vaulted ceilings and wide space of the cafeteria would keep the fire from spreading while the cinder block walls collected the heat like a kiln. In minutes, the fire would burn out.

"Melvin," Miranda said with a wheeze.

Like Shannon's burial, I won't describe her bereavement in detail. Grief should be a private thing, and I can relate with certainty I'd never seen grief so total as the sort Miranda experienced in that stifling little room. Horrifying as it was, there was something awe-inspiring about witnessing an emotion in so pure a form. Watching a man walk on water would've been less miraculous than the wailing she released. That's the best I can do. The only reason I offer the metaphor is because this is a confession. I don't want to leave an incomplete record.

Once she'd regained her composure, Miranda opened the medicine cabinet and produced a row of bandages and some ointment.

"Can you get that coat off without making it worse?" she said, gesturing to my hands.

Skin peeled from the palm of my right hand. My last two fingers were swollen and pink like undercooked pork. Some ointment couldn't hurt. I tried shrugging out of my jacket. The rough denim felt like raking glass over the scalded skin, but I freed my left arm without much trouble. The right sleeve refused to go over my hand without stealing my breath. Miranda stopped me, went back to the cabinet, and found some scissors to cut away the fabric. Afterward, she rubbed the ointment on my forearms. I hadn't realized I'd been burned beneath my coat, but I'd studied enough to know the real concern were those fingers on my right hand. There was the risk of shock from the trauma and, without real medical attention, the high possibility of infection. I already knew I'd never throw another decent punch or repair my machines again.

"You need a hospital," Miranda said as she bandaged my right hand. She sounded a little embarrassed to be saying this to someone with more medical knowledge.

The nearest hospital was an hour away in Charleston, but I couldn't linger in a burn ward. I planned to cross the state line by nightfall.

"We'll take Melvin with us," Miranda said.

"And Franklin?"

She wept again at the mention of his name. I wanted to touch her, but my dominant hand was already encased in the bandaged cocoon.

"Franklin said a true sacrifice should be something you love. The fire means he still loves us."

He only chose you after he couldn't find Alice, I thought, but there was no need for added cruelty.

The victims Alice had shown Carson were already in their graves, so I had no way of knowing the rituals that accompanied their end. Still, I hadn't expected the incinerating portraits and the brother's blood spilled on the canvases to be part of the spell. Alice had burned Franklin's art, but even after those cleansing fires, Franklin still chose flame for birthing his devils. The decision felt like a tribute to his lover. Both clearly enjoyed burning.

"Melvin warned me," Miranda said. "He told me once Franklin started down that path, there'd be no getting him back, but I wouldn't go without all of us."

"You did all you could," I said. I had to say something.

"I won't leave him. Even after this. He's still my brother."

Despite the speech, I could see her resolve waning. All she needed was an opportunity, and she'd cast off the burdensome obligations.

With the passage of some time, she might even delude herself into thinking the whole thing wasn't a betrayal, that saving herself was a bizarre manifestation of love not that much different from her brother's fire. She needed to be deceived. Luckily, there was the same deceiver in me as my father.

I handed over the truck keys. "Go start the engine," I told her. "If I'm not right out in a few minutes, you go on without me."

"He's my last brother," Miranda said.

Miranda took the keys. The old resolve was back. A hardness behind her eyes told me that even after such incalculable loss, she'd bear it.

Franklin was miraculously alive when I came back into the cafeteria. The fire was out, and he'd dragged himself from the cooling embers to the far wall. Even with his head lolling to one side and partially concealed by shadows, I could see that his eyes were shut around the burns, a thin liquid weeping from the sealed lids. Each weak breath wheezed in and out through the tear in his cheek. It would be better this way. The man wouldn't survive long enough to make it to a hospital. Better to die here and let me tell Miranda I'd done all I could. I remembered something Melvin had told me during our meeting at Wildcat's, a shy confession made while dripping rainwater and sipping martyr's whiskey about how I was right for the job because of a cold endurance during unpleasant acts.

Just sticking the needle in felt unceremonious. Kneeling over Franklin, I tried thinking of something appropriate to say, but he'd mostly been a stranger. He probably wouldn't hear any of it anyway, but decency dictated some final words pass between us.

Pretend he's someone else, I thought. *Someone with things left unsaid between you.* My first thought was Gabrielle, but that wasn't appropriate. The second possibility was my father, only I wouldn't waste words on the dead tyrant. While I debated, my mind conjured up an image of Brandon Flanders. Not Brandon's ghost, but the living man in his stark-white hospital room. The clinical smell in the antiseptic air. The gown he'd been wearing under the white sheets. I closed my eyes and, when I opened them, forced myself to see not Franklin but Brandon. Despite age, he would look the same as the day I'd beaten him with the lock. The child with the gap-toothed grin I'd demolished over boyhood teasing.

"You didn't deserve it," I said. "You didn't know what I was, and I'm sorry for it."

A little bubble of spittle popped in Franklin's mouth. Drool ran out of the hole, but I was still addressing Brandon.

"I'd take it back if I could. That's not a request for forgiveness. I just thought you should hear the why."

Even bandaged, my hand was steady and precise with the needle.

CHAPTER FOURTEEN

Emissaries from The Lighthouse greeted us at the church gate. Despite my protests, Miranda wouldn't let me go alone. She might've said her goodbyes in the cafeteria, but she insisted on accompanying her brother all the way. I didn't buy her claims. Some ulterior motive of revenge, or maybe even suicide, spurred her determination to look Logan in the eye. Perhaps my judgment was clouded by similar impulses. Our morbid peace offering felt foolish as I watched the guards come down the hill.

The first of the pair wore a plaid jacket and cradled a scoped rifle. The other was a young woman in a heavy winter coat. The headlights on Melvin's pickup were still busted, so I only got a dim look at the girl. Something about her shape, the way she wore the hood pulled up, convinced me it was Alice. I sat in the cab, feeling the tremble of the engine course through the vehicle's twisted metal. There was a mournful whine whenever I cut the wheel. Otherwise, it rolled along with a tired resolve I understood.

The man raised his rifle. I kept my hands on the wheel where he could see them as he approached my broken window. Miranda remained still as a stone in the passenger seat. Something about her posture worried me. She wasn't afraid of the gun.

"What's your business here?" the guard asked. He'd been days without sleep too. Wild-eyed and sweating in the cool night air.

"I'm here to see Pastor Logan."

My bandaged hand twitched. The spasms had started just after we'd left the school, and it felt like I was losing control of the appendage. The occasional throb pulsed up my burned forearm, but most of the feeling had left the digits entirely.

"Tell the pastor Harlan Winter is here."

The guard commanded me to stay put, and whispered something to the hooded girl before sprinting through the gate and up the hill toward the sanctuary.

Alice watched the man leave, then walked over to the truck, scraping her nails along the dents in the doorframe. Through the absent windshield, I smelled the scent of fresh arson trapped in her clothes, flammable chemicals trailing her like perfume as she walked to the covered tailgate.

Franklin lay in the center of the truck bed like a field-dressed deer. We'd wrapped his body in an old sleeping bag and covered the remains with a tarp from the art room. My third dead passenger in just two days. The sky had looked like rain when I departed the school, but showers didn't come.

Alice pulled back the trap to observe the body. She undid the sleeping bag and traced fingertips over the hole in her lover's cheek, clicking a nail against an exposed tooth.

Watching her goodbye, I couldn't help picturing what the couple might've been. I imagined other lives better suited for them. College kids flirting around the keg at a party. Maybe Franklin nervous and shy in an office break room as he invited this alternate version of Alice to the theater. A leather-clad Alice shouting a greeting in Franklin's ear over the growling amplifiers in a club someplace where downtown still existed. If they'd have been born in a time or place when rebellion consisted of power chords and nudes on canvas, would that have saved them from all the fundamentalist fire and ash? Art is only a tool. They'd been the ones who chose to wield it like a weapon.

"There are things that won't burn," Alice whispered. I didn't know if the valediction was meant for Franklin or the living.

Pastor Logan's footsteps crunched along the path. I watched him walk down to the gate, accompanied by the man with the rifle. I thought—and not for the first time—of the risk I was taking. The rifleman might gun us both down in the car, but I doubted that. As far as they knew, I still had *The Conjuror's Guide* and the money from Dalton Hardware. They wouldn't kill us without first retrieving their holy book.

"Did you know Franklin took the money?" I asked Alice. I needed answers before the pastor interrupted us.

"I didn't care about the money," she said. "I only cared about getting the book back."

"Alice," Pastor Logan called out, "come away from there. You don't have any further business with Mr. Winter."

Pastor Logan cupped a hand over her ear and brought his lips close. In the quiet, I heard the whispers.

"We don't mourn apostates," he said.

Hands cradling the sides of her face, Pastor Logan bestowed a kiss onto her forehead and sent her up the hill. After she was out of earshot, he came around the truck, lit a cigarette, and appraised me with cold eyes. Miranda stared right back, and I remembered the day at Eugene's gas station when she'd mocked me by shaking the bag of change in triumph. That grit was still present.

"You've seen some carnage," Logan said. "How are you maintaining?"

"Fine, assuming you've got a song that can raise the dead."

The pastor shook his head. "Still doubting after all you've seen."

"Until I see some results," I replied. "Aren't you going to ask what happened?"

"I know exactly what happened. This is the result of the songs we've been singing and the poems I've been writing. Each word and stanza and verse another thing bringing you closer to this inevitable moment. I chose you because you're the opposite of us. We create, and you destroy." As if to prove his point, Logan gestured to the beaten truck. "Destruction has its usefulness. Sometimes, the slate needs to be wiped clean."

There were uncomfortable truths in his statement. Whether conditioned on those nights with my father down in the basement, inherited in my blood, or just cursed by chance, I'd tried denying the violent birthright I earned on that long-ago school day when I'd beaten Brandon Flanders into a coma. I couldn't deny it any longer. Looking at Pastor Logan, I wanted to point out our similarities. That in all the infinite possibilities contained in the human imagination, with all those songs yet unsung and poems yet written, the only thing his congregation conjured up were the same old gods of wrath as our ancestors. Despite believing that words alone could fill empty bellies and mend broken hearts, his disciples managed nothing more than curses.

I might have said all this, but I was too tired to caution others away from the wrong path. Too wounded, too fucking burned.

"The only influence I'm following is self-preservation."

"Did you recover the money?" Pastor Logan asked.

I suppressed a laugh. No more talk of talismans or magic. In the end, the false prophet just wanted the cash.

"My uncle Abbott stole it. Why don't you curse him? Sketch up a nice picture where he's plagued with a tumor that rots his asshole."

"And our book?"

"That's my insurance policy. You leave the girl be after this, and I'll see it returned to you. If both of us aren't back within an hour, my associates burn it."

Logan nodded. "I figured you had it stashed. It wasn't at your home."

Pastor Logan stubbed his cigarette out on the back of his left hand. The flesh sizzled, but he didn't even grimace as he rubbed the cherry into the scarred flesh.

"You performed your duties, but I'm afraid your trespass here can't go unpunished. You won't be able to go home again."

Now I understood the smell of fire wafting off Alice and the parting comment she'd offered about how not everything burns. They'd torched my house. Had it not been for the thick bandage encasing my hand and the need to get Miranda away safely, I'd have strangled Logan while the guard put a round through my cranium. Instead, I bit down hard on my cheek and snuffed the anger until I could think properly.

"I'll return the book. All I want is an assurance that she's left alone."

"I've no further business with the girl now that she's not hiding the heretic," Pastor Logan said. "You have my word. Assuming she leaves here tonight."

"Nothing keeping me here," Miranda said.

Pastor Logan pulled back the tarp covering Franklin. After a moment of staring at the dead man, he gestured for the guard and another man who'd joined him. They took the corpse away. I wasn't sure Miranda would allow this, but she sat silent, just watching as her brother's remains were carried off by strangers. Logan offered his hand. A series of scars like puckered mouths trailed a line back toward his hairless wrist. I held up my own ruined appendage and just nodded. The pastor stepped aside.

"You'll bring the book back by tonight," Logan said. "If you don't return, we'll never stop hunting you."

I watched the gate shrink in the rearview mirror until it was out of sight. On arrival, I'd determined my odds of ending up dead or locked in a box near 70 percent. I had managed to extend my borrowed time by a few hours.

I decided to drive by the house. The rational voice inside knew nothing good would come of it, but I forced the beaten truck toward whatever remained of home. The sky wasn't filled with smoke as I crested the hill. No flickering firelights cast their glow through the trees. Only a faint scent of something burned hinted the pastor's words might be true.

The house had been reduced to a charred skeleton. I crossed the toasted grass, each blade crunching underfoot, until I stood inside the hollow perimeter. Just days ago, I would've been happy watching the leftover remnants of my boyhood burn. I'd thought of nothing but escape. Loading up the Mustang and fleeing. I wondered why I'd been born into a place where flight seemed like success and slinking back home from school felt like a failure rather than a comfortable return.

The garage still stood on the other side of the yard. The Mustang sat waiting.

I tossed Miranda the Mustang keys. "You're trading up," I said.

She caught them but didn't move toward the car.

"I know what you're gonna say. Just take it and don't come back."

I scooped up a handful of ash. Let it sift through the fingers of my unbandaged hand. The earrings my father had kept as trophies were still here somewhere. I wanted a final look at those diamonds. Behind me, the Mustang growled as the engine turned over. Miranda backed out of the garage. I could still hear the motor after she'd reached the bottom of the hill and put the throttle down hard.

At a distance, the campfires underneath Sergeant's Bridge resembled city lights. I'd expected all the fires to be extinguished by this late hour, but circles of people huddled around the flames, laughing and telling stories I tried deciphering from the exaggerated gestures cast by their silhouettes. A pack of children playing tag filled the night air with curses and accusations of cheating. Farther away, off in the near dark, I knew the tents would be filled with lovers making their own warmth.

I descended the hillside as I had days before and walked the dry creek bed toward the camp. The pain from my hand was a living thing that snaked up my arm, tunneling inside my ear until my teeth ached. When I tried moving my fingers, they refused to respond. It wasn't rational, but I feared that if I unwrapped the bandages, I'd see flesh falling from the bones like smoked meat.

No one greeted me this time. In fact, no one looked up from their conversations or meager dinners until I stood inside the perimeter of light. The first to notice me was a young man stirring a bubbling skillet with a wooden spoon.

"Any of you seen Arthur?" I asked.

The man with the spoon came closer, the forgotten utensil dripping juice in the mud. My knees buckled and I fell out in the dirt. Each blink seemed to be a longer moment, added effort necessary to pry my eyes open again. I heard voices debating. Finally, hands took up the weight of my body, and I was carried into a nearby tent.

I woke with Arthur sitting watch over me. Outside the tent, the sky shone a lavender hue that meant either coming dawn or dusk. I must have slept for an entire day.

"You need to eat," Arthur said, and handed me a chipped bowl. Steaming flecks of gray meat floated in the broth. I sipped, but when it hit my stomach, I almost gagged. The pain in my hand throbbed along with my heart. It had never left. I'd simply been too exhausted to stay awake.

"How long?" I asked.

"You've been in and out almost thirty hours. We gave you some pills and smoked you up a bit for the pain. Do you remember?"

Arthur gestured to a glass pipe near my pallet that stank of skunk weed. The idea that one of the tent-dwellers had wasted their stash on an outsider moved me. I tried sitting up. I put my bandaged hand on the ground to shift my weight but fell back into the pillows.

There was a sensation I couldn't describe underneath the bandages. I imagined legions of baby spiders crawling out some stigmata-like wound, their thousands of legs scurrying up my arm as their brothers and sisters dashed for the far corners of the tent. I could almost hear the crunching of the cannibalistic feast as the largest consumed their brethren. I pushed the thought away.

"I'm going to take these bandages off," Arthur said.

The dressings had already been changed once, the previous gauze wraps swapped out for lavender bed linens. Someone had cut up their best sheets for me.

Arthur sliced away the bandages with a small pair of cuticle scissors.

"You'd know better than me, Doc," Arthur said. "I think that without a hospital, you're in real trouble."

"Without a serious round of antibiotics, the whole hand will be gone in a few days," I told him.

"I'll try and find you a ride," Arthur said.

The hospital in Charleston would take one look at my wounds and bloody clothes and call the law. Maybe not The Lighthouse's bought sheriff but real law who'd file a report, take blood and skin samples, and ask hard questions for which I would have no satisfactory answers. I might luck out and keep the hand but spend the rest of my stay handcuffed to the bed. Afterward, I'd be the only guy in my cellblock who rolled cigarettes one-handed.

"No hospital."

"You know that's not an option."

"Always an option," I said. "Don't worry. I'll walk you through it."

Arthur shook his head. "No way am I doing that."

"Get some boiling water and that hatchet for firewood. It needs to be as clean as possible."

Arthur chewed his dirty nails.

"Everything needs to be sterile. Go wash up and get what I told you."

Arthur ducked out of the tent. Alone, I tried clenching my fingers into a fist one last time, but pain prevented me. Hopeless, I let the digits lay limp. The hand would never perform another healing act. In a sense, things seemed better this way. I'd split more lips than I'd ever set femurs.

Arthur came back inside with a tall man in dirty overalls. He wore a full black beard that trembled as he stood looking down at me. His arms were full of towels, water bottles, and a gleaming hatchet.

"This is Ross," Arthur said. "He's gonna—"

"Get a fire going and wash that hatchet. There's gonna be a lot of blood. You'll need to be ready to stop the bleeding. If that's not enough, you'll have to cauterize the wound with something."

Arthur swayed a bit, but Ross followed orders. Arthur leaned down close to me.

"Are you sure about this?"

"Just be quick," I said.

Ross returned with the hatchet, handed it to Arthur, who stood looking at the weapon with glazed eyes. I sat up, reached for one of the rags, and bit it. I leaned back, took a breath through my nose, and waited until I felt Ross's considerable weight pinning me. At first, I didn't think he'd be enough, but he kept me still when I tested his grip by struggling.

The hatchet sliced the air. The blade cut to the bone, pain enveloping my body until I bit down hard enough to chip a molar. Arthur pulled the blade back with a shaking hand and brought it down again.

This time, I felt instantaneous absence as my fingers fell away. A chill coursed through me as the blood poured. Arthur tightened a belt he'd looped around my wrist, but it did little to quell the tide. The scalding pan pressed against my stumps. The last thing I saw was Arthur plucking my severed ring and pinkie fingers up off the ground, one of the digits pointing at me like some unspoken accusation.

CHAPTER FIFTEEN

It took Alice a week to find me. The first few days I lay in the tent, consumed by fever sweat while the pain gods bestowed their visions upon me. My hallucinatory state transported me across the mountains to frozen plains, where Gabrielle braced a small child on her hip as she walked along the edge of a barren cornfield. Other times, visitors came to me. Brandon peeked through the slit in the tent one evening and watched me sleeping while the mustache of blood dripped from his nose. Speech felt impossible, so I invited him inside with a wave of my mutilated hand before he evaporated into the night.

The dreams had concluded by the third day, and I'd healed enough to assist with camp chores. The stumps of my fingers still ached, liquid draining from the wounds, but it was better than before, when sleep had been the only respite from agony. Arthur took up a camp collection. I received some donated clothes, including a single work glove to hide my deformity, and a used toothbrush. One of the members offered up some expired antibiotics they'd saved for their frequent ear infections. I took the pills as a precaution but wasn't much worried. Arthur's quick work with the hot pan had done the trick.

I'd always heard amputees felt their missing limbs. Apparently, ghost appendages like performing familiar tasks. Fingers lost to band saws will tie invisible knots. Feet blown off by land mines still tap along with the beat of favorite songs. This wasn't exactly what plagued me. It was more a sense of forgetting, reaching for something and remembering the absent fingers, or making a fist without all my prior flesh. I wasn't concerned. Eventually, I'd adapt to the loss like every other thing missing in my life.

On the morning Alice arrived, I'd kept busy with the duties of camp doctor. I examined a three-week-old infant, deeming the baby healthy despite the unsuitable conditions, attended an old man with a nasty cut along the sole of his foot, and set the broken fingers of a boy who'd fallen while playing in the creek. I was collecting kindling for the cook fire down by the same bend of that creek when Alice stepped out of the woods.

Her raven hair was woven into a single thick braid and tied with a piece of blue ribbon. The dark lipstick, black nail polish, and other artifices of her past appearance were gone. She wore faded gray jeans and a loose-fitting sweater that hung from her body like a cloak. The scent of fire didn't envelop her like before. Time had passed since her last occasion to burn.

"Good morning," Alice called out from her side of the creek. She didn't cross the deep pool where the commune washed its clothes, just stood on the bank, waiting to see if I'd come to her.

"What do you want?" I asked. I'd almost convinced myself I was safe hiding in the tent village, but her arrival revealed all the falsehoods in my plan. I knew Logan would be looking for me after my bluff with the book. They should've found me sooner. I imagined a small band of assassins dragging me back to The Lighthouse, or a bullet in my brain fired by a sniper in the hillside brush. A woman could pull a trigger as easily as a man, only Alice seemed concerned with something else.

She gestured at the water. "Either you're coming across or I'm coming to you. We've got things to discuss."

Water lapped at my thighs as I waded across. She looked weary, waiting on the other shore. Eyes underscored by puffy bags, the skin around her cheekbones tight and thin.

"Why the glove?" she asked.

"I'm short a few fingers."

"Can I see?" she asked.

Alice examined the empty fingers of my glove with the care reserved for fragile gifts. Aside from Shannon, she was the first woman who'd touched me in a long time. I wanted to pull away and let her caress every fire-sealed vessel at the same time.

"Shouldn't we be fighting?" I asked.

Alice released my hand. "I'm here for the book."

"That book is long gone. My uncle took it by accident when he stole The Lighthouse's money."

"Do you have any idea how dangerous it is in the wrong hands?"

"A witch like you is the wrong hands. You killed for it."

"If your uncle doesn't understand what he's got, he could do a lot of damage." Alice gestured at the distant tents. "I knew Franklin's creativity could be a catalyst for great things, but he and Logan didn't care about fixing life here. All they cared about was winning their private war. Just a couple of shitty bards, flinging satirical songs at one another."

"What would the pastor say if he heard such heresy?"

"Logan isn't responsible enough to have the book either. That's why we need to find it."

When The Lighthouse first appeared, I'd told myself that the fanatical rhetoric wasn't a real concern. Who had the time or energy to care about another chapter in the long line of American cults with people going hungry and the dollar crashing? I told myself it didn't affect me. I even turned a blind eye to the fires, not wanting to admit that eventually the flames might burn the things I loved. Standing on the shore with the witch and looking at my missing fingers, I realized what the avoidance had cost me.

Seeing my hesitation, Alice changed her tactics. “You help me find the book, and whatever money your uncle hasn’t already spent is all yours.”

“And how exactly are we supposed to find him?” I asked, throwing the kindling down at her feet. “He’s got several days’ head start and a bag of cash.”

“You must have a possession of his? Something he cared about?”

Jenny Long’s hummingbird earring was still in my pocket. I rubbed the outline it created in my jeans, the little wing tips cool even through the rough denim.

I didn’t want to be infected by Alice’s madness—didn’t want to tumble down into the trap of that zealotry—but I couldn’t deny the reality of the hummingbird earring received from a ghost or Brandon Flanders showing me the combination to the lock on Carson’s box days before in my basement. Whether or not I wanted to accept it, something beyond my reckoning had orchestrated recent events.

“If I agreed to your proposal—and I’m not saying I agree yet, but if I did—where would we start?”

—

Aside from the candles and small altar Alice had set up for the ceremony, the Prescott’s bridal suite looked the same as the night I helped Franklin hang his demon from the window. We sat facing each other on the scarred wood floor, a circle of white candles casting dim light that reflected off the mildewed rose wallpaper. I kept looking over Alice’s shoulder at the bits of broken stained glass.

Alice babbled an incantation like I’d heard from Franklin in the cafeteria. When she finished, she opened her eyes, held out her palm, and asked for the hummingbird. Clasping it in her hands, she chanted again. Finished with the recitation, Alice pulled her dress off over her head. I fumbled with my shirt buttons, eyes diverted from the pale skin and black dirt smeared across her thighs. When I wasn't fast enough, Alice unbuttoned the rest for me. She tried helping with my jeans, but I wouldn't allow it. We sat watching the flames flicker rather than look at each other's bodies.

Alice handed me the hummingbird.

"Clear your mind. Don't try to seek him. Just let the visions come to you."

Before I could respond, Alice pressed her palms over the candles. The fire died, accompanied with a small gasp Alice trapped in her throat. It reminded me of Logan extinguishing cigarettes on the back of his hand. Alice took me by the elbow and led me across the dark room toward the box. A series of little holes had been drilled into the lid like a child's jar for catching fireflies. Inside lay the sort of rough, unfinished boards certain to fill my bare ass with splinters.

Not for the first time, I wondered if I'd led myself into a trap. What would keep the witch from delivering me back to The Lighthouse like a parcel or leaving me to starve in the box? I pushed the idea away. If she wanted to betray me, Logan would've been waiting when we arrived at the Prescott.

"Are you sure there isn't another way to find him?" I asked.

"It's going to work," Alice said. "We're going to find the book. I believe that."

Alice steadied my body as I stepped into the box and helped me slide down onto my back. Once inside, she rubbed my cheek with her scorched hand and closed the lid.

My first night inside the box taught me the arbitrary nature of time. Seconds or hours passed at the same speed, with no light or sound aside from breath. If I slept, it was dreamless. There was no distinction between an aware moment and sleep anyway. The one surprise was how quickly the panic left me. After what felt like hours of hyperventilating, I gave in to the solitude.

The only physical presence with me was the little hummingbird. So long as I could feel the sensation of metal against my remaining fingers, I was present. My only other anchor to reality was Alice. Each night, she lay on the lid of the box, either whispering enticements meant for summoning spirits, or mantras that might open hidden parts of my mind. I didn't fully understand the magic in those days. It was just a comfort knowing I wasn't alone as she lay on the lid, weaving her spells.

Within days, I no longer feared death. How could the emptiness of nonexistence be worse than the stasis of this confinement? In death, I wouldn't be aware. That morbidity became a comfort after experiencing the way my mind raced inside the box. I was adrift in a river of thought, memories rising without cause or reason. I didn't analyze these intrusions, just let them float by and waited on the vision Alice had promised.

We didn't talk much in daylight. Just sat together at one of the banquet tables in the grand ballroom downstairs, eating canned leftovers she'd scavenged.

"It's never going to happen," I told Alice one morning as we dined on pears straight from the can. The thick syrup had congealed, forcing me to pluck bits of fruit from the jelly. I sucked each glob from my fingers.

Alice looked up from the journal in her lap. Maybe it was simply the proximity of so much time with a beautiful woman, or maybe I'd been indoctrinated into some sort of lovelorn Stockholm syndrome. Either way, I looked at her hair and lips, and thought about crossing the long table and letting her taste the old fruit on my tongue as we fucked on the ballroom floor.

"Do you still doubt?" she asked. "Even after all you've seen?"

"Of course. I certainly doubt I'm the right man."

Alice nodded in understanding. After all, she'd admitted practically the same thing to Carson. Those chosen for greatness were marked from the beginning. I'd seen that truth in all other aspects of life. The beautiful grow up knowing their beauty after the first adult gaze in a mirror, just as virtuoso musicians hear innate talent with their earliest chords. It had been that way the first time I healed a body. The maladies had succumbed to my abilities with minimal resistance. I knew my calling. The same was also true the first time I threw a punch in anger.

"We'll give it another day or two," Alice said.

Perhaps she'd let me leave, or perhaps I'd end up tricked into a shallow grave like The Lighthouse's failures—a sacrifice in her new garden of disappointments instead of a creator. Even with my compromised hand, overpowering a man like myself would be hard, but Alice didn't need to worry about that. She could lock me in the box or, if she missed the flames, light it on fire while I lay sealed inside. For some reason, this didn't alarm me. I was too focused on finding my uncle regardless of the cost.

—

On the day the vision finally arrived, I was thinking about the future Gabrielle built without me. A certain relief came with knowing she'd found happiness, but it mingled with bitter disappointment that our contentment couldn't exist together. After she'd told me about her brother throwing his ex-wife from the window, I'd secretly hoped that if my past was ever disclosed, the history of familial bloodshed would act as a bond. Instead, she'd sniffed out the way violence had marked me. Gabrielle had remained determined to be different from the men of her upbringing. I'd taken the combination lock to Brandon Flanders.

As I wondered why we'd followed such different paths, the darkness behind my eyelids filled with a pale-orange glow. I opened my eyes expecting the box's darkness but found myself standing in Alice's apartment. I looked over her belongings. Secondhand furniture with rips in the fabric. A beanbag chair procured from some yard sale. A kitchenette with an oval table and four mismatched chairs. Whether this was the actual interior of the apartment or simply my impression from Carson's description, I didn't know. Either way, the room felt real. I smelled the gasoline in the carpet. Wetness squished between my bare toes as if I'd been transported to the moment before Alice struck the match.

The Garden of Eden mural covered the far wall, but the garden was on fire. Tall flames burned up the high savanna grass like lit fuses. Low-hanging branches caught, and fiery leaves drifted back to the ash-laden ground like slow-falling comets. The animated flames darkened the expanse of blue sky with smoke. I expected the fire to spread off the wall and ignite the gasoline, but something kept the two worlds separate, reinforcing the border between art and reality despite the recent cracks I'd witnessed.

Behind me, Brandon Flanders sank into the beanbag chair. He wore the same white hospital scrubs as always, blood forever staining his upper lip.

"You're running out of time," he said. "They've already found him."

I didn't understand what he meant but no longer doubted his knowledge.

"Just tell me where," I said.

Had the ghost plotted revenge, no conceived punishment would've been worse than the one fate had already assigned me. Missing fingers and allowing myself to lie naked in a box, awaiting mystical instructions I hadn't believed in only a week ago. Each bit of his assistance had led me deeper into these dark waters of bizarre belief, but I felt no animosity from Brandon. If anything, he looked at me with a certain pity.

The ghost's nose dripped. "You're going to wake up in a moment. When you do, you'll know where to find him. Just don't let her have the book."

Behind me, the flames warmed my bare skin until I stepped away from the mural. Brandon rose as if to leave.

"Wait." I raised my hand with the missing fingers. I held it out like a penance for my mistakes. "I'm sorry. For what I did."

Another slow bleed filled the half-moon shape inside his ear. Watching him, I understood the pointlessness of my apology. Our connection in life had little to do with these spiritual interactions. The dead harbor no malice. Some unknown force had assigned the ghost as guide on my journey. Brandon performed the role with indifference.

Still bleeding down his cheek, Brandon reached out and touched the burning wall. The fire released from the painting, spilling like lava onto the floor, where it ignited the gasoline in the carpet. It spread around me, engulfing the beanbag chair. I expected heat, but as the fire traced its way up my legs, I felt nothing at all. It rose higher, my legs both pillars of flame yet strangely unharmed. The pain must be coming. Soon, my testicles would roast, flesh peeling from my thighs until I was nothing but skeleton. The heat pressed against my lips. Fire poured past my tongue. I felt it slide down my esophagus like warm milk. I gagged, ready to spit flames like a dragon, when I opened my eyes to the blackness inside the box.

My mind was filled with new images. A small country cottage, a dirt road with a deep fork in the woods.

I knew where to find my uncle.

I slammed my fists on the lid, shouting for Alice.

CHAPTER SIXTEEN

We took special precautions before departing. I reloaded the .38 with some shells Alice had scavenged during her arsons. She packed one of the Prescott's kitchen knives and a travel can of gasoline. A quiet pall settled over us as we drove across town. The ragtop Jeep ate up the country road beneath us, the path changing from asphalt to dirt as we turned down a final hollow and up the mountain path.

None of the flashes from my vison were cohesive, just quick bursts without connection. I saw a wooden swing on a barren front porch. A tight cluster of dead trees. A red wooden door with no peephole or windows. By the time Alice pulled me from the box, I'd convinced myself it was nonsense, but the mention of the red door made her eyes light up.

"I used to bring people there," she said.

I understood it was the same place she'd ambushed Carson in his story. Uncle Abbott wouldn't be hiding in any mountain shack of his own free will. If he really was there, The Lighthouse had found him. A part of me hoped the bastard was dead already. The rest of me wanted to find him alive so that I could finish him myself. As much as I wanted the money, what really drove me was the desire to wrap my hands around his throat.

Ahead, the road narrowed to a foot trail. Alice parked the Jeep. We'd brought no flashlights for the dark, so she led the way. I couldn't help thinking of Carson following her on this same path. Had Alice sensed his reticence and offered a reassuring smile to string him along? What did it say about my circumstances that I trusted such a woman?

The path was dark in the thicket of trees. I trailed behind, matching her footsteps, navigating more by sound and proximity than actual sight. We emerged into a small clearing. The cottage sat on the other side of the field. Carson's flattering description of the cabin hadn't prepared me for how much time had stolen its luster. The dark stain on the wood resembled dried blood. The flower boxes overflowed with dead azaleas and weeds. The glider on the porch swung in a lazy arch, its rusted chain creaking in the wind.

We crossed the high grass, the night's prior rain painting our pantlegs. I took the pistol from my waistband while Alice peered through the corner window. I knelt by the front entrance, careful not to brush the glider.

I couldn't open the door and hold the gun at the same time, so Alice set the gas can down and grasped the handle. Our eyes met. She mouthed a count of three, and we came through the front door at the same time, her low and me high with the gun ready.

Another box lay in the center of the room with the same chain and padlock. I hammered the lock off with the gun's handle. Alice unwrapped the chain.

Uncle Abbott wasn't entirely nude in the box. He wore a long dark robe, the tie at the waist undone and hanging past his pale knees. Judging by the stiff muscles and his eyes sealed shut against the faintest light, I guessed he'd been inside for days. Pointing the gun with my left hand felt awkward, but I stuck the barrel against the back of his head, pressing down hard to assert my resolve. I thumbed back the hammer while my uncle tried catching his breath.

"One sound above a whisper and I'll scatter your skull across the floor."

"Harlan?" Uncle Abbott said.

His voice sounded like something dried out in a smokehouse. He was nude under the open robe. A deep gash perforated his stomach just below the ribs. The wound was days old. Whoever slashed him had also stitched him up, the cut slathered in brown Betadine and sutured with some type of thin twine. Not the best job but a solid-enough field dressing to keep his guts from spilling out.

I looked at my uncle's exposed body to avoid his eyes. The tiny, dime-size nipples and uncircumcised prick hidden in a nest of pubic hair. The stink off him was tremendous, like a truckload of road-killed dogs rotting on a summer afternoon.

"Keep your voice down," I said. "Who's here?"

"The big one with the red beard. Sometimes the pastor comes at night."

"How long have they been gone?" Alice asked.

"I don't remember. He tells me I've only got days left to receive a vision. I tried telling him I'm no artist, but he doesn't listen."

Uncle Abbott looked up at me, rheumy eyes dripping over the black, sunken sockets down into the craters of his cheeks. The tears should've inspired sympathy, only I couldn't find any pity for my uncle. I remembered Shannon bobbing in the full tub, the weight of her and Carson as I placed them in the grave. Maybe Uncle Abbott didn't deserve languishing in the darkness of the box, but my finger kept testing the tension in the trigger, hungry to pull it.

Keeping my left hand gripping the gun, I fished in my pocket with the remaining fingers on my right hand and produced Jenny Long's earring. Uncle Abbott's eyes widened when he saw it. He reached for the little bird, but I refused to hand it over. When it was apparent that I wasn't giving him the hummingbird, Uncle Abbott dropped his hands back into his lap.

"You killed Shannon and Carson," I said. I wasn't sure why I bothered relating his transgressions from a life almost over. The wound should've already ended my uncle, and even after surviving days of torture, I planned on shooting him in the yard as soon as we secured the cash. "The book and the money. I want them back."

"The money's all gone. Logan made me burn it."

"Don't bullshit me." I pressed the gun harder into his temple. "Why would he burn his own money?"

Uncle Abbott shivered until his teeth clacked. The shaking reminded me of a molting tarantula I once saw as a kid, the spider lying on its back, all eight legs spasming as it shed its skin.

"Logan said it was part of the sacrifice. They cut me when I refused to burn it." Uncle Abbott reached for me. I stepped away, and he collapsed forward onto his hands and knees. "Don't leave me here with him. I can't go into that box again."

Alice drew the knife. Her eyes slid past Uncle Abbott groveling on the floor toward something in the shadows in front of me. Redbeard and Pastor Logan stood at the open back door. Redbeard held a dead chicken by its broken neck. His face was still swollen from tumbling down the basement stairs, the left eye closed by a purple bruise and a knot like a tumor underneath his eyebrow. An unlit cigarette, frozen on its way to his lips, hung in Logan's right hand.

I raised the pistol. Redbeard didn't look concerned. Just placed the dead chicken on the counter by the sink. Pastor Logan smiled his alien smile at me.

"Where's the book?" I asked.

"It's close by," Logan said. "But you'll never touch it." He looked down at my uncle. "New terms, Abbott. Either you go back in the box or your nephew and this apostate can take your place."

Uncle Abbott grabbed my ankles and pulled my feet out from underneath me. I fired two rounds from my prone position as my uncle clawed for the gun. The first hit Logan just below the collarbone. The bullet spun him around into the doorframe. The second struck him between the shoulder blades and pushed him out the open door, where I heard him collapse against the boards of the porch. My third shot went past Redbeard's head. The giant was already crouched low, his height now similar to a normal man's, as the bullet whizzed by and blew out the window above the kitchen sink.

Alice plunged the knife through Uncle Abbott's shoulders, pinning him to the floor of the cabin like an insect on a corkboard. Redbeard charged, and she fled out the front door. I squeezed off another round, missing the man completely.

Redbeard kicked the gun from my hand. It clattered under the nearby stove as the giant lifted me overhead and tossed me at the far wall. I hit the kitchen table and kept rolling until I crashed against the lower cabinets. I tried standing, but pain kept me down. Thick fingers coiled around my throat. My vision blurred at the edges as I lost oxygen. In a few more moments, I'd be gone.

Glass shattered as Alice smashed the front window and splashed gasoline inside. Fumes filled the room until I could almost taste high test on my tongue. Uncle Abbott squirmed, trying to reach the knife in his back. Alice doused gasoline over the kitchen until Redbeard released me. The giant stumbled around the overturned table and fallen chairs. Alice let the last dregs from the can pool near his feet and took a Zippo from the pocket of her jeans. She backed up to the front doorway and tossed the burning lighter as she stepped outside.

The overturned table kept the fireball from melting my face. The burning giant forgot about me completely, staggering after Alice with his back and shoulders erupting in flame. He came at her screaming, the sound of it some inhuman mixture of rage and pain. Redbeard tripped over Uncle Abbott's box, collapsing in the broken glass underneath the front window. I crawled for the pistol on hands and knees. My neck ached from the throttling; no doubt some vertebrae were damaged. I tried taking a deep breath, but the stench of bubbling fat hung too heavy in my nose. I grabbed the gun from underneath the stove and put the last two bullets into Redbeard's face.

Alice dragged Uncle Abbott onto the front porch. I crawled out the back door, where Pastor Logan lay dead in the grass. By the time I found my feet and walked around the side of the cottage and into the ash-heavy wind, Uncle Abbott and Alice lay tangled together in the tall weeds of the yard.

I sat beside them and watched while the fire lit up the night.

"Last chance," I told Uncle Abbott. "You refuse, I bury you out here."

The torn stitches of his wound sagged open like a mouth. Blood loss was taking him.

"On the edge of the field, buried underneath the big pine. You'll know it."

"Watch him," I told Alice, and went to find the tree. The book was right where he said, covered by a pallet of stones. I unearthed it; held the rough, worn leather in my hands; and cracked the pages open. I touched the brittle paper, thinking about how many horrible secrets lay inside. A wiser man would've cast it into the fire.

When I returned with the book, Alice sat alone. She told me Uncle Abbott's final words had been an apology. I doubt this was true but like believing she made something up to soften the man's selfishness.

I took Jenny Long's hummingbird from my pocket and caressed the little wings, the long stiletto beak and ruby eyes. I gave it a final chapped-lipped kiss and tossed it into the fire.

IV

The Occultist

CHAPTER SEVENTEEN

Alice and I spent weeks reading *The Conjurer's Guide*. Completely immersed and absorbing every word like scholars. Alice brewed elixirs that guarded against hexes from the remaining members of The Lighthouse and wove charms guaranteed to ward off spirits. We waited for some retaliation after killing Logan and Redbeard, but none came. Eventually, Alice went by the church and found it empty. Without Pastor Logan, the remaining members of The Lighthouse simply drifted away.

It wasn't long before I grew bored and moved into the book's darker pages promising necromancy, conjuration, and escape into other realities. During those early days, I deluded myself into thinking this was all harmless inquiry, theoretical knowledge that wouldn't cause harm. The warnings that escaped the crypt of Brandon Flanders's mouth should've been all the deterrent I needed, but each night I slipped away from our squatters' suite in the Prescott and perused the forbidden pages while Alice slept.

One morning after our second month together, I woke to find Alice gone. No goodbye note or other explanation. She'd simply disappeared. I wasn't surprised or upset. She wasn't going to stay with me forever. The truth was, I barely noticed her absence and was mostly relieved she hadn't tried taking the book with her. By that point, I was completely under its spell. I'd killed for it. If killing Alice had been necessary to keep it, I wouldn't have hesitated.

Time passed, as it must, and the economy gradually improved. America entered another war that devoured its youth but fed the corporate coffers. Politicians passed a sizable stimulus package for the crumbling banks and corporations but nothing for working people. Coopersville received none of this aid. While the cities slowly regained their vitality, we became the sort of place where only the trapped abide. I barely noticed. The only communion in my newfound isolation came from those seeking treatment. I set up a clinic in the Prescott's old barbershop. I mended dislocated bones, stitched lacerations, broke fevers, and even delivered a set of twins—a boy and a girl. Holding the squalling newborns, I thought of Uncle Abbott dying in the field while Redbeard's cabin blazed, and of Miranda driving off in the Mustang, her future as uncertain as my own.

The remaining residents of Coopersville whispered new rumors, and my patients dwindled as my legend grew. The previous points of discussion—both the fear surrounding my family lineage and the disappointment of my wasted talents—were replaced with genuine distrust. With Alice gone and The Lighthouse dormant, I became Coopersville's monster. Children spun campfire tales about my rituals until their bikes detoured the long way around the Prescott even in daylight. Only the truly desperate still sought my treatment. Eventually, I closed shop.

I kept expecting a visiting pilgrim from The Lighthouse. I saw Deputy Smith patrolling downtown one day. I was ready to duck into an alley if she chased me, but the lights on her cruiser never illuminated. She drove on by as if she had no recollection of our encounter and no desire to avenge her church. Maybe it was the charms I'd made with the book. Maybe she just didn't care.

Things proceeded that way for months. My nocturnal hours were filled with the brittle pages from *The Conjurer's Guide*. I dusted my doorways with blessed chalk; drew protective symbols on the concrete floors; and brewed potions of boiled animal fat mixed with my blood, all manner of roots, and other remnants of nature's pulp. The spells promised to exorcise ghosts, but I still felt Brandon's presence. Stairs that no one climbed creaked, and unseen eyes watched me in the dark. Once, an invisible body brushed by me in an empty hallway.

It might have gone on that way forever if I hadn't come downstairs for my midnight work and found Brandon Flanders sitting in one of the lobby's chairs. He looked alive, face lined with wrinkles and hair receding, until I saw the blood drying along the side of his scalp. He wore the soiled white hospital scrubs. The smile he greeted me with was almost sincere.

"Quite the collection you have here," he said.

Brandon surveyed the far wall, its built-in bookcases stuffed with leather-bound medical journals I'd saved from the garage and spiral notebooks filled with my findings from *The Conjurer's Guide*. A paisley rug in the center of the room covered one of my protective sigils. According to the book, no harm could befall me so long as I stood upon it. I'm sure the ghost felt its presence but knew I couldn't stand there for an eternity. There were a few other options, incantations I might try or an elixir I might grab if I could reach the far side of my abandoned clinic in the barbershop, but none of this was likely to do more than enrage Brandon.

"You aren't welcome here," I said.

A small sheet of thin paper materialized in Brandon's hand. He held it out from the chair. Tiny newspaper font, too small and tight on the smeared page to read at a distance. Two steps would've been close enough, but I didn't move from the protection of the rug.

"You'll have to do better than that," I said.

Brandon looked insulted. With a wave of his hand, the paper sailed across the distance, stopped inches from my nose, and floated as I read. The article documented the three-month disappearance of an acclaimed writer from Seattle. When the author failed to appear at a dinner engagement, a friend reported her missing, but police found no signs of a struggle or forced entry at the residence. A suitcase was absent from her belongings, along with some books. The friend didn't believe the author would just leave without making any arrangements. For one thing, a beloved Persian cat had been left behind. The author wouldn't have abandoned the animal without a caregiver.

"How many has she taken?" I asked.

"This author, a sculptor in Rochester, and a fledgling director from a film school in Indiana. He is powerful, but she'll take more."

"I haven't seen Alice in months. You've got to have better leads."

"She's covering herself with a spell of some sort."

"And you want me to find her?"

"You've shared a home and broken bread with her. You've got personal possessions she left behind."

"I don't care anymore," I told the ghost. "I'm finished with you."

"She'll take more," Brandon said.

I remembered the little garden of talent in the woods behind The Lighthouse.

I imagined Alice lying atop the kidnapped writer's box in some rented dungeon, whispering her late-night lullabies of the glorious coming world. The promise of poems that would reduce heaven itself to ash and the new clay they would mold into a better, kinder paradise. She wouldn't mention the sacrificial blood necessary to mix that mortar.

"None of this is my responsibility anymore. I'm done with your hauntings."

Brandon bit into his wrist. "This will hurt," he said, and let the blood cascade onto my forehead. The flow didn't follow natural laws, only pooled until I felt as if an entire ocean weighed upon my brow. Just when I thought the weight of one more drop might drown me, the blood ran into my eyes. In my momentary blindness, I witnessed secret moments from each life Alice had touched and some that she'd extinguished. Lies told to lovers as they lay together in bed. Friends betrayed for money, cowardice, or sport. I saw Nathaniel Logan kneeling above his father's grave. One hand held the headstone to steady himself; the other clasped a small notepad, in which he'd scrawled an inelegant, poorly rhyming poem about God's mercy that he recited. Uncle Abbott cradling Jenny Long's silver hummingbird, the hole in his heart aching with each beat over his unrequited love. All those lifetimes of pain distilled down into a feast Brandon poured into me.

Afterward, Brandon placed a cold palm against my neck. The tiniest squeeze followed, as if he might pull me forward by the throat and conclude our business with a kiss.

—

The next morning, I retrieved some of Alice's hair from the brush in the bathroom closet. There were other items I could use: a toothbrush left in one of the vanity drawers; an old pair of jeans abandoned in the upstairs closet; or the single, unmated glove I found in the floorboards of the truck that must've fallen from her coat pocket while driving to town one cold morning. There was even a dried tampon I kept in a Ziploc bag in case blood was required, but the hair would suffice. It was a simple curse.

I took a walk under Sergeant's Bridge, hoping someone might need treatment, but all the tent flaps stayed closed. I could see people inside through the thin membrane of curtain, bodies huddled together in darkness, waiting on me to pass by. No one came out asking for help, and the few people near the water didn't greet me with smiles or call me "doctor." No one approached me at all.

I stood on the edge of the water. That morning, I'd wrapped a combination lock with the strands of Alice's withered hair, spilled blood from my palm over the dial, and said the necessary words. I remembered that Carson had said Alice kept her own box. Once bound by my spell, Alice's new box would permanently seal the next time she climbed inside. Distance and time wouldn't matter. She'd remain trapped. I could leave her like that, but it would take days to die of thirst. I owed her better. If I only dipped the lock in the shallows, she'd drown.

As I moved my fingers over the lock, I recalled Gabrielle's stomach all those years ago during our anatomy lesson. *Here is the spleen,* I'd said, never telling her I knew just how to punch and make it quiver. *Here are the lungs,* I'd said, never acknowledging my joy at them emptying each time I plowed a fist into some boy's sternum. *Here is the heart.*

With no more bodies to please, heal, or wound, I tossed the lock out into the dark water, restoring order where I could.

ACKNOWLEDGMENTS

Many people are responsible for making this book a reality. First, my incredible agent and friend, Noah Ballard, who has been a fine champion of my work and the best partner I could have in this business. Thank you, Noah.

My sincere gratitude to my brilliant editor Megha Parekh for believing in the book and giving it an excellent home at Thomas & Mercer. My thanks to Megha, Clarence Haynes, and everyone at Thomas & Mercer for their support of the novel.

My thanks to the teachers, workshop members, writing mentors, and other writers who have supported my work over the years, including Belinda Acosta, Jonis Agee, Joy Castro, Sean Doolittle, Megan Gannon, Smith Henderson, Gabriel Houck, Ted Kooser, John Van Kirk, James A. McLaughlin, Devin Murphy, Bernice Olivas, Raul Palma, Rachel and Joel Peckham, Casey Pycior, Ron Rash, Timothy Schaffert, Bradford Tatum, Chris Harding Thornton, Anthony Viola, Stacey Waite, and Nick White.

Finally, my thanks to my family and loved ones. I hope to keep making you all proud.

ABOUT THE AUTHOR

Photo © 2022 Raphael Barker

Jordan Farmer is the author of *The Poison Flood* and *The Pallbearer*. He was born and raised in a small West Virginia town, population approximately two thousand. He earned his MA from Marshall University and his PhD at the University of Nebraska–Lincoln. For more information, visit www.jordanfarmerauthor.com.